Doug and Carlie: Lessons in Love

by Lisa Smartt

Books by Lisa Smartt:

Doug and Carlie Series:

Doug and Carlie

Doug and Carlie's Love Conspiracy

Doug and Carlie: Matchmakers on a Mission

The Smartt View: Life, Love, and Cluttered Closets

The Smartt View 2: Life in Progress

www.lisasmartt.com
Copyright 2014
ISBN 978-0-9914856-1-1
Front and back cover photo by Yana Godenko,
shutterstock.com

To every person imprisoned by regret,

There is hope.
There is love.
There is home.

Chapter 1, CARLIE: Freedom, Sweet Freedom

Prisons scare me. It all started when Pappa was unlawfully imprisoned in Commerce, Georgia, on September 19th of my third grade year. Pappa and Meemaw had taken me to the county fair that Saturday because my mama thought fairs were complete nonsense. She said, "Those carnival people smell like they haven't had a bath in ten years and all that food on the midway will rot your teeth!" But I didn't listen. I didn't listen because Mama also thought the mailman smelled bad just because he had long gray hair pulled back in a ponytail. But I'd gotten up close to the mailman plenty of times and he just smelled like Old Spice and Cheetos.

Mama also thought nearly every food and drink known to man would rot my teeth. Anytime she didn't want me to do something, she would say, "Carlie Ann, that will rot your teeth." When I was eleven, I asked for a puppy for Christmas. She said, "No. That'll rot your…" But then she caught herself and realized a professional educator could not in good conscience tell me that a Golden Retriever would cause the decay of my molars. Even Mama had a twinge of conscience now and then.

Back to the story of Pappa's imprisonment. We were walking down the midway on that fateful day. Meemaw held my left hand while I held a paper cone of cotton candy in my right hand. The mass of light pink cotton candy was bigger than my head and sometimes a piece would fly off and get caught in my blonde braids. Pappa would laugh and pull it gently out of my hair. When I finished the great mound of sugar, he placed his favorite monogrammed handkerchief under a water faucet by the corn dog stand so he could wipe my sticky hands. In the process, we got up real close to the corn dog man. I wanted to call my mama right then and tell her he didn't smell like he hadn't had a bath in ten years. He just smelled like corn dogs and dried ketchup. But when Pappa was bent down at the faucet, well, that's when all heck broke loose.

Our mayor, a red-headed middle-aged man with thick black glasses, walked up behind Pappa and said with a loud shout, "Arrest this man! Go ahead, Horace, arrest him!" Horace was the preacher at First Methodist and I didn't even know preachers were allowed to arrest people. But Horace did the mayor's bidding. He held Pappa's hands behind his back and began to walk him toward the big pavilion where we had just left a big jar of Meemaw's bread-and-butter pickles. We felt certain Meemaw would win first place this year 'cause Cora Dempsey was down in her back and living with her daughter in Nashville.

I shouted at the top of my lungs, "No, he's my pappa! He's my pappa! He would never do anything wrong!"

Pappa grinned and said, "Honey, it's okay. Really. It's not what you think."

But it was what I thought. My pappa had been arrested by a Methodist preacher right there on the midway next to the corn dog stand. Now I realized why Mama and Daddy always said Mayor Clawson wasn't worth shootin' and that he was only the mayor because his daddy had been a fine high school principal.

I had to run in order to keep up with Pappa and the preacher. I made another failed attempt to secure his freedom, "Mr. preacher man! Mr. preacher man, please let my pappa go!"

The skinny young preacher just laughed and patted me on the head. When he did, I smelled a horrible stench coming from under his arm. Oh, the irony of it all. I knew Mama would never ever say the Methodist preacher smelled bad because he graduated from college and his hair was cut military style.

We soon arrived at a make-shift prison right next to the Chamber of Commerce booth in the big pavillion. A chubby white-haired lady came running straight toward me. "Here, Sweetheart! A free balloon courtesy of the Chamber!"

I shouted with disgust, "No ma'am! They're putting my pappa in jail!"

The smelly preacher put Pappa into an old rusty cattle trailer and locked the outside door with a combination lock that was just like the one my middle school neighbor, Miranda, had on her locker at school. I knew for sure because Miranda sat on her front porch the whole first week of August practicing opening that lock. One time she threw the lock down and yelled out a cuss word and her mama made her brush her teeth with a bar of Lava soap.

Mayor Clawson stepped up on an old yellow wooden platform and yelled out with way too much enthusiasm. "William T. Bookman has now been imprisoned!! Yes, imprisoned! Sonny Davis of Davis Insurance Group made a $100 donation to the Commerce Quilting Guild to assure his capture. He will now need ten fine citizens to donate $5 each to the Guild in order to secure his release!"

Meemaw reached down and took my hand, "See, Honey? It's not real. It's just a way of raising money. Your pappa is fine, just fine."

But I thought the whole thing was beyond ridiculous. And I couldn't imagine how my poor pappa felt all locked up in that old rusty cattle trailer. I put my arm through the grates and said, "It's okay, Pappa. I'm here!"

Thirteen minutes later enough people had donated to the stupid quilting guild to secure my grandfather's pardon. He walked out of the trailer holding up his arms and yelling, "Thank you, one and all! I never doubted you would come through for me! The ladies of the quilting guild acknowledge your kind-hearted generosity!"

He knew I had been terribly worried, so he knelt down beside me, looked into my eyes and said something I will never forget. "Carlie Ann, I was never scared. I wasn't. It takes more than metal bars to imprison a man's spirit."

Chapter 2, CARLIE: Sharon Recap (If you've already read the first three books, you can skip this chapter. But I wouldn't, 'cause skipping chapters gives you that weird feeling of incompletion that may cause you to lose sleep at night.)

Other than Pappa, the only person I know who has been in prison is Dusty McConnell. Years ago he did time for stealing cars and for what he would call "overall misguided mayhem." But now Dusty is happily married, the father of four great kids, and a business owner.

I guess I need to back up and fill you in on my wonderful, albeit sometimes bizarre, life here in Sharon, Tennessee. My husband, Doug, was raised here in Sharon. He graduated from the University of Tennessee in Knoxville but, years ago, he returned to his West Tennessee home to work at the First National Bank of Sharon. At the time, I was working at the Dollar General Store in Commerce, Georgia. We met through his great uncle. By the time we married, I had become a best-selling author. That story is recorded in a book called, "Doug and Carlie." I've now had three books on the New York Times Best Sellers list which proves that some people get tired of high-minded literature and prefer to read a chubby country woman's ramblings about, well, about most anything. Our son, James, is five years old and beginning Kindergarten in a few weeks. He can't sit still at all so I hope they do a lot of "active" learning. Parents of boys always hope for a kindergarten teacher who understands the importance of "active" learning.

The best part about being a writer? Last year we got a Christmas card from the Queen of England. I know. She probably never even touched that card. Plus, I'm sure they sent out thousands. But still. Oh, and the answer to your next question is no, I'm not sure why she always carries a purse, especially in a Christmas picture. And yes, I'm surprised no one has written a book pretending to be one of her dogs. Note to self: Write a book from the perspective of the Queen's Corgi. Hire a linguist so it will sound sufficiently British.

Clara McConnell is Dusty's wife and one of my very best friends. She was my roommate in Commerce, Georgia, years ago when I worked at the Dollar General. I fixed her up with Dusty and they got married a few years ago, adopted three great kids, and then had a baby last year. Well, I can't really claim to be their matchmaker. Long story. No time to tell it. That whole beautiful tale is recorded in a book called "Doug and Carlie's Love Conspiracy." Much to my chagrin, they named their new baby Beauregard. Thankfully, in honor of his future on public school playgrounds, they call him Beau. Everyone loves Dusty and Clara and all four kids. And only my mama refers to Dusty as "that nice mechanic who did time in the slammer."

When my first book was made into a movie, I became even more famous and that's also when I met one of my other best friends, Ashley Harrison Robertson. Doug and I first met her when she was our waitress at a diner in Hollywood. But then she ended up being the star of the movie based on my book, "A Single Woman's Guide to Ordinary." She even got an Oscar nomination for that role. The year after that she got another Oscar nomination for a movie called, "Over the Hills." When she talks about her journey from waitress to famous actress, she uses the term "surreal." If you don't know what that means, don't bother looking it up. It kind of means surprisingly blessed. But the most amazing part is that she ended up marrying one of our best friends, Dave Robertson. Dave was a widower and father of a beautiful little boy named Collin when he married Ashley. That story is recorded in a book called, "Doug and Carlie: Matchmakers on a Mission." Now Dave, Ashley, and Collin split their time between

Hollywood and Sharon, Tennessee. That's called diversifying one's geographic portfolio. Or that's what I call it anyway.

Okay. So everyone should be caught up on the players in our diverse little community. Well, I also should tell you about Doug's Uncle Bart and Aunt Charlotte because they're just, they're just beyond words really. Aunt Charlotte is a combination of Aunt Bee from the Andy Griffith Show and LuLu Roman from Hee Haw. Uncle Bart is like a combination of your favorite high school shop teacher and the gruff old man who changes your oil at the Shell station. Jerry Conner is one of our local law enforcement officers. He's in his late 20's and loves telling about all the times he's been called upon to protect Ashley from misguided fans. Jerry keeps getting a crew cut down at the barber shop even though it makes his face look rounder. Oh, and then there's Chester and Ida who remind you of really sweet, really old people everyone thought would be dead by now, but who keep on living. They say it's because they put out a garden every year. Note to self: Eat more fried squash.

Chapter 3, CARLIE: Who in the World is Matthew Prescott?

Some people with a criminal record spend their whole lives trying to hide it. Embarrassment, I guess. But not Dusty McConnell. Oh, no. He's spoken about his time in prison at most every Rotary and Kiwanis Club meeting in West Tennessee. He even spoke at an all-school assembly at the high school last year. It doesn't seem like Dusty is trying to forget about his past. Seems instead he's trying to use it to help other misguided youth. I know. There aren't very many misguided youth in the local Rotary Club. I think his goal there is to help old people who aren't misguided...to understand those who are and maybe show a little compassion.

Well, anyway, last Wednesday night, he stood up at prayer meeting and made an announcement, a big announcement, an announcement that ended up causing quite a stir in Sharon, Tennessee. He cleared his throat and then smiled real big as though we were in for a real treat. "My good friend, Matthew Prescott, will be arriving here in Sharon this Monday. He'll be living in Chester and Ida's guest room for a while until he finds a place of his own. And he'll start working for me at the shop on Wednesday. I hope you'll all pray for him and I expect you'll be plenty nice to him 'cause that's what you do. It's what you did for me."

Dusty didn't say it out loud, but it didn't take long for the folks of Sharon to find out that Matthew Prescott wasn't just a friend from high school or a second cousin from St. Louis. No. As Mama would say, "They met in the slammer." As word started spreading, the folks of Sharon weren't quite as understanding as Dusty had hoped. Uncle Bart said the men at the barber shop were rightfully concerned about Chester and Ida's safety. Jerry Conner even talked about setting up 24-hour surveillance around Chester and Ida's house. Of course, we all knew Jerry Conner had just been hoping for a chance to use the word "surveillance" ever since he started watching "Walker, Texas Ranger" on Netflix.

Uncle Bart even cornered Doug at the Farmer's Market Saturday morning and said, "Ol' Chester ain't got the sense nor the eyesight to fend off a young fella like that if he was to turn mean on 'em. What if he was to knock both of 'em in the head one night and run off with ever' thing they got?"

Doug laughed, "And what do Chester and Ida have that he could want?"

"They might have money hidden under the mattress or somethin'. Plus, you remember when Chester won that rifle in the raffle a few years ago."

Townspeople started coming by Dusty's shop, questioning his judgment, wondering if he'd pressured Chester and Ida to take in Matthew Prescott. So Dusty, well, Dusty did something, something completely surprising. He took out an ad in the Weakley County Press. The top line said something like "Dusty's Shop in Bradford Hires on New Mechanic from Nashville Area." And it wasn't long before that ad was passed all over the county. According to the ad, Matthew Prescott was 35 years old and a well-trained car mechanic. He also had a bachelor's degree from some university we'd never heard of in California. Then, well, the most surprising thing of all was the last two lines of the advertisement. "Matthew has spent the last fourteen years in prison. The friendliness of our beautiful area will be a refreshing change of pace. We hope you'll come by and welcome Matthew Prescott to Dusty's Shop and to West Tennessee."

I think Dusty was trying to shame all of us. I mean, I think he was hoping all the Rotarians and Kiwanis folks and Lions

Club members and, well, everyone in the area who knew him would trust his judgment. Hadn't they all given him a standing ovation? Weren't they anxious for their kids to hear his story at the high school last year? If they appreciated Dusty's story so much, why would they not embrace Matthew and his story? But I think Uncle Bart hit the nail on the head when he said, "Truth is ol' Dusty ain't told none of us what this new fella done. Must have been pretty bad to do fourteen years. Prolly killed somebody."

Chapter 4, CARLIE: Welcome, Matthew! Oh, And What Exactly Did You Do?

Doug and I invited the McConnells and Matthew and Chester and Ida to Monday night dinner. James was busy in the living room setting up every Lego set he owned so that Will, Mandy, and Molly would be impressed.

As I pulled brown pieces of Romaine lettuce out of the salad, I whispered in Doug's ear. "Okay. Aren't you curious? Even a little bit?"

"Curious about what?"

"Doug, please. About what he did. I mean, fourteen years. That's a pretty long time."

"I figure he'll tell us if he wants to tell us…when he wants to tell us."

"You are the best person in the world. Seriously. You should be married to a woman who is willing to rip all your clothes off tonight and make mad passionate love to you."

He started laughing, grabbed my rear end, and whispered, "Lucky me."

The doorbell rang at 6:05. I quickly removed my apron as Doug headed toward the door.

"Dusty, hey! Come in. Will, you've grown like a foot in the last week, man." All nine dinner guests filed through the door. Well, Beau didn't file in. He rode in on Dusty's shoulders.

Chester carried an old lemonade container with a torn paper label barely clinging to the outside. He shook his head and spoke with hesitation, "Charlotte wanted me to bring you this buttermilk. Don't know the source. Don't want to know. Just doin' what I'm told."

I quickly grabbed the old jug. "No problem, Chester. Thank you."

Clara took the older kids into the living room where James was beckoning their approval of his various Lego projects. Doug had helped him make Hogwarts Castle and they all testified of its majesty.

Dusty removed his camo cap and said, "Doug, Carlie, I'd like you to meet one of my very best friends. This is Matthew Prescott. Matthew, this is Doug and Carlie. They're not friends. They're family."

Doug extended his hand, "Welcome, Matthew. Welcome."

I reached out to hug him because that's what I do. I hug strangers. Matthew hugged back but not in a clingy scary way. No. He hugged back like an old college friend who felt comfortable being reunited with us. And he smelled like that expensive cologne my cousin, Jim, always wore. Canoe or Shipwreck or something like that. "Matthew, welcome to our home. It's chaotic but it's home. Doug will take you into the living room where Lego magic is happening before your very eyes."

He laughed. "Thanks. I'm glad to be here." He glanced into the kitchen area. "And something smells wonderful."

He looked nothing like I envisioned. It was crazy for me to have envisioned Matthew Prescott in the first place. Dusty had never given us a physical description. But somehow I had pictured a large brawny man with scars, a hoarse voice, and hair on his back.

Matthew looked like a young Hugh Grant instead. He looked like someone who, ten years ago, could have played a teenager on a Disney TV show, even though he would have been 25 at the time. He wore dark blue jeans and a forest green long-sleeve shirt that looked vaguely familiar. I soon realized they were Dusty's clothes.

Matthew followed Doug and Chester and Ida into the living room as I discreetly pulled Dusty into the kitchen and whispered, "Aren't those your clothes?"

"Yes."

"So, he doesn't even have his own clothes?"

"No. Not yet. Clara and the kids are taking him shopping in the morning. We have to get school clothes for the kids anyway. We'll just pick up some things for him then. I've got plenty of work clothes he can have. He'll just need clothes for you know…" Dusty smiled and winked. "…for the many social things he's gonna get invited to around here."

"What about family? Does he not have anybody?"

"Yes, Carlie. He has people. He has me. He has Clara. He has the kids. He has us."

I could tell Dusty was getting impatient. He had declared Matthew Prescott one of his very good friends. Instead of trusting him, I was giving him the third degree. "I'm sorry. Really. He seems nice."

"He is."

I ran into the living room and announced, "Come and get it while it's hot! Chicken spaghetti, one of Sharon, Tennessee's signature foods. Noodles and butter and yard bird! What's not to love, people? Oh shoot, I left the garlic bread on broil!"

As I ran toward the kitchen, James bumped into the coffee table and accidentally knocked over Doug's tea glass. The tall glass made a piercing sound as it shattered on the hardwood floor. Matthew jumped from the couch and shouted a string of obscenities.

James yelled, "He said bad words, Daddy! He said bad words!"

When I returned to the living room, Matthew's face was as red as Aunt Charlotte's homegrown tomatoes. He reached down to pick up some big glass pieces and said in a quiet voice, "Sorry about that. Just a little jumpy, I guess."

Dusty put his arm around him. "No worries, Man. We understand. You're among friends."

But Chester and Ida didn't look like they did understand. In fact, Chester's face turned several shades lighter than his normal pasty white. He looked like he was regretting that night Dusty took him and Mrs. Ida to the Sonic in Greenfield for mustard burgers and cheese tots. It sounded like such a great idea when Dusty first told him that Matthew could help with the yard work and the housework. But perhaps all that grease and sodium had dulled Chester's senses. Matthew Prescott had spent every day of the last fourteen years in a state prison cell...and now he was going to be living in Chester and Ida's guest room with Ida's silverware and all the Christmas decorations stored neatly under the bed.

Doug ran toward the kitchen and then briefly glanced back. "Look, this is no big deal. I'll grab the trash can in here. Carlie, can you get a big towel? We'll just make quick work of this."

But all of us had forgotten one simple fact. James is five. And five-year-olds, well, they act like five-year-olds. All the time.

As Matthew was picking up big chunks of glass, James tapped him on the shoulder. "You are in BIG trouble with my daddy, mister."

"Am I?"

"Yes. My daddy is gonna make you take a bath or go to bed or put all your toys in the closet."

"I've already had a bath. What if I just help clean up this mess? Do you think that would count?"

James looked puzzled and then shook his head. "No. That won't count."

Doug broke in, "James, Matthew is our guest and he will not be taking a bath or going to bed while he's here. He'll be eating with us. You're the one who knocked over the glass. We're not fussing at you, are we?"

"No."

"Right. We're not fussing at you and we're not fussing at Matthew either. Accidents happen. Let's just move on."

By the time we all gathered at the table and started eating, calm had been restored once more. Other than two loaves of black garlic bread eternally stuck to a pan on the counter and a pile of broken glass in the trash can, it was a nearly perfect night. But like most seasons of calm, it was all temporary.

We could all hear Uncle Bart and Aunt Charlotte's loud voices as they scurried onto the porch. As they've gotten older, their talking has become increasingly louder out of necessity.

"Now, Bart, don't go embarrassing none of us! We don't know he killed somebody! He might have jest maimed 'em or took somethin' or robbed a bank!"

"Well, he done somethin' bad if he served fourteen years! And I aim to find out what it was!"

Aunt Charlotte knocked on the kitchen door and yelled out, "Yoo Hoo! Anybody home?"

Doug excused himself from the table and opened the door. "Well, look who's here." He smiled and spoke in a tone that was half friendly and half scolding, "Uncle Bart and Aunt Charlotte, what a surprise! I hope this is a social call. Tell me you brought some of your famous magic pickles for our newest Sharon resident."

Aunt Charlotte blushed with embarrassment which was rare. "No, we done forgot the pickles, Hon. But yes, we did figure on meetin' Chester and Ida's newest boarder."

Aunt Charlotte was wearing a bright pink, floral, sleeveless muumuu. She ran toward Matthew and extended her hand. When she did, her arm jiggled so much it put Santa Claus' belly to shame. "Charlotte Nelson. Pleased to meet ya. And this here's Bart. I gotta say you don't look nothin' like I expected."

20

Matthew wiped his mouth and smiled. When he smiled, I couldn't help but wonder if they had provided teeth whitening strips in prison. I guess he had plenty of time for brushing and flossing. Or is floss considered a potential weapon? Not sure. He stood. "And what did you expect me to look like?"

"Well, I watch all them cop shows and that show about the way criminals think. And, well, they all look like criminals. You look like...I don't know." She wrinkled her brow and turned toward the door. "Who does he look like, Bart?"

"He looks like that fella on Channel 6 news, the one that does all the investigatin' of bad contractors and plumbers and stuff."

Aunt Charlotte beamed. "Don't he though?" She turned toward Matthew and put her hand on his shoulder. "Honey, Bart's right! You look just like that fella on the 10 o'clock news. And he's a good lookin' fella too. Sarah Simpson is set on marryin' him even though she ain't never even met him. And she's a respectable third grade teacher at Sharon Elementary."

Matthew sat back down and laughed as though he felt comfortable playing along. "Well, that's the greatest compliment I've received all day, all year even."

I pulled two chairs from the bar to the table. "Won't you two join us for a little spaghetti?"

Uncle Bart grabbed a cherry tomato from the salad bowl and said between chews, "We already ate. You ain't got no ice cream, do ya?"

"No. No ice cream today. We have Tiramisu in the refrigerator for dessert. How 'bout that?"

"Tira-ma-what? Gall darn it, Carlie, you know I don't eat that crap I can't even pronounce."

I patted his back. "I know. What about a graham cracker?"

"Got any marshmallow crème?"

"I do."

Uncle Bart looked at young Matthew as though he were interviewing him for a job. "Chester and Ida here are good folks. You're mighty blessed they saw fit to take you in."

"Yes, sir. I think it's gonna be a good situation for all of us. I like doing yard work and fixing things. I hope I can help them out while they're helping me."

"You like fixing stuff, huh?"

"I do."

"Where did you learn to do that? Your daddy?"

"No. My dad hired everything out. I don't think I ever saw his hands dirty. No. I learned how to fix stuff when I was in school. And I did a lot of work around the prison too." Matthew looked straight at Uncle Bart when he said it. It's like he wanted it all out on the table. Front and center.

Uncle Bart spooned a huge glob of marshmallow crème onto a graham cracker and when Matthew said the word "prison" the graham cracker snapped and Aunt Charlotte reached out to help gather the crumbs. She spoke loudly because she only has one volume really. "Yeah, I 'spect you had a lot of time on your hands. Yes, sir."

22

Matthew leaned back in his chair. "Yes ma'am. I did have a lot of time. Mr. Nelson, I have a question for you. What's the best thing about living here in Sharon?"

"I don't rightly know. I lived here my whole life. So I don't know if it's better or worse than other places. I know er'body in town. Maybe that's the best thing. I know people. Good people."

"I figured that's what you'd say. And I understand, at least a little bit. Mr. Chester and Mrs. Ida have fixed up a nice room for me." He patted his flat stomach. "And if Carlie keeps cooking like this, I'm going to gain ten pounds. Seems like a good place to be."

Aunt Charlotte chimed in, "Where are your people, Honey? Your family?"

"California."

"Then why ain't you in California, Baby?"

Doug stood up and put an end to the interrogation. "I think we've asked Matthew enough questions for one night. He just arrived in Sharon today. We'll have plenty of time to get to know him. Why don't we eat some of that Tiramisu in the living room? Plus, I know Dusty and Clara's oldest three want to recite their parts for the Soybean Festival Breakfast over in Martin. We can't wait to hear that, kids. Really. I've always wondered about the history of the soybean. Haven't you, Matthew?"

He smiled. "Absolutely. I'm all ears."

I couldn't help but respond, "Save your ears for the Sharon Corn and Music Festival. That's when it really breaks loose around here."

Chapter 5, CARLIE: Friday Night is for Rednecks and Movie Stars

If Ashley isn't shooting a movie, the Robertsons come to Sharon at least twice a month. I know. You're wondering why a famous movie star and her ridiculously good-looking husband and child would come to a place that doesn't even have a movie theater or a Home Depot or even a KFC. That's easy. People. Plus, they own a modest little log house here that Dave bought back before they were an "item." After they married, they decided to keep the log house because, well, because it's in the woods and because it's near all of us. Plus, everybody knows people buy places out in the country just so they can run around in their underwear and not get caught.

Ashley was scheduled to shoot a romantic comedy in late October, so they decided to spend most of August and September in Sharon. Dave is busy writing a book about the connection between grief and addiction. I read the first ten chapters and cried like a baby. Between the graphic details of his personal story and the helpful counseling advice, it's destined to be a best-seller.

Dave asked Homer Crittenden to cater a big fish fry at their place the Friday night after they arrived. Everyone was to bring sides and desserts. Friday morning Chester walked down to the bank just to ask Doug if he thought they should bring Matthew to the fish fry. Poor Chester. Such a long life. So little wisdom. Doug assured him that, unlike a hamster or a goldfish, which would be inappropriate to bring to a fish fry, Matthew was an actual person and, therefore, was absolutely invited.

That evening, when we pulled into Dave and Ashley's long driveway, we could see Matthew, Chester, and Ida already sitting on the front porch with Dave and Ashley. James started yelling, "Where's Collin, Mama? Where's Collin?"

"Oh, I'm sure he's around here somewhere." James' sandy brown curls bounced as he ran to the back yard in search of his light sabre-wielding comrade.

Dave ran from the porch and jumped on Doug like he was an intruder. "Hey, old man! Who invited you and your clan?"

Doug put Dave in a pseudo-headlock and said, "The law sent me to make sure things didn't get out of hand out here. Said some poor citified California sap was likely to set the woods on fire."

Dave struggled free and lightly punched Doug in the gut. "Uh, yeah, they should be worried. My good looks are producing a lot of heat out here, brother. A lot of heat."

Doug rolled his eyes and reached for the cooler in the back seat. Doug will absolutely under no circumstances consider eating potato salad at an outdoor summer event unless it's been chilled to a temperature that would make Antarctica shiver. I may burn a lot of food, but I know to never leave stuff at room temperature because of Doug's now-famous "1997 Fourth of July Potato Salad Salmonella Story." Really. It should be translated into a book. A horror story that would make Stephen King blush. So, now our potato salad has to be transported in a huge cooler with massive blocks of ice guarding the health and well-being of everyone we love.

Dave leaned in and spoke in a quieter voice. "We met Chester and Ida's house guest. Seems like a good guy."

"Yeah, he does. I guess you know...I mean, you know the situation, right? That he's Dusty's friend from..."

"Prison. Yeah. I know. Chester called and talked to Ashley for 30 minutes explaining the whole thing and asking if we were worried about him casing the joint. He literally used those words. It was like a line out of 'Matlock.' God bless the old man. I really expected him to show up in a seersucker suit."

Doug laughed. "We should be more worried about Chester driving after dark and owning a firearm and eating pinto beans and cabbage after 6 pm than we should worry about Matthew Prescott." Doug put his arm around Dave and whispered as we approached the porch. "I'm glad he's here anyway. Matthew. I'm glad he's found a home here. Speaking of homes, I hear ya'll are staying a while this time. Good. We like it when our charm lures the famous people back home."

I liked Dave and Ashley. We all did. Love them? Sure. But maybe more importantly, we liked them. Ashley was chatting with Matthew like an old friend. She broke conversation just long enough to give me a hug before I sat down in an old wooden rocker. "Matthew tells me he likes Sharon so far. I guess you guys haven't scared him too much. At least not yet."

"Well, Uncle Bart and Aunt Charlotte aren't here yet."

She spit out some of her sweet tea. "So right, Carlie. So right."

"Matthew, how was work? I mean, are you liking it? Dusty's Shop can get pretty busy. Everything goin' okay?"

"Yeah. I like it. It's busy. But that's better than being too slow. And it's a lot better than...well, it's better than where I have been workin'."

I wasn't sure what to say. I just smiled and nodded. I took a moment to look at Matthew. I mean, really look at him. In so many ways, Aunt Charlotte was right. He didn't look like someone off an episode of "Cops." But he did possess a nervousness, a slight tic almost. He rocked back and forth in the old rocker but it wasn't a relaxed rocking motion. More fast-paced. His dark hair was short, but not military style. It laid down on one side a bit. His skin was clear except for a small shaving cut on his chin. He looked younger than 35. I found that odd because I figured, well, that prison would have aged him. But no. Somehow he had persevered. About 6 ft. tall. Thin, like Dusty. Brown eyes. His blue jeans were new but the faded kind. He wore a simple black t-shirt with no writing on it, which also looked new. His hands were clean but in the way a working man's hands are clean. Not lily white clean. No. Rough and scarred a bit.

When Homer Crittenden's nephew, Jacob, set off some firecrackers about ten feet from the porch, Matthew jumped out of his chair and looked around like a wild animal being hunted. Ashley leaned over the porch railing and told Jacob not to set off any more fireworks because it might scare the kids. But we all knew the truth. It made sense. Fourteen years in prison. Matthew had PTSD.

He apologized. "Sorry. Just been a while since I've heard fireworks, I guess. When I was a kid though, I loved it. My dad took us to this huge fireworks display in San Diego every Fourth of July. I used to tell him that someday I was gonna work for that company. I told my sister that when she grew up, she'd be sitting at the park watching the fireworks and I'd be the one down at the pier making it all happen." He picked up his water glass and smiled as he pointed toward James and Collin who were engaging in some serious "active learning" with two light sabers. "She was so naïve. She probably believed me."

28

I saw this as an opportunity, not to find out what he did, but to find out who he is. "You have a sister, huh?"

He stood and pretended to be in a hurry. "Yeah, Mary, two years younger than me. Ashley, I need to use your restroom."

"Absolutely, first door on the right after you go through the living room."

When the big front door closed behind him, I had to ask. "So, Ashley, what do you think about our newest Sharon resident? He seems like a good guy, huh?"

"Yeah. Plus, I love the fact that he had no idea who I was. I just said, 'Welcome, Matthew! I'm Ashley Harrison Robertson.' And he said, 'Nice to meet you. Do you work at the bank with Doug?' I smiled and said, 'No. I'm busy being a mom to Collin most days.'"

"That was humbling and a little bit wonderful, yes?"

"Yeah. He seems nice though. Sure, a little nervous. But that's to be expected. Fourteen years...well, it's a long time. Think of the life experiences you had between 21 and 35. Isn't it weird to think about being locked up that whole time? Every day. I can't even wrap my brain around it. When Chester pulled up, Matthew got all their stuff out of the car, helped Mrs. Ida with her cane, and helped us set out chairs under the oak tree. It was sweet really."

"I don't guess he said anything about...about what he was in for?"

"No. You mean you don't know?"

"I don't. I'm embarrassed to ask Dusty. He already feels like Matthew is under the gun. I don't want him to think I'm not giving him the benefit of the doubt. Dusty says he's a good guy. That's enough for me or it should be enough anyway. Doug always says, 'He did his time and that's the end of it.' But is it the end? I don't really know."

Dusty and Clara approached the porch as Matthew swung open the front door. They were smiling in that embarrassed way that parents of one-year-olds smile. Beau was screaming at a glass-breaking decibel and squirming to be released from Clara's arms. Dusty looked at him with stern commitment, "You can't play with the big kids, man. You can't even walk yet. Here, we'll set your flying saucer thing up here."

Ashley jumped up from the rocking chair and flung open her arms. "Welcome, McConnells. Welcome!"

Dusty shouted back, "You may not want us today, Ashley!"

"Are you kidding?" She pointed her finger straight at Beau. "I'm not scared of this little guy! I can take whatever he can dish out."

Matthew put out his hand to shake Dusty's, even though they'd been working together less than two hours before.

"Matthew, I thought you'd be sound asleep by now, man!" Dusty wrapped his arm around Matthew's shoulder and loudly declared, "This man put in some kind of day today, Ladies! He's a work horse!"

Matthew's face turned red as he put his hands in his pockets. Out of the corner of my eye, I saw Sarah Simpson's mother, Deloris, carefully placing a 3-layer coconut cake on the food table. Sarah was walking up the driveway carrying a huge

Tupperware tray of deviled eggs that Doug, of course, would never eat even though we all trusted the Simpsons' general commitment to food safety.

"Deloris! Sarah, come on up to the porch!"

"Be there in a minute!"

I can't help being a matchmaker. Lord knows I've tried to not be one. I'm not even saying I'm a good one. I've had more failures than successes. But even if I only had failures, I'd still be a matchmaker. It's kind of like how Aunt Ruth couldn't help sweeping the front porch every day. It was an obsession. Even when Dr. Harris said she was less than a week from death, Aunt Ruth still hobbled out to that porch and swept it every day because sweeping, well, it was part of her identity. I understand that completely.

Plus, just because a man has done prison time, it doesn't mean he doesn't need love. It doesn't even mean he's not willing to do whatever it takes to maintain love. I don't know Sarah Simpson that well but I trust her. She's a third grade teacher. She also teaches James and Collin's Sunday School class and she never seems angry or impatient. Sarah calls their hyperactivity "boyish charm." I mean, come on. Any woman who believes Collin and James are full of boyish charm is alright in my book. She's also one of those women who's not ridiculously good-looking and not ugly either. It's weird. Kind of like, well, like Sigourney Weaver or the actress who plays the nerdy woman on "The Big Bang Theory." You know, the one who used to be on the TV show, "Blossom."

Sarah is about 5'6, straight brown shoulder-length hair, brown eyes, and an average figure. Sweet smile and disposition. A little more in the behind than in the boob area, but again, that's probably the national norm. I noticed she was wearing make-up tonight and cute white capri pants that looked like they came from one of those expensive boutiques. Her solid pink top was made out of a thin billowy material that made everything look as good as it could up top, without being immodest. Push-up bra, maybe? Hmm. I wonder if someone told her that Matthew Prescott is the spitting image of the Channel 6 investigative reporter.

"Sarah, hey! Glad you could come! Have you met our newest Sharon resident? Sarah, Matthew Prescott. Matthew, this is Sarah, the best third grade teacher at Sharon Elementary School."

Sarah laughed and when she did, I noticed she had gotten that chipped front tooth fixed. And she was wearing some serious mauve lip gloss, probably from Emma's bi-monthly Mary Kay party at the Community Center.

She put out her hand to shake Matthew's. "Nice to meet you, Matthew. Actually, I'm the only third grade teacher at Sharon Elementary so I guess it's not hard to be the best one, huh?"

Matthew looked even more nervous than when James broke the glass. He smiled ever so slightly and said in almost a whisper, "Nice to meet you, Sarah."

Sarah grabbed Dusty's arm. "I hear you're workin' for this guy right here. You could definitely have done worse when it comes to bosses. Probably could have done better too...but still."

Dusty pretended to push her off the porch. "Well, if Sarah here had been my third grade teacher, I'd have been even worse off."

"Yeah, 'cause I'm a teacher, not a miracle worker."

Matthew silently leaned against the porch post during the exchange. He hardly moved a muscle. When Dave announced we were gathering out under the oak tree to eat, Matthew stepped off the porch and walked quickly toward the tree never making conversation or looking to see if anyone was beside him. I guess he was used to filing through the meal line, not worrying about social graces. Dave shouted, "Let's pause for a word of thanks! Dusty, would you do the honors?" Dusty ran forward and put his arm around Matthew. He thanked God for friendship and love and for Matthew Prescott coming to town. Then Matthew picked up a paper plate and walked through the line as though he were not one bit worried about being first. It was odd. When he got to the end of the table he just nervously stood there. Ashley said, "We've got these tables set up. Just sit anywhere, Matthew."

He sat at the table closest to the dessert table and looked over both shoulders before he picked up a piece of fish and started eating. That's about the time we heard Aunt Charlotte's loud declaration as she trotted up the driveway. "We're here! We're here! Lord, have mercy! You won't believe what we been through. But we're here now! Bart's parkin' the truck. Hope he don't get stuck out there." She had on a light green house dress with cap sleeves and a John Deere apron. She wore suntan knee-hi hose and those comfortable tan shoes old lady teachers wear from the SAS store. As she ran up the driveway, her arm fat and large breasts moved in rhythmic motion, almost like a synchronized swimmer. Well, like a synchronized swimmer carrying a lard bucket of magic pickles and an extra-large loaf of Bunny bread.

Dave ran to retrieve the pickles and bread. "Welcome, Aunt Charlotte! Glad you made it!"

"Oh Lord, Dave, you won't believe what we been through. Billy Smith, you know…Carl's boy, not the smart one but the one who don't got no sense. Well, he done killed our calf! Right there in the street! Killed her dead! I reckon somebody left the backyard gate open and Sunshine got out and into the street. 'Fore we knew it, tires was squealing and the calf was bawling....oh, it was...." Aunt Charlotte broke down in sobs as Dave grabbed the pickle bucket and loaf of bread. She lifted up the edge of her apron and blew her nose. It sounded like a foghorn on a big cruise ship beckoning everyone back on board.

Uncle Bart came strolling up the driveway wearin' a white t-shirt and overalls. "Quit blubberin', Charlotte. Ain't no cryin' gonna bring that calf back." He looked down at the gravel driveway. "What's done is done."

When they approached the food table, everyone shared their heartfelt condolences. Ida spoke with unusual enthusiasm. "A few years ago that Smith boy hit a cat on our street and Cora Belle ain't never been the same since. Said she always felt that calico cat was her grandmother come back to earth in cat form to look out for her and her sister."

Chester jumped in. "People don't come back as cats, Ida. You know that. Cora Belle ain't got no room to talk. She's more 'an half crazy. Always has been."

Every social event is an opportunity for education, that's what I always say. The Friday night fish fry at Dave and Ashley's was no exception. By the end of the evening, here's what I'd learned: Sarah Simpson got her front tooth fixed and wore new capri pants, which makes me think she's ready for my matchmaking services. Tom Hanks plays Ashley's wealthy uncle in the upcoming movie. Aunt Charlotte is now mourning the death of a calf she wasn't supposed to have in the city limits anyway. Cora Belle Mathis pretends to believe in reincarnation even though she's a Baptist. And Matthew

Prescott? He has a sister named Mary. The rest of his life is a complete mystery.

Chapter 6, CARLIE: Matchmaking Principle #1: Don't Get the Cart Before the Horse (Principle #2: Ignore Principle #1 As Needed)

I don't like to match people in ignorance. So, in honor of my desire to help Sarah Simpson, I headed out to Dusty's Shop Monday morning for an oil change and some undercover detective work concerning Matthew. I'll be the first to admit that my matchmaking attempts are not always successful. Last year I set up Bill Cline, the primary school principal, with Macy Snider, the girl who runs the animal shelter. Turns out he's allergic to pet dander and was offended that she called her dogs her children. According to her, his last words of the evening were, "I work with children every day, Miss Snider. And trust me. These wiener dogs are not children." Boom. That closed the casket on any possible relationship. And I reluctantly buried that matchmaking attempt in the backyard.

When I pulled into the parking lot of Dusty's Shop, Matthew was carrying a tire from the shop to an old truck in the back lot. I waved and he nodded. I realized right then and there why so many women like "worker men" types. I don't know. There's just something about a man wearing work boots and greasy coveralls that makes some women swoon. Of course, I'm happily married to a banker so I make it a point to swoon over khaki pants and a navy jacket myself.

"Matthew! Matthew, how's it goin'? I'm sure you're ridiculously busy!"

He shouted back, "Just about to take a break!" He dropped the tire next to the truck and pulled a red shop rag from his back pocket, wiping his hands as he headed across the lot. "What brings you to Bradford, Carlie?"

"Just an oil change."

"We can fix you up."

"Speaking of fix-ups..." Ooops! Had I just said what I said when I didn't mean to say it yet?

He smiled as he put the rag back into his pocket. "Fix-ups? Were we speaking of fix-ups?"

"Well, I mean, uh...people probably haven't told you yet...I mean, why would they? Uh...I'm...well, I'm..."

"Famous. Yeah, I know. Dusty told me. You sold a bunch of books and made a movie and everything. You've been on TV and have met a bunch of famous people. And he told me that Ashley's famous too. I didn't watch much TV when I was...I'm more of a reader. And I read history books mostly. So I guess I missed your books. And I don't care much about movies so I missed out on Ashley's fame too. Sorry about that."

"Oh, please! No worries. Really. Neither of us care much about being famous so it doesn't bother us when other people don't care either. In fact, it's refreshing."

"Nobody has called me refreshing in a long..." He laughed. "Well, nobody has ever called me refreshing."

"I'm sure! Well, here's the deal and I'll just cut to the chase. I wasn't talking about my fame. I was saying people probably haven't told you I'm a matchmaker. And I was wondering, wondering if you're interested in meeting people, people in our area?"

"Yeah, sure. I liked going to that thing at Dave and Ashley's. I went to the barber shop Saturday, met the mayor and a guy who works at Farm Bureau."

"Well, I'm thinking more along the lines of female people. Dusty says you're a good guy and I'll be honest with you. There aren't a ton of eligible bachelors around here. Are you interested in…"

"Meeting a woman? Yeah. Eventually." He straightened a pile of tires by the front door and avoided eye contact. "The question is probably, 'Is a woman interested in meeting me?' And I can't see that she would be. Not right now anyway."

"And why is that?"

He glanced up at me as he squatted down to pick up a candy wrapper that had blown onto the sidewalk. "You're kidding, right?"

"No. I'm not kidding. Look, you did something bad. You're not the only one, y'know? Our mailman takes a nap every afternoon on Mrs. Eula's back porch. The mayor threw a bottle of syrup at his wife at the Rotary Pancake Breakfast last year. Seriously. It was a full bottle too. The middle school lunch ladies swear up and down they're still findin' sticky spots on the ceiling. The high school football coach got suspended for tackling an official during the Play-offs last year. I mean, put him on the ground and punched his lights out too. And evidently, Cora Belle has paid no attention to her spiritual training because she believes dead people can turn into cats. Stand in line, Matthew. Really. You're not the only messed-up person around here."

He stood up and looked right into my face. It was the first time I had really seen him up close and personal. Up close, he did look 35. Deep lines around his dark brown eyes. I doubted they were laugh lines. He shook his head and spoke quietly, "You guys have no idea. Throwing a syrup bottle? That's embarrassing, yeah. But it's not a felony." He looked down. "I'm a felon, Carlie. That doesn't go away." He turned and pointed toward the service bay. "Go ahead and pull your car in right here. I'll get it taken care of."

"Thanks." I turned to get into my car but quickly turned back around. "Oh, and guess what, Matthew? The mayor? Re-elected the very next year. Seriously. It was a landslide. Wanna know why?"

He laughed as he wiped his sweaty forehead. "Do I have a choice?"

"Not really. Y'see, Mayor Perkins, he got on the radio the very next morning. Apologized to his wife, Gloria, to the people of Sharon, the Rotarians, the children of the area, school officials. Said there was no excuse for such an angry outburst. Real humble like too. Ida said it made his mama cry. And the people 'round here? Well, they forgave him, even re-elected him." I slid into the car seat and rolled down the window. "So really, whatever you did, you didn't do it to the people around here. Nobody's cleaning syrup off the ceiling 'cause of you, Matthew. And even if they were…well, they might be more forgiving than you think. Just remember that."

He grinned as he directed me into the service bay. "I'll try."

Chapter 7, CARLIE: Aunt Charlotte vs. Billy Smith

The Sunday potluck was more crowded than usual even though Dave and Ashley decided to skip out on it. Ashley always drew such a crowd so she sometimes skipped out on Sharon social events to help maintain decorum. (I've always wanted to use that word "decorum.") Aunt Charlotte was busy organizing the dessert table, but she paused and whispered, "Bet they're all here to get a look at Matthew. Don't ya figure?"

I nodded my head in his direction. "And yet, there he is. Looking normal. Disappointing, I'm sure."

Aunt Charlotte rarely picked up on my sarcastic chiding. She shrugged her shoulders. "Well, I reckon it might be for some."

"I was joking. I think there's just a lot of people back in town because school's starting. That's all."

Matthew approached us, looking like a fraternity kid in his khaki pants and navy polo shirt. "Ladies, prepare to be amazed."

Aunt Charlotte yelled out, "Do tell!"

"These are the one-and-only famous peanut butter cookies of my childhood. My neighbor's recipe. Made by yours truly. Yes, with my very own hands in the pleasant but outdated kitchen of Chester and Ida Miller."

I clapped with enthusiasm, "Here, here, my boy! I must give them a taste!"

Aunt Charlotte scolded, "Not till Brother Dan says the prayer, you won't. Mama used to say the food would rot in your stomach if it wasn't blessed."

"Look at these cookies, Aunt Charlotte! And look at this fine young man who prepared them. They're blessed alright. Blessed for sure." I picked out a small one and broke it in half. Aunt Charlotte reluctantly participated in my debauchery.

Her eyes widened and she smiled so big, we could see her missing molars. "Oh Honey, them are some kind of wonderful. What's your secret?"

Matthew winked and set the plate on the table. "If I told you, it wouldn't be a secret anymore, would it?"

Jerry Conner ran up to Aunt Charlotte like the house was on fire and then spoke more quietly than usual. "I'm not supposed to do this on Sunday, Charlotte. But I figured you should know. Carl's boy? He's suing you. Suing you for personal harm, fatigue, damage to a vehicle. I don't know all the legal terms. I'll be bringing the papers by sometime next week. Just wanted to give you a heads-up. Might want to think about getting a lawyer."

Aunt Charlotte broke down in loud sobs. "Suing ME? He's the one who done killed Sunshine! And no, sir. I ain't gettin' no greasy lawyer, Jerry. You can forget about that."

"Look, I understand. I do. Just lettin' you know."

Matthew handed Aunt Charlotte a napkin from the dessert table. "Maybe I can help."

She removed her glasses and wiped her eyes. "I thought you was a mechanic."

"I am. But I spent years studying law too. Couldn't sit for the bar. But I know a lot about the legal system. I could at least do some preliminary work."

"Oh Baby, that would mean the world to me. Carl's boy's a snake though. A snake, I tell ya! Who else would kill a woman's calf and then turn 'round and sue her? Only that Smith young'un. Good Lord, he needs to focus on goin' to drivin' school, not suing an old woman like me."

"When you get the papers, let me know and I'll come help you."

"Oh, thank ya, Darlin'! I'll even cook supper for ya. Surely you're tired of Ida's Shepherd's Pie by now. I ain't never seen people who like Shepherd's Pie more than them two. And not an ounce of fat on either of 'em. Must be that horrible lowfat powdered milk they get from that store...oh, can't think of the name of it. Where all them green beans are three for a dollar 'cause the cans are dented."

Matthew laughed. "It's a deal."

Chapter 8, CARLIE: Hollywood Comes to Sharon

Ashley invited me to come sit on her porch Sunday afternoon
while the boys took naps. We call these little meetings
"Friend Therapy."

"Where to next, Carlie?"

"Philadelphia next week, speaking to a university group about
the connection between writing and rural life. What about
you?"

"I was scheduled to meet with my agent on Thursday in LA.
But I convinced her to come here. She's never been to
Tennessee. I told her she was culturally deficient. That got to
her, I guess. We're picking her up in Nashville on
Wednesday."

"Well, look at you. Ordering people around. The perks of
stardom, eh?"

"The only stars I care about right now are the ones in the sky."

"And that's why we all love ya. Oh, I forgot to tell you the
bad news. Guess who's gettin' sued?"

"Jerry Conner?"

"Probably should be, but no. Aunt Charlotte. It's all about
that whole calf-in-the-street fiasco."

"You're kidding!"

"I wish. Seems Billy Smith is suing for personal distress,
injury, and destruction of property. Or something like that.

But Matthew said he'd studied the law a lot when he was in prison and he'd be willin' to help her with her case."

"A mechanic and a lawyer, huh? Sharon's very own Renaissance man."

"I don't think he's an actual lawyer. He said he couldn't sit for the bar exam, but he knows a lot about the law and could at least do a preliminary assessment of her case."

"Poor Aunt Charlotte. Bad enough to lose Sunshine and now this."

"Okay. Changing the subject, but I have a question for you. What do you think of Sarah Simpson?"

"I like her a lot. Collin loves her. Why?"

"Well, I've been thinkin'. You know, she turned 30 last year. And there's something about her 30th birthday party you probably didn't know 'cause it didn't exactly make the front page of the newspaper."

"Yes?"

"Jerry Conner asked her to marry him."

"No."

"He did. On her actual birthday too. We were all over at her mama's house having cake in the backyard and listening to her little brother play Kenny G. songs on his saxaphone. All of a sudden, it was like Jerry had wasps up his britches. He got all nervous and twitchy and ran up to the cake table and just blurted out, 'Sarah, you're the best thing that's ever happened to me. Will you marry me?'"

"He did not."

"He did. Oh, it was pitiful to watch. I mean, they'd been out all of five times maybe. And he just blurted out a marriage proposal. Right there, in front of everybody. And there was Sarah, mouth open, face turning the color of school glue. The crowd was just silent and Jerry's face grew redder by the minute."

"And?"

"Well, finally, Sarah's mama broke the silence by saying, 'There's more ice cream inside, everybody! Let's all go inside and give these two their privacy.' Whew! That Deloris sure knows how to swoop in and save the day. Of course, we were all glancing out the window every few seconds. But we tried to be discreet about it. Five minutes later Sarah came running in the house and locked herself in the bathroom. We could all hear her crying and flushing the toilet every 30 seconds. So we knew that was our cue that Sarah Simpson's 30th birthday party was officially over. Well, everyone understood that except Uncle Bart. He thought we should stay and find out what happened between her and Jerry. Plus, he kept saying, 'But Deloris promised us Butter Pecan ice cream.' Doug finally promised to bring a whole half gallon to his house if he'd leave. He did. And Doug had to drive all the way to Martin to find a store that was still open."

"So I take it her answer was 'no.'"

"Yeah, and Sarah being the sensitive type, I think it just crushed her to embarrass him like that. Word travels fast around here. She knew everybody would find out."

"But he embarrassed himself, didn't he? Proposing in front of everybody? And when they'd only been out five times?"

"Thank you. Yes, that's what I tried to tell her. But I don't know. She felt sad about it. Plus, she later told me a part of her thought about saying, 'Yes.' She was 30. Jerry was a decent guy. Maybe she should have just decided to love him, to make it work."

Ashley looked at me. "But you're glad she didn't decide that?"

"I am. She's right. Jerry is a decent guy. But, I don't know. He's not right for Sarah."

"Wait a second. You're not planning one of your matchmaking things, are you?" Ashley started laughing. "I thought you learned your lesson with that principal and pet dander debacle."

"Hey, I can't be responsible for a man with dander issues." I smiled as I looked out on the lake. A family of ducks had formed a perfect line on the water. "And yes, I am matchmaking. Kind of. Maybe."

"And who's the lucky bachelor? You wouldn't keep a secret from one of your very best friends, would you?"

"No. Not normally. But yes, this time I'm keeping a tight lip. I just need a little time. Besides, I don't want you to accuse me of jumping the gun. I'm not Jerry Conner, y'know."

Chapter 9, CARLIE: Shayla McGuire Comes to Town

I like giving tours of our farm. I especially like giving tours to people who haven't spent much time on a farm. Such is the case with Ashley's agent, Shayla McGuire. According to Ashley, Shayla spent most of her life in Toronto and moved to LA five years ago. She, Ashley, and Collin were to arrive at 9:00 am. I made blueberry muffins (from a box) and strong coffee and then sat on the porch. James played on the swing set, enjoying his last days of summer freedom.

They pulled into the drive at 9:20. Ashley immediately began her apology tour as she opened the car door. "Oh, Carlie! Sorry we're late. We just...well, there were just..."

A blonde woman, wearing jeans and a gray t-shirt shouted, "It was me! Just couldn't get going this morning."

"No worries! Come on up!"

Collin ran to the swing set as Ashley and Shayla approached the porch.

"Carlie, this is my agent and friend, Shayla McGuire. Shayla, this is the famous Carlie Jameson."

Shayla put out her hand and as she did, I noticed she had on very little make-up. Blonde hair in a ponytail. Green eyes. A regular girl, but beautiful in a natural way. Unpretentious. She had perfect eye contact but sounded almost nervous. "It's an honor to meet you. Really. I love your work. The books as well as the movies. And if Carrie Blackstone ever doesn't do right by you, well, I'm available to represent you."

I laughed, "Never let an opportunity pass you by, eh? I like that. Thank you. I've gotta ask. You're way younger than I expected. How did you become an agent so young? Must be a go-getter."

"I hope so. But I did get some big breaks. My dad has been in the business for forever. Ashley was my first big client. I was lucky. She signed on with me before, well, before…"

"Before she became an A-list celebrity?"

"Exactly. And now? Now I'm left catering to her constant diva demands." She smiled and placed her hand on Ashley's shoulder. "It's a burden. A cross to bear really."

"Oh, I'm sure! You wouldn't believe what she's always demanding of the Sharon folks! Why, she asks for lemon with her water nearly every time we go to the diner downtown. Uptown Sally. That's what we call her. Pretty soon she'll be asking for biscuits without gravy. Oh, and if she gets another Oscar nomination, no tellin' what kind of nonsense we're gonna have to tolerate around here."

Ashley shoved me in the shoulder. "Look who's talkin'. Shayla, you'll have to see this diva's shower in the upstairs bathroom. It even has surround sound."

I attempted to set the record straight. "Only to pipe in romantic music to keep the marital flames burning. Priorities, people! It's not common knowledge but REO Speedwagon and Lionel Ritchie can literally change the direction of a marriage." I laughed. "Seriously. They have that kind of power. Okay. You gals, have a seat on the swing. I'll bring out some muffins and coffee and we can chat before the tour."

It's weird how I kept getting images wrong. I'd envisioned Matthew as looking like a thug. He didn't. I'd envisioned Shayla as looking like Kim Kardashian, complete with leopard print leggings. But she didn't. She looked like us. Like Sharon people. Well, not exactly. Mabel, down at the coffee shop, does wear tight leopard print leggings. But Mabel looks nothing like Kim Kardashian. At all. Trust me. No relation.

I came back out to the porch carrying a tray. I learned that from the movies. No one in my family ever carried a tray to serve guests. But I had seen it in "Guess Who's Coming to Dinner" and even though I wore mom jeans, I was determined to live with the same style and grace as Katharine Hepburn.

"So, Shayla, tell me your life story. Really. Start at the beginning. Or wherever you'd like."

"You're not making book notes. Are you?"

"Who me? Absolutely not. I've got nothing more than a coffee spoon in my hand. But I should warn you. I have a pretty good memory."

She grabbed a muffin and smiled. "Yeah, I was afraid of that."

Ashley put her arm around Shayla. "Look, it's only right that I should warn you about something. Carlie's not just a best-selling author. Oh no. She's a matchmaker. A really bad matchmaker. But still. You've been warned."

Shayla laughed while I spoke calmly, "Ashley's just jealous that she doesn't have my gift. A great actress? Absolutely. But she'll never have the keen insight I do. She'll never understand why the organist at First Methodist and the retired postmaster are meant to be together. She'll never have the courage to make that happen. That's where I come in. Yep! The people around here depend on me, Shayla."

Shayla leaned back in the porch swing. "I'm definitely looking for someone with insight. I'm on a project, Carlie. A project you might be able to help me with."

"Oh, I love projects. I mean, especially projects that other people have to accomplish. How can I help?"

"You may have heard about the reality show called, 'Standing My Ground.' Ever heard of it?"

"No. Can't say that I have."

"Yeah. It tanked after only three episodes. It was supposed to be about these seismologists and how they can predict potential earthquakes. But evidently the general public doesn't really want to get to know seismologists and they aren't as interested in earthquakes as the network thought."

"So, what does that have to do with you?"

"Daddy and I helped with the casting. Oh, the network is not blaming us. They said the show was their idea. But we're kind of wanting to pitch something, something that might make up for it. Something fresh. Something people would be interested in watching."

Ashley sat her coffee cup on the table. "Tell me you're not wanting to cast Carlie in a matchmaking show. I love the woman. I do. But the postmaster is like 100 years old and he'll never tolerate Ms. Eula's constant complaining about her arthritis. He'll be out by the second date."

Shayla spoke with half humor and half seriousness. "I don't know. That might be pretty interesting to watch though."

I jumped to my feet. "I've got it! I do! An idea."

Ashley looked frightened. "Yes?"

"Shayla, what about, well, what about an ex-convict who runs a small business and hires an ex-convict and then puts an ad in the paper telling everyone in the community that the new guy is an ex-convict. And everyone has to come to grips with it all and the small town rallies around the man…or doesn't rally…and the guy, uh, well, I don't know. I mean, I don't know how it's gonna finish 'cause it hasn't finished yet. It just got started."

Shayla leaned forward. "Is this real? I mean, you're not saying you know of a real life situation like this?"

"As a matter of fact I do."

"And you think they'd be willing to tell their story? I mean, on a TV show?"

"Uh, well, no. I'm not sure they'd be willing. But we won't know if we don't ask, right?"

Shayla responded as though she'd won the lottery. "This sounds marvelous. Really! Where do we find these guys?"

"Well, we could find them down the road in Bradford. But let's not disturb them during work hours. No. Let's make a plan that will be much more conducive to a 'yes.' What are you doing for supper tomorrow night, Shayla?"

She grinned. "Well, I do believe I'm meeting you and a couple of ex-convicts, Carlie."

"Yes, ma'am. Yes, you are."

Chapter 10, Carlie: Hollywood Comes Knockin'

The very next morning the big news around Sharon was that
Billy Smith had decided not to sue Aunt Charlotte. Seems
Matthew Prescott went to visit him yesterday afternoon,
explained some things about liability and well, I don't
know…about hitting a calf in broad daylight, I guess. It seems
to me that most reasonable people know that a person who hits
a 100 lb. calf in a 30 mph zone in the middle of the afternoon
is a brick shy of a full load anyway. I'm not sure if that's
what Matthew Prescott said. But I do know his successful
efforts merited an invitation to a chili supper at Aunt Charlotte
and Uncle Bart's house last night. I saw Mrs. Ida at the Dollar
General Store this morning and she gave me the whole scoop.
She was buying TUMS, and telling everyone in the store that
poor Matthew was up half the night with heartburn.

We usually got together with the McConnells on Friday night
anyway. So a pizza party at our house wasn't the least bit
surprising to Dusty and Clara. Inviting Dave and Ashley and
their out-of-town guest, Shayla, wasn't surprising either.
When Dusty asked if Matthew could come, well, it all seemed
to just be falling in place. But if there's one thing I've learned
it's that things that seem to be falling into place sometimes go
Kaboom! Just ask the primary school principal and the girl
who runs the animal shelter.

Dusty, Clara, Matthew, and the kids arrived early. James
asked if he could put gel in his hair before they arrived. I later
learned he wanted the gel because it made his hair curlier and,
in his words, "Molly just loves my curly hair, Mama!" Lord,
help us. Seriously.

When Dave pulled the Escalade into the driveway, James and
the kids ran out to greet Collin. When Shayla got out of the
backseat, she looked almost nothing like the young girl of

yesterday. She had on a bright blue blouse tucked neatly into fitted black dress pants. Her blonde hair hung loosely around her face and she wore make-up. Not too much, but enough to show she meant business. She was beautiful. I had to wonder if Matthew would notice. Of course, he would. Would her beauty complicate the project? I had no idea. Truthfully, it was too late to care.

"Welcome, Robertsons! Shayla, you too, friend!"

While Dave and Ashley were giving instructions to Collin before he hit the swing set, Shayla walked onto the porch alone. Dusty, Matthew, and Doug rose from their chairs because that's what gentlemen do when they meet a woman.

"Doug, Honey, this is Shayla, Ashley's agent, friend, and confidante. Oh, and Shayla, this is Doug, the love of my life. And this is Dusty, our friend for what seems like forever. His wife, Clara, who has been my friend since leg warmers were in…and this is our new friend, Matthew. Matthew Prescott."

Shayla shook Doug's hand, then Dusty's. Finally, she shook Matthew's hand and looked into his eyes. "Nice to meet you. All of you."

Dusty spoke up, "Welcome to Sharon, Shayla. What brings you to our beautiful neck of the woods?"

"Ashley just wouldn't take 'no' for an answer. I'd never been to Tennessee and she shamed me and convinced me such neglect was almost un-American." She laughed. "But I'm glad she did. I like it here. It's beautiful."

We did all the regular stuff we do on Friday nights. The pizza man brought pizza. Doug let James drink orange soda, which made him burp so loud the neighbors probably heard it. We

53

felt we should scold rather than laugh. But everyone knows a curly-headed burping five-year-old is one of life's amusing treasures.

Beau took his first real steps, right there on the porch. We all took pictures and video. Clara cried and called Aunt Charlotte with the news. Y'see, Beau is eighteen months old and they were beginning to wonder if he'd ever let go, step out...trust himself. It's a scary thing. Not being afraid. Letting go. Just ask Matthew Prescott.

I knew the kids would soon get cranky and everyone would make plans to leave. So I made an announcement. "Oh, guess what? I have news. Big news! And it involves all of you, or it could anyway. Let's go inside and let the kids play in James' room and we can all sit in the living room."

When everyone had found a comfortable spot, I made my introduction. "Shayla McGuire is our guest tonight. Yes. But she's also here to pitch an idea. If you hate the idea, I think we all should blame Shayla and Hollywood in general." They chuckled. "But if you love the idea? Well, if you love it, I'm happy to take partial credit. Shayla, you have the floor....even though it's covered with toys!"

She leaned forward as though she were a teacher telling her class they could all get into the prize box and retrieve a toy. "Carlie has given me an idea, a great idea. But it involves your cooperation, your willingness to see it through. My dad and I are wanting to pitch a new reality show to A & E. And we may have found our subjects right here, in Sharon."

Dusty hollered out, "Oh no! Aunt Charlotte and her magic pickles are gonna be famous! Weakley County will never be able to recover. Wal-Mart will be selling 'Uncle Bart's Buttermilk' shirts by the end of the year." He looked straight at Shayla. "Tell me it's not true. And tell me she won't have to give up those knee-high hose and housecoat dresses!" Everyone laughed.

Shayla smiled. "Sadly, I haven't met Aunt Charlotte yet. So, no. The people I'm talking about are here, in the room right now. Dusty, from what I hear, you're pretty vocal with your life story. Why not take it to a national audience? I promise we'd treat it with respect. Ex-con overcomes all kinds of tragedy and finds new life in a sleepy southern town. People love stuff like that."

Dusty looked confused. "What are you talking about?"

"I'm talking about you, your shop, and well, about Matthew here too. I'm talking about a show that tells your story. But don't decide right now. And no, it won't make you look bad or dumb or I don't know. I'm talking about a story that gives people hope. Isn't that what you want to do? Give people hope?"

Shayla may only be in her late twenties. But good night. The girl is good. I'm thinking she could sell a sun lamp to the mayor of Phoenix.

The room was quiet. Deathly quiet. She raised her right hand and spoke again. "Look, I am friend, not foe. I promise. Matthew, what do you think? I mean, wouldn't you want to turn your life story into something that would help people?"

He looked up, making direct eye contact with Shayla. For a moment, he looked just like Beau when he finally let go of the porch rocker and started walking. Fearless. "Is that what reality TV does? It gives people hope? 'Cause I don't know. I'm not a big TV watcher, but the reality TV I have seen doesn't seem to give hope. It exploits people's mistakes, their bad days. So, no. I wouldn't want to turn my life into a twenty-minute TV episode every week. I doubt that twenty minutes would change anyone's life, not for the better anyway. Dusty, do what you want. But count me out. My family has been through enough."

Dusty cleared his throat. "I don't understand. I thought you were an agent. You're saying you're a producer too?"

"No. But my dad and I, we pitch ideas sometimes. He's friends with a producer and he's looking for a new show. They just had one that flopped. Look, I'm not out to exploit anyone and neither is my dad. At least come to Hollywood and talk to him about it. He's excited about the idea. He doesn't want something sleazy. And you guys are anything but sleazy. I mean, look at you. You're successful and happy. What could go wrong?"

Doug was always the voice of reason. "How about everyone just go home and sleep on it? Shayla, when do you go back to California?"

"Monday morning."

"Okay. Well, that gives them the weekend, right?"

She looked like she'd been hit by a truck. "Well, yes. But honestly, I can't see the hesitation. Do you know how many people would love to have their own reality TV show?"

Matthew stood. "No. How many?"

For the first time, she looked nervous. "Well, tons of people."

Matthew picked up his water glass and headed toward the kitchen. "Then maybe you should contact them."

She followed after him like a puppy wanting attention. "At least think about it. Can you do that?"

He turned around and smiled. "Sure. No man was ever hurt by thinking."

"And what about you, Dusty? Can I tell my dad you're at least going to consider the possibility? The trip to California?"

"Things are busy at the shop. I can't see takin' off any time soon. But as for the show, yes, I'll think about it. Matthew's right. Nothin' wrong with thinkin'. We better round up the kids." Ashley and Clara headed down the hallway. Dusty smiled, put his arm around my shoulder, and said with an air of chastisement, "Carlie, are you saying this was your idea?"

"Uh, yeah. Hello! I'm a writer. I'm always looking for a story. And yes, it was my idea because, yeah, I think it could help people. It's helped me. It's helped the people of this community. Clearly, it's helping Matthew."

Shayla picked up her bright red purse that cost twice as much as Dusty's work boots. I found myself wishing she had worn jeans and the gray t-shirt to the living room negotiations. Maybe it all would have gone better. She tried to put a happy spin on it. "Well, thanks for thinking about it. If you have any questions, I'm at Dave and Ashley's all weekend. Oh, and when you're thinking about it, think about this. Look at Ashley and Carlie. They're famous. Do you think their lives help people? Their work? Matthew, do they look exploited to you?"

He hesitated. "I don't know them well enough to know. Let me get back to you on that."

Chapter 11, CARLIE: The Hard Sell Never Works or Does it?

Shayla was smart enough to leave Dusty and Matthew alone on Saturday. Dave and Ashley took her on a pontoon boat tour of Reelfoot Lake. According to Ashley, Shayla flirted with the good-looking park ranger, took tons of pictures, ate fried fish at Boyette's, and never once mentioned her business proposal.

But come Sunday morning, I had a feeling the recruiting gloves were back on. Matthew wore his standard khaki pants to church but this time with a white button-down oxford shirt that had been ironed. Had he ironed it himself? To try to impress Shayla? Or had Mrs. Ida ironed it for him because she didn't want her new boarder to look like an ex-con? I didn't bother asking.

Matthew sat next to Uncle Bart and Aunt Charlotte during the church service. That made perfect sense to me. Aunt Charlotte attracts young single men like a magnet. Oh, not for that reason. My word, no. She's old enough to be Matthew's grandma and her breath smells like pickles and Fun-yuns.

People are attracted to Aunt Charlotte because she found a crippled bird on her back porch and took care of it until it could fly. She cried when the high school principal was forced into retirement because he had Alzheimers. When Dave went to rehab, she sent him cookies and cheese crackers. She went to the sheriff when Dusty was falsely accused of drug dealing and pleaded his case. I don't know. It's like Aunt Charlotte wears a sign that says, "Free hugs" or "No condemnation." Yeah. I think it's that last one. Matthew was drawn to Aunt Charlotte for the same reason all of us were. She had assaulted him. Assaulted him with unconditional love.

Dave, Ashley, and Shayla sat on the pew right behind them. It was quite a Sunday too. Mabel led the kids' choir in "Leaning on the Everlasting Arms" complete with hand motions. But on the very last verse, Tyler Mathis grabbed himself and yelled out, "Granny, my pee pee gots to pee pee! My pee pee gots to pee pee!" His grandma was completely mortified because Sally Mathis is the kind of woman who gets mortified pretty easily. She still talks about the day she forgot to paint her eyebrows on and I ran into her at the Dollar General. I never would have even noticed had she not tried to hide behind that big pallet of dog food.

Thankfully, Sarah Simpson saved the day as well as the dignity of the closing song. Tyler was a student in her Sunday School class along with Collin and James. Oh, and Tyler fit right in too…considering he had plenty of hyperactive "boyish charm." Sarah whisked Tyler off stage all the while whispering, "It's okay, Honey. We'll get you to the bathroom." That made me like Sarah even more. I glanced across the aisle at Jerry Conner and for a moment I felt sad for him. Not only had he humiliated himself at her birthday party last year, but he had actually quenched any possible future with her.

Aunt Charlotte laughed as Sarah discreetly escorted Tyler away. Then Aunt Charlotte shouted, "Keep praisin' the Lord, Mabel! Keep praisin' the Lord!" That's when Mabel cued Mr. Dickenson to continue on the piano and they finished the song. Matthew smiled and put his arm around Aunt Charlotte. I wondered if it was his way of saying, "You are a breath of fresh air." I felt certain it was.

After service, Shayla acted completely enamored with Matthew Prescott. Was it a form of salesmanship? Or was she one of those gals who always liked men she knew her daddy wouldn't approve of? I had no way of knowing. She wore a black pencil skirt and a silky white blouse that accentuated all the positive aspects of being a natural beauty. She touched him on the arm and leaned back laughing as they recounted the Tyler Mathis scene. He smiled but never in a flirty way.

When I approached them, Shayla said, "What a great service! Really. And not just the closing song either. No. The whole thing. It was beautiful." She turned to Matthew. "Are you a church-goer, Matthew? I mean, is this your thing normally?"

"Not growing up, no. But yes, I went to services a lot in prison."

She placed her arm carefully around his waist and leaned in. "But I'm sure it wasn't as exciting as that last song, huh?"

He smiled and said nothing.

Sarah Simpson seemed unusually shy as she walked up the center aisle. Aunt Charlotte reached out and grabbed her by the arm. "Here's the woman who saved the day right here! Shayla, this is our very own Sarah Simpson."

"Nice to meet you, Sarah. What do you do in this lovely community?"

"I'm a teacher. And of course, a transporter of kids to the bathroom. Obviously."

Matthew laughed and said, "It's an important job. At least it was today."

Sarah started blushing. "Thanks." She held out her arms as though she were addressing a large crowd. "I live to serve the bathroom needs of kids everywhere."

I jumped in. "Sarah, come to lunch with us. Please. We're stuck with all these yahoos. We'd love for you to join us. Doug's just pickin' up chicken. There'll be plenty."

"Okay. Sure."

Sarah was dressed appropriately for a porch picnic. She had on bright blue cotton pants and one of those stylish shirts that looks like a big multi-colored silk handkerchief. Uh, I don't know how to describe it. But I got the definite feeling Sarah Simpson had been shopping at the boutique downtown because she even had on a bright red and white beaded necklace, which could be referred to as a "statement piece." If you don't know what a "statement piece" is, you should watch some episodes of "What Not To Wear." It's on Netflix. It also looked like she'd gotten highlights and curled her hair with a big curling iron.

Truthfully, Sarah's appearance was a bit out of character. At her birthday party last year, she wore long ugly denim shorts and a green t-shirt she'd gotten free from the Soybean Festival Fun Run. But today? Well, today she looked like a woman trying to do the best she could to get a man's attention. Attention in a good way, not like the kind Beyonce gets the morning after a music awards show.

For just a moment I was mad. Mad at the system. The system that hadn't really changed since the beginning of time. Sarah was funny and kind and she was definitely trying. Trying to be beautiful. Engaging. But Shayla? She didn't have to try at all. It was effortless. Maddening.

Chapter 12, CARLIE: Winner, Winner...Chicken Dinner

After most of the chicken had been consumed, Aunt Charlotte clapped her hands together. "I have an announcement! I do! That was my last meal right there. My last decent meal anyway."

Doug stopped cleaning up the boxes. "What do you mean? Is something wrong?"

"Yes, somethin's wrong! I'm fat, Doug! Ain't you noticed, Hon? I'm fatter than a polar bear or one of 'em big fat seals. What are they called? Sea lions, yeah. I'm fatter than a dad gum sea lion." She grabbed her inner arm. "Look at this flab! This right here could keep an Eskimo alive for a year. I'm on the wagon. I gotta be. Doc Wilson's gonna shoot me if I gain another pound."

Dave put his arm around her. "I have never seen a sea lion wear a John Deere apron. And I've been to SeaWorld a lot too."

"Well, apron or not, I'm done with eatin'. Or done eatin' the good stuff anyway. I'm announcing it 'cause I need your help. If you see me eatin' somethin' greasy or sweet or good tastin', just pop me on the hand real good."

Doug laughed, "You'd pop us back, wouldn't you?"

She grabbed his arm and grinned. "I just might. But you gotta love me enough to try it anyway. Okay. That's the end of my rantin'. Anybody else got news?"

Shayla cleared her throat and straightened her tight-fitting skirt as she stood. "I do! I'm trying to convince Dusty and Matthew here to become famous and I need your help. My dad and I think we can get them a reality show about two ex-convicts and their lives in a small rural community. But they're both hesitant. And I need you folks to help me convince them."

Uncle Bart yelled out, "Them two is smart to leave well enough alone. Last thing we need is a bunch of camera men 'round here. Bad enough with all of Ashley's fame and nonsense." He turned to face Ashley. "Sorry, Darlin'. You know we all think a lot of ya."

Ashley nodded and pursed her lips together to keep from laughing.

Shayla continued, "But don't you think they have a great story?" She put her arm out toward Matthew's shoulder like one of the pretty girls on Price is Right pointing to a new refrigerator or jet ski. "Don't you think people would be inspired?"

Matthew stood. "I'm sorry. I've gotta go. I told Mrs. Ida I'd mow and trim this afternoon. Dusty, can you give me a ride?"

Before Dusty could respond, Sarah said, "I'm going right by there. And I need to get home too. I've got some lesson plans to work up."

"Thank you. I'd appreciate it." He put his hand out toward Doug. "Doug, thanks. Carlie, it was a great meal." He spoke quieter now. "Shayla, I need a little more time."

Shayla stood and leaned in close as she patted him on the back. "Just don't take too long, Matthew. Sometimes opportunity knocks only once."

Aunt Charlotte ran up to give him a hug. "Come see me soon, Baby. I'll make some of that chili again."

Matthew's face turned red. "I'm not man enough for that chili, Aunt Charlotte." He turned toward Shayla, "Dusty and I will talk about it and get back to you."

Chapter 13, SARAH: Rose Bushes Always Have Thorns

"I'm the blue Ford Focus. Right here. The one that really needs to be washed. Oh, and let me move all those school books. Occupational hazard, I guess."

"Looks fine to me."

Matthew smiled and it made me nervous. He reminded me a lot of Jim Faulkner. Jim was the quarterback of our high school team and all the girls wanted to date Jim and be up close to Jim and get attention from Jim. Me? I never even tried to get his attention. Why waste the effort?

"It gets me where I'm going, I guess."

"Where are you going exactly?"

"Well, in the morning, at a really godless hour, I'll be going to Sharon School to work carpool line. If you mean in life, I hope I'm going a direction that helps kids and teaches them their times tables, at least."

He started laughing as he slid into the front seat. "No. I mean, where are you going right now? Like where do you live?"

"Oh, sorry! Good night! Yes, well, I live just two streets down from you actually. Yeah. Right across from the gas station. Yellow house that needs a paint job. Rows and rows of beautiful rose bushes. That's me."

"Yeah. I know that place. I walked to the barber shop and I would have passed right by you, yes?"

"Right. Speaking of the barber shop, I guess you got an earful of all the Sharon news there."

"I don't know enough people here to have understood half of what they were talkin' about. But yeah, they do like to talk. That's for sure."

"I've lived here my whole life. It never really changes. Just the names change, I guess. Of course, you fixed all that, Matthew. Really. Some of the women's groups should pay you for the excitement you've provided."

He stared out the passenger window but I could still see him smiling. "I do what I can."

"Of course, if you had a few more tattoos or piercings, it would have added some credibility to your story. Mabel is still not buying the bit that you were in prison. She said we'd be able to see it in your eyes."

We were at the only stop sign in town, when he looked at me and said in a quiet voice, "See what?"

I could feel my face growing warmer. "I'm not sure really. You'll have to ask Mabel. I guess she expected to see more, more pain, I guess."

"And pain shows up in the eyes, huh?"

"According to Mabel it does." I'm not sure why I said what I said next. But I'm glad I did. "How's it been? Bein' here in Sharon? The adjustments and all?"

We were sitting in front of Chester and Ida's house now but he didn't touch the car door handle. He looked at me again.

66

"Are you asking what it feels like to spend fourteen years in prison and then move into Chester and Ida's guest room?"

"I guess."

He stared out the front window. "It feels like...like the way you feel when you've worked hard outside all day and someone brings you a glass of lemonade. Or like you've heard about the beach for years... and then one day you're standing there, at the edge of the water...and you still can't believe you're there, able to put your feet in the water and everything."

Something about his words and the way he said them almost brought me to tears. "Who knew Chester and Ida's little guest room had so much power, huh?"

He chuckled, "Yeah. I'm convinced it's that paisley velvet wallpaper."

"You know how people always say, 'If walls could talk...' well, if Chester and Ida's walls could talk, I think they'd reveal that not much has changed in that house. Probably pretty much the same routine every day for the last 50 years."

He smiled. "They're pretty set in their ways, yeah. But I like them. Both of them. No pretense."

For some reason, I didn't want him to touch that door handle. So I pulled a desperation move. "And how's your work? You like workin' for Dusty?"

"It's Dusty. Who wouldn't like working for him, right?" He tapped his fingers nervously on the door panel. "Dusty came to visit me a lot. Sent letters. Told me all along I'd have a job when I got out. But you know, people talk. Not Dusty though. He came through."

"Oh, and what about your impending fame? From Chester and Ida's paisley guest room to reality TV star, huh?"

He shook his head. "I don't know. But I trust Dusty. I'll probably do it if he wants to. Of course, that means everyone will find out...you know, find out more about me."

"Carlie always says nothing good comes from secrets. Or something like that."

"There aren't secrets anymore anyway. Not really. Anybody can google my name. I figure some people already have." He looked at me like he was asking a question. His eyes were so brown they looked black. His hands looked rough as he nervously moved them about. I wanted to touch them. Hold them.

"I haven't."

He reached into his pocket to retrieve his keys and then opened the door. He stepped out but stuck his head back in. "Maybe you should. Teachers shouldn't be seen with known felons anyway, right?"

"I spend every day with third graders. Life can't get more dangerous than that."

He laughed. "Livin' on the edge, huh? Maybe Shayla McGuire needs to talk to you about a reality show and leave Dusty and me alone."

"For sure. Look, I know you're new in town. So if you need anything, I mean, information or something about…something, anything." I was drowning. "You can call me."

"I don't have a phone yet. But thanks for the ride. I appreciate it."

"Oh, no problem. Bye!"

"Bye."

He waved, turned and walked toward the front door. I realized now why I never tried to get Jim Faulkner's attention. It was because of this feeling. The feeling of my face getting warm but the other guy walking away without my phone number. Without even caring. Matthew Prescott was 35 years old. He didn't own a house, a car, or even a cell phone. He'd spent the last fourteen years in prison. A miserable flight risk, to be sure. Sadly, I didn't care about his past any more than he cared about my present.

Chapter 14, SARAH: Carlie's Right About Secrets

Of course, I did it. Anyone would have done it. I unlocked the front door and went straight to my laptop. Matthew Prescott. Nevada insurance salesman. No. 2004 Rigby High School Science award. No. Investment banker. Co-anchor Seattle morning news. No. No. Matthew Prescott. January 12, 2000, The Tennessean. Prescott Sentenced to 25 Years. Click.

The Tennessean- Tuesday morning Matthew Prescott, son of California software mogul, Jonathan Prescott, was sentenced to 25 years in prison for the deaths of his sister, 19-year-old Mary Prescott, and her roommate, 21-year-old Caroline Fitzgerald, both of San Diego, California. Both women were Vanderbilt students at the time of death.

In November of 1999 a jury found Prescott guilty of two counts of vehicular homicide related to a one-car accident on I-40. According to police reports, in the early morning hours of September 2, 1999, Prescott was driving a 1997 BMW at approximately 85 miles per hour when he hit a guard rail. Both women were ejected from the vehicle and declared dead on the scene. Prescott sustained a broken leg, broken arm, and a bruised rib. Hospital tests later revealed the presence of multiple prescription drugs in his system. His blood alcohol level was over the legal limit. Prescott's license had been suspended four months earlier related to a DUI charge.

In a story that drew national attention, both of Prescott's parents testified vigorously on behalf of the prosecution and later told reporters that their son's drug use was out of control. A tearful Emilia Prescott told CNN reporter, Julie Hilton, "Matthew's drug use was getting worse. He'd just flunked out of his first year of law school. But now his drug use has taken our beautiful baby girl. And we'll never get her back. She's gone forever. She never caused us one moment of sorrow. Never brought us anything but joy."

Judge Mary Kathleen Baker sentenced 21-year-old Prescott on Tuesday morning in a courtroom filled with reporters and family members. He was immediately taken into custody and is expected to serve the majority of his sentence in Nashville. Reporters asked his father, Jonathan Prescott, for a comment as he exited the courtroom. He spoke three words. "Justice was served."

I'm not sure what I'd expected to find when I went searching for Matthew Prescott's name. But I hadn't expected this. His tragic error in judgment hadn't just cost him fourteen years of freedom. No. That was only a tiny part of the cost. He'd lost his sister. He'd even lost his parents. His life.

Chapter 15, CARLIE: What Have I Done? (Sadly, I Have To Ask This Question a Lot)

I agreed to ride with Ashley and Shayla to the Nashville airport. We wanted to take James and Collin to the Children's Museum anyway, so it was perfect timing really. But first, Shayla requested a stop at Dusty's Shop in Bradford.

Dusty was washing down the concrete floor with an old water hose when we got out of Ashley's Escalade. He started laughing. "Let me guess. You gals and you two little fellas just happened to be in the neighborhood and you wanted to bring Matthew and me some doughnuts from Sally's. Ol' Sally makes a mean doughnut. Sure does. Plus, we need to fatten Matthew up anyway. So bring 'em on, ladies! Bring 'em on."

Shayla was wearing tight-fitting black jeans and a bright red t-shirt. Her high heeled sandals clicked on the pavement as she pulled out her pointer finger. "No doughnuts for you, Mister! We gotta keep both you guys looking slim. The camera adds twenty pounds! Remember?"

Dusty turned off the hose and walked toward us. Matthew walked up next to him. They both wore light blue work shirts with their names proudly emblazoned on the patch. Dusty spoke with zeal. "Oh, we're all about image, Shayla. Yes, ma'am. It's funny you should walk up 'cause Matthew and I were just saying we needed to work on our social media business. Weren't we, Matthew?"

"Uh, I think we were saying we needed to place an order for Pennzoil 30 weight today."

Dusty laughed. "Oh yeah! That's what it was. How can we help you ladies? Oil change? Tire rotation?"

Shayla smirked. "No. You can tell me that you're willing to at least shoot a pilot. Look, that's all we're asking for. One 40-minute pilot. A crew comes here, spends a few days, and it's over. I mean, what can that hurt? Right? We don't even know the network will want it."

Dusty looked more serious. "We're open to it. We are. But we have a question. What kind of editing control do we have? What if we think the pilot makes us look like idiots and we want to pull the plug?"

"You'll have the freedom to do that. But you won't want to. I've tried to explain we're not trying to do a Jersey Shore thing. Seriously. We want it to be inspirational and funny and real. It's worth a try, right? I mean, if the folks in California decide it's a go, I can tell Daddy to get the papers to you next week, yes?"

Dusty put his arm around Matthew. "What do ya think, brother? Think we should try our hand at the biz? Carlie and Ashley here are starting to think they're the only ones worth makin' a deal over. Let's give 'em a run for their money. What do ya say?"

Matthew smiled. "I'm in."

Shayla jumped up and down like Publisher's Clearing House people had arrived at her door with a dozen roses. "Yes! Oh, yes! You won't regret this! You won't!"

She shook Dusty's hand but then reached up and kissed Matthew on the cheek. He tried to hide his embarrassment by turning to open the second garage door.

She spoke quickly as she turned to get in the front passenger seat. "Look, I've gotta catch a plane. But I'll be in contact. I will. You guys have a great day. Oh, and stay away from the doughnuts."

On the way to Nashville, Shayla talked non-stop about the project. "So, what do you think about Matthew? I mean, viewers are just going to eat him up, right?"

I patted her arm. "He's a sweetheart alright."

"He's positively dreamy."

Ashley spoke with an air of caution, "Shayla, you're not…I mean, you don't have a thing for Matthew, do ya?"

"Ashley! I'm a professional! Of course not! Just because I'm looking doesn't mean I'm buying. But I've gotta admit he does have a certain presence. It's a good thing I don't live here or I might find myself tempted to mix business with pleasure."

"Your last boyfriend was an investment banker who lived in Beverly Hills and looked like Orlando Bloom. And you're saying now you're interested in a car mechanic in Bradford, Tennessee? A car mechanic who was just released from prison?"

"No. I'm saying it's tempting. And the whole ex-con thing, well, you've gotta be honest, girls." She lowered her voice. "There's a certain mystique to that. And that's what I'm counting on."

We dropped Shayla at the airport and part of me felt relieved. We spent most of the morning and early afternoon at the museum. The boys slept on the way home and I kept thinking about Shayla's words. Was there really a mystique to Matthew's years of imprisonment? And if the TV show took off, what complications would that bring? I started wondering if I'd made a horrible mistake by suggesting the show in the first place. I also wondered if Aunt Charlotte would be able to live without fried food. No woman on earth loved to crank up the Fry Daddy more than she did.

**Chapter 16, CARLIE: (one month later) Aunt Charlotte
Lost Three Pounds and Hollywood Came to Sharon**

Aunt Charlotte acts like she's lost 50 pounds. But she hasn't.
She's lost three. Yep! Three pounds in four weeks. She told
Uncle Bart she felt like a new woman. Uncle Bart said, "I
don't need me a new woman. I'm used to the old one."

Collin and James have been in Kindergarten for two weeks
now. Doug and I didn't cry on the first day of school and
neither did James. He was so excited about showing his
teacher his Spiderman lunchbox, that he hardly noticed us slip
out the door. And while James and Collin do sometimes cause
a little bit of classroom mayhem, neither have been expelled
from Sharon Elementary School. We count that as a win.
Sarah swears up and down that Miss Molly testifies almost
daily in the teacher's lounge of their utmost adorableness.

Oh, and everything got worked out for the reality show too, or
at least the pilot show. Shayla and the camera folks arrived
two days ago. But it wasn't a whole big crew of people.
Shayla said the trend in reality shows is to make it look
natural, like a college kid shot the footage on his phone or
something. Chester asked Dusty if he could sit in the office at
the shop every day during filming. Of course, Dusty agreed
because no one likes to deny the requests of really old people.
Do you want someone to say "yes" to something? All you
have to do is send a really old person with the request. When
people think someone will probably be dead within a year,
they'll agree to almost anything.

Everyone in town knows Matthew's story now too. Herb
Donaldson called in to the local morning radio show a few
weeks ago, saying he remembered why Matthew's name was
so familiar. Then, right there on the air, he read an article he
found on the internet. And that was that. Uncle Bart said it

76

was good to get it all out in the open. But I think he was just relieved to find out Matthew wasn't in prison for knocking an old person in the head or stealing something from under an old person's bed. No one denied the absolute horror of what Matthew did, but most people realize he certainly didn't set out to murder his sister and her roommate.

But today? Today the big news in Sharon is that Matthew Prescott is going to be speaking at a big community youth rally downtown. Mabel thinks the whole thing was set up by the TV people. But Mabel also thinks the government has hidden cameras in the diner to try to monitor everything she does. Of course, that's ridiculous because Mabel doesn't do anything the government or anyone else would find remotely interesting.

By 5:30 the park in Sharon was starting to get crowded. I later found out some of the high school teachers had agreed to give extra credit to students who came. Mabel and the folks at the diner set up a booth to sell hamburgers and all the civic organizations had their banners up. Some of the high school girls wore dresses and high heels because they hoped to be on TV. Suzie Bowman even dressed up like one of the characters from "Frozen" and then did a full gymnastic routine in the parking lot of Sharon Furniture and Appliance. Her great-grandma walked up to one of the young cameramen and said, "What about that? Now that right there is real talent." He just nodded his head and said, "Yes ma'am. It sure is!" Of course, he said that because he was probably raised by good parents who taught him to always say 'yes' to really old people.

Dusty and Clara arrived early and set blankets on the ground near the grandstand. Ashley thought her presence would be a distraction so she asked the Rotary folks to video the proceedings, which they had planned to do anyway. Ashley and Dave also agreed to keep James and Beau so there would be fewer distractions.

I asked Sarah to meet us there and she agreed. Sarah had eaten lunch with us every Sunday for the last four weeks. So had Matthew. Of course, there were always other people there too. But still. I kept thinking he'd ask her out. I think she thought so too. But every Sunday was the same routine. They would visit with all of us on the porch and then he'd say he needed to help Chester and Ida. She'd volunteer to drive him home. He'd thank her and they'd be on their way.

Rotary president, Mitch Smith, approached the microphone. Mitch is about 30 years old. Married with two kids. He's lived in Sharon all his life. His MeeMaw always said he was as pretty as any girl in town and she was right. His blonde hair was always perfect and usually he wore khaki pants and an oxford shirt with the sleeves ironed so crisp they could cut a piece of bologna. But tonight he had on a full suit and tie. "May I have your attention? May I have your attention, please?"

As he spoke, I scanned the crowd, looking for Sarah. Eventually I saw her leaned up against the back of Mabel's hamburger stand. She had on a beautiful peach-colored summer dress that was tied at the waist with a tan cotton belt. Her hair was pulled up in the back with loose strands around her face. I knew she had gone home after school to change. She was starting to look less like Sigourney Weaver and more like, uh, like a shorter Anne Hathaway except with more in the caboose than Anne Hathaway. Oh, and Anne Hathaway has way bigger teeth than Sarah too. But it was like Sarah Simpson was going through a transformation. She waved and shrugged her shoulders, indicating she couldn't get through the crowd to sit with us.

Mitch cleared his throat a few times. "This is a very big night here in Sharon. We have many honored guests in the audience but we won't start introducing them or we'll be here forever. I know you've all come to hear our guest speaker. I won't make you wait any longer. Matthew Prescott moved to Sharon six weeks ago. He works as a mechanic at Dusty's Shop in Bradford. He wasn't here long when his story started making the local news." He smiled and pointed at Dusty. "His boss, Dusty McConnell, even put something in the paper about it, about him. But tonight? Tonight you'll get to hear the story from the person who lived it." His face grew more serious as his voice got stronger. "And young people, we want you to know we're not here tonight to glorify Matthew's story. We don't want you to live it. We want you to learn from it. It's my privilege to introduce Matthew Prescott."

Matthew walked to the podium like a confident lawyer with an open and shut case. He had on new, dark dress pants and a maroon dress shirt with thin, navy blue stripes. He'd gone to the barber shop this afternoon and even though Jimmy had taken a little too much off the back, he still looked handsome. He pulled a handkerchief from his front pocket and wiped his face a bit. He placed some note cards on the podium and then made eye contact with the crowd and smiled.

"Thank you. I know speakers are always supposed to say, 'I'm glad to be here.' But I'm not really." He hung his head and his voice cracked slightly. "Truth is I wish I were anywhere but here right now. I wish the story I'm going to tell was someone else's story." He looked back up. "My life was always easy. Growing up, I had very little hardship. So, no, this isn't a story of a poor boy who endured so much pain and suffering that he turned to drugs. No. No excuses. This is a story about bad decisions. And selfishness." He moved in front of the podium and spoke more personally to the crowd. "I was probably like a lot of you, growing up. Except I lived in San Diego and my parents had a ridiculous amount of money." The crowd laughed as Matthew shook his head and smiled. "But don't get me wrong. There's nothing wrong with money. Most of us could use a little more of it, huh?" He pointed to Dusty. "I mean, if Dusty here wants to give me a raise tomorrow, I'll be all over it. I will." The crowd laughed. Then you could hear a pin drop. They were with him.

"And my parents were nothing but kind to me. They shared their blessings. They had faith I could handle their generosity. But I couldn't....or I didn't anyway. I made good grades. School wasn't hard for me. I went to college and that wasn't hard either. Then I got into law school. Right up the road here. Vanderbilt. My parents were proud. So was I. Maybe that was the problem. I thought I was special. Untouchable. My roommate got involved with prescription drug abuse. It started when we needed to stay up late to study. Then we needed something else to wake us up. We drank excessively on the weekends. And pretty soon, well, it was over. For both of us. For the first time in my life I had failed at something. Failed out of law school. It should have been a wake-up call, right?" He held his hands over his head. "It should have been a big sign saying, 'Matthew, change directions. This is not working.' But addiction isn't always like that, is it? It does shout to us. Loudly, most of the time. But then the very same addiction, the one that shouts so loudly is...well, it's the same one that gives us something to keep us from listening. It throws us on the ground and then it kicks us until we stop feeling. I've been going to Celebrate Recovery meetings with Dave Robertson. I know a lot of you know Dave's story. He's helped me a lot. Oh, and Dusty..." He pointed to Dusty, wiped his eyes with his handkerchief, and dropped his head. "Dusty has been...I can't even tell you what he's been. He's been a friend."

"I guess most of you came tonight to hear the story of how I went to prison for so long." His voice began to crack. "I killed my best friend. That's how. My very best friend in the whole world." He dropped his head and started crying. He wiped his eyes with the handkerchief and recovered some before speaking again. "Mary and I were always close. She was good and kind and she did what my parents said." He smiled. "I was a little more stubborn. But she loved me. When I came to Vanderbilt, she decided to apply to come the next year for her undergrad. English major. Ridiculously smart. Always loved to write. But by the time she came, I had already flunked out of law school, living on Mom and Dad's dime in Nashville. I know. You're right. They should have cut me off. Or I think they should have. I don't know. I'm sure they question that every day. Anyway, Mary and her roommate went to a party with me and some friends. They both drank a little too much. I decided to be the big brother. You know, save the day and all. But I was high and drunk...and I killed both of them. Right there on Interstate 40. Some of you may be tempted to say, 'Well, it was an accident.' But it wasn't. Getting high is not an accident and I'm not here to make any excuses for it. Most of you know that my parents..." His voice broke again and he paused. "Well, during the trial, they stood...they stood with Mary, for Mary. And they should have. I served fourteen years but I should have done life. And that's my story. If there's a moral, it's this. Don't think you're smarter than everyone else. Don't get high. And don't give up. God has a purpose for your life that's bigger than your addiction. Thank you."

The crowd erupted in applause. Aunt Charlotte yelled out, "We love you, Darlin'!" The cameramen ran here and there getting footage of the response. Matthew stepped away from the podium. He wiped his eyes and face with the handkerchief and then put it in his front pocket. Mitch thanked all of us and dismissed us, encouraging us to grab a hamburger from

81

Mabel's stand before heading home. The Westview High School band played marching music as the crowd dispersed.

Sarah walked over to our blanket, dabbing her eyes with a Kleenex the whole way. "That was…wow. Sad. Powerful. I don't know what else to say."

Doug nodded his head. "Brutally honest. No excuses."

Even though the mayor was having what looked like an in-depth conversation with Matthew, Dusty ran up on stage and threw his arms around him. Sarah watched the whole scene in silence. Then dabbed her eyes some more with the wadded-up Kleenex.

I determined to move things along. "Sarah, Doug and I were getting ready to grab a burger at Mabel's. Why don't you join us? Clara, are you and your clan in?"

Clara smiled and began gathering up the blankets. "No. These guys have some serious math homework, so we better pick up Beau and get back to the house."

"Gosh, I'm glad you reminded us!" I wrapped my arms around Doug's waist. "Honey, we have a school kid now. We better go get him and help him get started on that Physics homework, eh?"

Doug laughed. "You can never start 'em too young. But he does need a bath and he needs to get to bed early. In honor of Miss Molly's sanity, I think we'll have to make a sandwich at home and hope that Mabel will forgive us."

I patted Sarah on the back. "Sorry, friend. How 'bout a rain check?"

"No problem. Really."

Dusty and Matthew walked toward our small group. But soon
Matthew was overtaken by well-wishers. The principal of the
high school thanked him profusely. A group of high school
girls giggled and said a bunch of encouraging things about his
speech. But ultimately, we all knew they were flirting with
him, which was a million miles from appropriate. Mary
Miller's mama even pulled a desperation move. She
approached the group of girls and told Mary it was time to go
home and feed the cows. As she grabbed her daughter's arm,
she turned and said with a scowl, "Cows or no cows, you
teenage girls best get on home too."

It was that term "teenage girls" that stung the girls' pride and
caused their faces to turn bright red as they turned to leave.
Did Mary's mama say it for their benefit or for Matthew's?
We'll never know.

Shayla came running through the crowd with a cameraman
close on her heels. She was wearing a little black dress and
silver wedge sandals. She grabbed Matthew and hugged him
like he was her husband returning from battle. "Matthew! Oh
Matthew, you did it!! My word! You did it!"

"What did I do?"

"You're kidding, right?"

"No."

"You wowed them! That's what you did. You wowed this
crowd! And pretty soon you'll wow all of America too! Get
ready for your life to change, Mister. This is no seismology
show. No, sir! Forget earthquakes! This one's a winner!"

Dusty put his arm around Matthew. "Hey, be careful with the guy. Just remember he's a person, not a product."

Dusty pretended he was joking, but I knew he wasn't. I felt confident Shayla would never do anything to intentionally hurt Matthew Prescott. But with or without bad intentions, people can still be hurt. Badly. Just ask Matthew.

Chapter 17, SARAH: Learning to Take Chances

After the Jamesons and McConnells left the rally, Matthew was still being approached by members of the community and even some media folks from Jackson. That's when Jerry Conner pulled me aside to give me some late-breaking news. Turns out it wasn't really news at all. He twitched and stammered like he was hesitant to share it. But then he shared and kept on sharing. "Sarah, I'm not sure about this guy. This Matthew Prescott. I know for a fact his parole officer is worried. Really worried. If this TV thing gets big, well, a life of fame could just throw him back into a life of crime. You know? That's what the parole officer's afraid of. It happens, you know. It does."

"I have no doubt."

"Oh, and Bart Nelson says you and Matthew both have been eating Sunday dinner at Carlie and Doug's place a lot. You know Carlie. She's a matchmaker even when it's dangerous. So be careful. Oh, and there's probably something else you don't know too."

"But I'm sure you're gonna tell me."

"Well, yeah, 'cause you need to know. Matthew Prescott will never drive a car again. Never. License suspended. For life. Yep, forever. I reckon poor Matthew will be toted around like a fourteen-year-old boy for the rest of his life."

"I figured as much. I mean, it makes sense, right? People died, Jerry. That part of the story didn't escape me."

"Look, I just wanted you to be clear about who you're dealing with."

"I don't know Matthew Prescott well. But neither do you. So I'm guessing neither one of us know who we're dealing with, right? And no one has asked us to testify on his behalf either, so you and I don't have to determine his trustworthiness. Not today anyway."

Jerry's countenance fell. "Just lookin' out for ya, Sarah. Just want ya to be careful."

"Thanks. I've got stuff to do. I better get home."

Mabel hollered out, "Jerry Conner, I got a burger with your name on it if you got three dollars in your pocket! Jerry turned toward Mabel's booth. I walked past the railroad tracks to look for my car.

"Sarah! Sarah!"

I recognized the voice and it made me feel nauseous, like a school girl with a crush on the new football coach. Maybe I was really no different than those high school girls who clamored around him a few minutes ago. But it wasn't just his looks or the fact that he was new. I was now enamored with his story. Not his story really. I was enamored with his willingness to tell it. To put all the weight of it on himself. No blame games or excuses. I turned my head just as Matthew was wiping sweat from his face and walking toward me. Sadly, he didn't look at all like a fourteen-year-old to me. No. He looked like a man. "You haven't lost your car, have you?"

"Uh, maybe. Verdict is still out."

He smiled and looked around. "Or maybe Jerry's security wasn't as good as he promised. It could have been stolen, y'know."

I laughed, "Yeah. I'm sure there's a run of car thieving on dirty Ford Focuses here in Sharon. But with all the ex-cons in town now, hey, you never know, right?"

He put his hands in the air and smiled. "Don't blame me. I was busy all evening." He ran up to walk beside me.

I stopped and faced him. "I guess you need a ride, huh?"

"No. Chester brought me. He's still doing interviews with the camera guys. Who knew, huh? Chester...the new Phil Robertson."

"Yeah, except Phil Robertson actually knows how to wield a gun. Chester needs to stay away from his."

"That's what I hear. Yeah, that's what I hear."

"What you said tonight...it was perfect. I don't mean your story's perfect. I get that it was terrible. But the way you shared it, it meant something to this community. It meant something to me. Thank you."

"Thank you for saying that." He looked back over the town square. People were still chattering and standing in line to buy hamburgers from Mabel. "I'm certainly not proud of it. And there's no merit in it. Any of it. But there's something about telling the truth. Maybe it will be a warning."

"Can I ask you something?"

"Sure."

"Your parents, have you talked to them at all?"

"No. I know they were notified about my getting out on parole. But no. I haven't spoken to them since…since the morning Mary died."

"Do you want to talk to them?"

"Can we change the subject?"

"Yeah. Sorry. Do you want me to tell you all about eight-year-olds? Because I can. I'm an expert on eight-year-olds, Matthew."

He smiled and looked down as he gently kicked a big rock. "Why don't you tell me about your parents. I met your mom. She seems nice. Where is your dad?"

"He died when I was in seventh grade."

"Oh, I'm sorry. Seventh grade's bad anyway. But that must have been rough."

"It was. Car wreck out on 22. Mom never married again. I knew she wouldn't. You know how they say you go through these phases of grief. She never finished. The phases, I mean. She still hasn't. Every day it's like he died yesterday."

"What happened? With your dad, I mean."

I was getting nervous. "Someone crossed over the median. Head on collision. He died instantly."

Matthew's face grew pale and he gently touched me on the arm. It was the first time he'd ever touched me. "And?"

"And the difference is…Jim Hill…he never did time. Never did one day in jail. Put my mom in prison for the rest of her life, but never spent one day in there himself."

"I'm sorry. Would it make you feel better if I told you he hasn't slept one whole night since then?" Matthew looked down the railroad tracks like he was looking for an escape route. "That he's probably never walked through a store without wondering if people were pointing or wishing he'd been the one who died."

"Mr. Hill died two years later. Refused to even go to the doctor. Sclerosis of the liver, I guess. According to the men at the barber shop, less than ten people were at his funeral. His daughter didn't even come in from St. Louis."

"And your mom? Did she forgive him?"

"No. She didn't. She still hasn't."

He looked into my eyes. "Then you understand why I haven't had contact with my parents."

Recalling Daddy's death brought tears to my eyes. "Yeah, I guess so."

Chester was almost completely out of breath as he crossed over the tracks. "Matthew! Matthew! They're gonna put me on TV! Can you believe it?"

Matthew smiled and shouted, "They know a star when they see one!" He turned and said quietly, "Do you want me to help you find your car?"

"No. I see it now. Over there by Bart and Charlotte's Good Times van."

He shook his head and looked at the ground. "That van is perfect for them, isn't it?"

"It is. We call it the lime green good times machine." I turned back toward town. "Hey Chester! Don't you and Matthew go gettin' into any trouble tonight, y'hear?"

"We won't! Ida's got us shuckin' corn as soon as we get back to the house!"

Matthew moved in just a bit closer and touched my arm again. "I hope we can finish our conversation another time. Looks like corn shuckin' is in my future."

I'm not sure why I did what I did next. Overcome with emotion, I guess. I leaned in and gently placed my arms all the way around him. When I did, he put his arms around me too. For a brief moment, I placed my face against his chest. I could hear his heart beating. He moved his right hand gently to the back of my head. Sheer bliss. I whispered, "Thank you. Thank you for sharing what you did tonight."

He pulled away and when he did, I saw that his face was red. He looked directly into my eyes. "No problem. Really."

I stood there as though I were paralyzed. I watched every detail as Matthew and Chester walked back toward town square. I could hear their friendly banter and occasionally Matthew would pat Chester on the back like they were old friends. Life is funny like that, I guess. Matthew Prescott was raised in a wealthy family in the San Diego suburbs. Smart. Gifted even. Never wanted for anything. Chester only finished the 8th grade at Palmersville School. His mama and daddy lived in two rooms until their death. And here they were, the two of them…friends. Friends on the way to shuck corn.

Chapter 18, CARLIE: Who Needs CNN? We've Got Aunt Charlotte

The morning after the rally, Matthew Prescott was the talk of Weakley County. Mitch Smith even called into the morning radio show to give a blow-by-blow report of the evening. On the radio, Mitch sounded just like my brother, Bennett, the year he got a full-size air hockey game for Christmas. Pure excitement filled the air waves as he spoke. "The TV stations from Paducah, Jackson, and even Memphis were there covering the story. And of course, the A & E camera crew was filming the whole time. It was the most excitement Sharon has seen since Ashley Robertson was nominated for an Oscar." A few times, the radio host had to interrupt Mitch's exciting story to take a phone call about a lost gray cat on Main Street or the broken water line in front of the Assembly of God. But other than those few interruptions, Mitch Smith took up nearly 30 minutes of air time. The host finally had to cut him off when it was time to give the high school sports scores.

Aunt Charlotte was at our house by 9:00 am to report to me about the report that had been reported on the radio. (You'd have to live in a small town to understand that sentence).

She fanned herself with her apron as she poured a cup of coffee. "Good night! This place is goin' plum crazy over that young'un. Bless him! I started to go by Mabel's and have a sausage biscuit in honor of it all. But then I remembered I ain't supposed to eat hog meat. You don't got anything good to eat 'round here, do ya?"

"Define good."

"Somethin' that would taste like a sausage biscuit but have the calories of a carrot stick."

I turned my back toward her. "Look at my rear end, Aunt Charlotte. Does it look like I have anything like that?"

She laughed, "Oh child, you and me's got the same problem, I reckon, 'cept you not near as big as me and you're tall and all gorgeous and everything."

"I love you forever...even if you eat hog meat."

"Love you too. Here, I'll make some toast while you sit right here at this table 'cause I'm gonna tell ya what happened after you left last night and you won't wanna miss a thing."

"I already heard it all on the radio."

"Oh no, Baby. You ain't heard this. No. I promise Mitch Smith didn't report nothin' about it on the radio. Seems Sarah and Matthew was gettin' all up close and personal over by the railroad tracks last night. Yes, ma'am. And I heard it from more than one person too."

"I doubt they were gettin' too up close and personal. I've watched them sit on that porch every Sunday for the last month and it's like watchin' molasses being poured from a frozen jar."

"Well, you wasn't there. But that's not all. That little Shayla McGuire stopped by Chester and Ida's last night around 9:30 too. Said she was lookin' for Matthew. Ida told her he'd done gone to bed, that he was a workin' man who had to get up early. She asked Ida to wake him up but Ida refused. God bless her. And then little Shayla stomped off the porch and Ida was so nervous over it, she didn't sleep a wink."

"Shayla's probably just not used to people goin' to bed that early."

"Well, I think that gal has more than just a TV show on her mind. That's what I think."

"I'm sure it's none of our business."

Aunt Charlotte laughed. "And that's comin' from the gal who has invited Matthew and Sarah to Sunday dinner every week for the last month! I figure it's your business alright. You done made it your business."

"If I give you a sausage biscuit, will you stop trying to make me seem nosy?"

"Honey, if you was to give me a sausage biscuit, I'd give you my last litter of speckled pups."

Chapter 19, CARLIE: That's a Wrap

Shayla McGuire and the camera crew did just what they said they were going to do. They shot footage for the pilot in only four days then high-tailed it back to California. The producer said it would require a week of editing and then they'd do the preliminary presentation to the network big wigs. Of course, everyone in Sharon was on the edge of their seats, waiting for Dusty and Matthew to get the call as to whether the show was a go. Dusty and Matthew seemed far less concerned. They went to work every day and came home every night.

But then came Thursday. On Thursday something completely odd happened. According to Dusty, Thursday morning he went by to pick Matthew up for work, but Ida said he'd gone. He called a taxi the night before. Said he borrowed a suitcase and seemed pleasant enough. Hugged them both and said he'd be back on Sunday. She handed Dusty a note that said, "I'm sorry. Something important has come up. I'll be back and ready to work Monday morning. Matthew"

Jerry Conner said the parole officer was tight-lipped about where Matthew was going but that he did check in and go through the proper procedures for leaving the state. Clearly, Matthew's strict adherence to the conditions of his parole disappointed Jerry Conner.

Sunday afternoon found Sarah sitting on our porch swing without her usual after-lunch companion. "Those burgers were great, Doug. Thank you. Carlie, I loved that red Jell-O stuff too. My grandma used to make it just like that. Called it Jell-O salad even though it was sweeter than cake."

"Yes! My MeeMaw did the same thing! How did southerners convince themselves a syrupy liquid could ever be called a salad?"

94

"Or that lard could be a 'flavor enhancer'?"

I leaned back in the rocking chair. "True. So true. Okay. So, about that elephant in the room, any ideas?"

"Ideas about what?"

"You know what. About where Matthew is. Look, I know you're curious. We're all curious."

"No. I've no idea. I mean, I guess he's probably in California. Maybe Shayla wanted him to be part of the pitch to the network. That makes sense, doesn't it?"

"Yeah, but why wouldn't he just say that? Why wouldn't he just tell Dusty he had to go spend a few days doing something about the TV show?"

"I don't know. Why does any man do what he does?"

"Right. I asked Ashley if she knew anything, if she'd had contact with Shayla. She hadn't."

"I'm sure it's all fine. He told Dusty he'd be ready for work in the morning. He will."

And Sarah Simpson? She was right on the money. Dusty went by Chester and Ida's house at 6:15 Monday morning and Matthew was waiting out on the stoop, carrying a brown paper bag which contained two meatloaf sandwiches, two uncut fresh tomatoes, and a salt shaker. He apologized for missing work Thursday and Friday. Promised to make it up to Dusty. And that was that.

Chapter 20, SARAH: Mysterious Matthew Prescott

When I was 17 I used to drive by the new band director's house nearly every evening. He was only 25 years old and all the girls at school thought he looked just like Alan Jackson. He rented a little white house from Maude Jenkins, just down from the appliance store here in Sharon.   I'd drive by just, I don't know, just to see his old El Camino parked in the gravel driveway, I guess. I was hoping to see him outside washing his car or walking the dog...or pining for me. Young girls and their silly dreams.

When I left Carlie's place Sunday afternoon, I drove by Chester and Ida's. And yes, I got that same stupid, giddy feeling I got when I was in high school. Of course, Matthew Prescott doesn't even have a car, so there's no way I could even know if he were at home or still, still wherever he was. Chester was sitting on the front porch swing and reading the paper. Ida, cane in one hand, broom in the other, was sweeping the walk. I waved and Chester shot up from his rocking chair and beckoned me with both arms to pull in the drive. I rolled down the passenger side window. "Hey! Looks like Mrs. Ida's doing all the work and you're taking it easy!"

Chester grinned and walked toward the car. "It's a day of rest, Sarah! A day of rest. But you know ol' Ida here. She's gonna wear out, not rust out."

"Yes, I feel certain."

"Guess you heard that our boarder took flight last week."

"I did. Is there anyone in Weakley County who hasn't heard that news?"

Chester pulled out a dingy handkerchief and wiped his bald head as he laughed. "No, I reckon not."

"And no, I'm not gonna ask you where he went either. I don't see it's any of my business."

"Well, I wouldn't know if you did ask, Sarah." He sighed as he bent over and leaned into the window. "No idea. Lord knows we've put our heads together. He got a phone call 'bout supper time and was gone within two hours. He didn't seem troubled. But he didn't seem excited neither. Just said he'd be gone a few days."

Mrs. Ida stopped sweeping long enough to call out. "Sarah, come in and see the quilt! Finally got it all pieced together."

"Sounds great!" Chester and Ida's house smelled like Lysol and canned cinnamon rolls and old furniture. As we walked down the hallway to the sewing room, I glanced into the small guest room. Yes, the velvet wallpaper was atrocious. But the bed was made neatly, and I noticed a stack of books, at least ten, sitting on the end table. "Matthew must be a reader."

"Oh, he is. That child reads more than anyone I ever seen. But he's not a hermit. I mean, he don't just sit back there in his room at night. Usually he sits with us in the living room. I crochet and Chester watches the news channel. And Matthew, he reads books about the Civil War and the Holocaust and books about presidents. And I don't know what else. Smart fella though. Smart fella."

"So, it's workin' out, huh? Him being a boarder, it's workin' well?"

Ida's face lit up like a child's face on Christmas morning. "Oh, it is! It is. He's so pleasant and well, we've both, we've missed him these few days. Sure have."

The front door slammed and a voice called out. "I'm home!"

Ida turned and almost ran down the hallway. The green shag carpeting was so worn down, it hardly moved under her shuffling feet. I walked slowly behind her. It was like I'd finally gotten caught driving by the band director's house, except I didn't care because I wasn't seventeen anymore. Matthew had on new blue jeans, fancy brown western boots, and a blue and white plaid western shirt but not the kind with the pearl buttons. Just the regular kind of buttons. He set his suitcase by the front door just as Ida threw her arms around his neck. "Welcome home, stranger!"

"Thank you. Good to be back." He shook Chester's hand. "I missed you two." He smiled and winked at Ida. "Oh, and I definitely missed the good cookin' 'round here."

Chester spoke with enthusiasm. "We got us a visitor today! Yeah, reckon we missed you so bad, Matthew, we went out and got another young person to fill in for ya!"

I couldn't bring myself to move forward. It's like my feet were glued to the edge of the green shag hallway carpet. Matthew looked over and paused for just a moment. Then he smiled. "Well, if you do decide to replace me, she'd be a good one. Absolutely." His words became softer. "She's a good one alright."

His eyes met mine and I realized he'd gotten even better looking. In just four days. When a man goes away for four days and comes back way better looking than when he left, it can only mean one thing. My heart sank.

98

I finally moved and extended my hand like I was his new insurance representative or someone interviewing him for a job. "Welcome home, Matthew."

"Thanks! Good to be back."

Ida completely forgot about that lavender and purple quilt with all the states on it. She forgot she was walking me back to the sewing room so I could ooh and aah over its intricate details. Instead she became laser-focused on making food for her weary traveler, the son she never had.

"Chester, take the young folks into the living room. I know this one here hasn't eaten a thing and I'm gonna make him that omelet he likes so well. You'd like that, wouldn't you?"

He reached down and gently kissed her cheek. "Sounds great, Mrs. Ida. Thanks."

Chester led the way to a crowded living room filled with a combination of junk and antiques. Old Coke crates. Fancy doilies. Blue and green candy dishes. Too much furniture. Matthew immediately removed his boots and sat in the old brown vinyl chair which faced the door. "Sarah, Chester and Mrs. Ida and I have assigned seats in here."

"Do you?"

"Chester has this old green recliner. Mrs. Ida sits in that floral wingback chair and this is mine, by the reading light. But we're leaving the best for you. The big wooden rocker. Mrs. Ida was rocked to sleep in that rocker."

"Oh my. Well, I don't want to…"

Matthew spoke like he'd lived there his whole life. "Oh no. It's fine. Have a seat. You can't hurt it. She says it was made back when people knew how to make furniture, when they took pride in their work."

He jumped from the vinyl chair and handed me an orange throw pillow. When his hand touched mine, I smiled. I wanted to reach out and hug him. But I wasn't Mrs. Ida and Matthew Prescott wasn't my boarder either. So I just sat down in the old wooden rocker and rubbed my hands on its intricate carvings. "Thanks. It's lovely. Comfortable too."

Chester pulled the old recliner handle and it snapped back with a loud thud. "People 'round here been real curious, Matthew. Real curious about where you been."

"It's funny. Growing up in San Diego, no one would have even known if you were gone for a month, but around here I guess people...they notice."

Chester wasn't surrendering. "Most people figure it was somethin' havin' to do with that TV show. Then there's some who figure it had to do with that little blonde thing throwin' such a fit on our porch the other night. And of course, there's always a few wantin' it to be the worst...I won't tell ya what they said 'cause it's not fit to tell."

Matthew looked at me like he was trying to keep from laughing. He winked. "Thank you for sparing me, Chester."

Chester continued, "But I, I told 'em it wasn't none of their business what you was doin'. You wasn't breakin' the law and they needed to just mind their own affairs...uh, not that you was havin' an affair of any kind 'cause Ida and me, well, we swore up and down it wasn't any kind of nonsense such as that."

"Thank you for defending my honor. Thank you."

Silence fell over the room. Chester grabbed his glasses and pretended to be looking at the TV Guide. I pretended to be examining the needlework on the orange throw pillow as I rocked back and forth in the antique rocker. Matthew just leaned his head back in the brown vinyl chair and gently closed his eyes. And Mrs. Ida made an omelet, an omelet for a good-looking ex-con who left for four whole days and not a soul in Weakley County knew where he had gone.

Chapter 21, CARLIE: We're All Gonna Be Famous (Lord, Help Us)

It's been a week since Matthew Prescott's disappearing act and nobody seems to care anymore. The only thing people in Sharon are talking about is the fact that the TV show got approved by the network big wigs. A picture of Matthew and Dusty made the front page of the paper too, along with a detailed story about how Sharon and Bradford were gonna be famous towns now. Homer Crittenden called into the morning radio show and said, "I have an important announcement. An emergency really. If you live in Sharon or Bradford, you need to take more care with your lawn and house upkeep, seeing as how we're all gonna be on TV now. Some of ya'll need to throw away those dead chrysanthemums and broken flower pots. And if your car ain't runnin', see if you can at least tow it 'round to the backyard so as not to embarrass the rest of us." Then he listed seven or eight people by name, people he considered the worst violators. Of course, then he said, "If you need help with the cleanup, just call my nephew, Jacob, at 514-0022. He graduated last year and is doing mighty fine yard work now." The radio host immediately accused Homer of using the call for free advertising. The whole exchange made for some pretty exciting radio.

Shayla said they'll send the camera crew out again in a few weeks. Mabel swears up and down the diner will be getting so much business, she'll have to hire a security guard. But Mabel has always wanted to hire a security guard for the same reason Jerry Conner has wanted to conduct a surveillance mission. I like to call it "Enthusiastic small town overkill."

It had been a few weeks since we'd invited Uncle Bart and Aunt Charlotte to Sunday lunch and Doug was feeling bad about it. I think he was feeling bad because Aunt Charlotte came by the bank and said, "Doug Honey, I don't never see you 'cept when I come in here and wrangle you to the ground."

We hadn't invited them in a while because we wanted to give Matthew and Sarah a chance to get to know each other without Aunt Charlotte's loud and overbearing interference. But clearly, that strategy had been flawed from the get-go. Maybe Aunt Charlotte's loud and honest declarations were what was needed to light the fire. When it comes to people, Aunt Charlotte is definitely like a good piece of kindlin'. Good or bad, she's sure to get things started.

After church, Doug picked up two huge sandwich platters from Sammy's. Sammy's Sandwich Emporium also sells used "items of interest." If you're wondering what would happen if Goodwill and Subway went in business together at an old gas station location, well, you don't have to wonder anymore. Just go to Sammy's Sandwich Emporium in Sharon, Tennessee, and you'll know for sure.

Matthew helped Doug carry the sandwiches onto the porch as I retrieved two gallons of sweet tea from the kitchen. Matthew seemed unusually happy and I didn't know if it had to do with the TV show, Sarah Simpson, his trip last week, or the fact that Sammy threw in a huge bag of kettle chips for free.

Aunt Charlotte set a big platter of sugar cookies on the picnic table, declaring that she read in a Reader's Digest article that all dieters should take one day a week off, and that Sunday would be her day. But then Uncle Bart yelled, "Well, what about all them cookies you ate last night, Charlotte?"

"Well, maybe I'm doin' the days like Jewish people, Bart! Ever thought about that? With the real Sunday beginning

Saturday night? Lord, sometimes you ain't got no culture. No culture at all."

Uncle Bart just laughed and threw up both hands as though he were surrendering. Sarah Simpson sprang up the porch steps like a teenager who'd just been asked to the prom. She had on the cutest, most flattering denim dress. And I don't mean that ridiculous tent-like denim jumper all teachers and pregnant women wore in the 90's. No. This dress was tailored with a red leather belt. She wore shiny red sandals too. She sat down in her usual rocking chair on the porch. Matthew sat on the porch swing facing her. The McConnells and Robertsons were at the swing set watching over their brood. Uncle Bart and Aunt Charlotte sat at the picnic table. I knew it was so that Aunt Charlotte would have ready access to the sugar cookies, seeing as how the sun would be setting within hours.

Soon, Doug would call everyone to the porch. We'd pray. We'd eat. And I figured, well, I figured it would all go exactly like it went every Sunday. But I was wrong.

Chapter 22, CARLIE: Who's Afraid of the Big Black Car?

Most everybody was at least half-way through their sandwiches. The bag of kettle chips was gone and only a half-gallon of sweet tea remained. James and Collin were already eating ice cream sandwiches or rather, ice cream sandwiches were eating them by the looks of their shirts. That's when a big black car pulled into the driveway. It wasn't a limo. It was like those big black cars that senators or congressmen ride around in because they don't want their constituents to think they would waste money to ride around in a limo. Of course, that's dumb seein' as how they waste so much money on expensive muffins and bad haircuts.

Doug walked toward the porch steps just as a gray-haired man dressed in a black suit stepped out of the car.

Doug threw up his hand. "Hello there."

The man moved toward the porch but didn't extend his hand. Clearly, he wasn't at all like the Farm Bureau guy who comes by the house every year to do a property assessment. The Farm Bureau guy always talks about high school football and whether our relatives are all in good health. But the man who got out of the black car didn't seem interested in the health of our relatives at all. "I'm Edgar Morgan and I'm looking for Matthew Prescott."

"I'm Doug Jameson. Nice to meet you, Edgar. Won't you join us for lunch? We've got plenty."

"I'm looking for Matthew Prescott."

"Yes, I heard that. What's…"

Before Doug could finish his sentence, Matthew moved forward and spoke calmly. "I'm Matthew Prescott."

"Yes. I've been commissioned to deliver a message to you personally."

"Okay."

"It's from your father, Jonathan Prescott."

"My father?"

"Yes. Do you have some way of proving that you're Matthew Prescott?"

"I have an ID, yeah." Matthew nervously removed an ID from his billfold and held it up for the man's inspection. "Not a great picture, but yeah, that's me."

"Is there somewhere we can go in private?"

Doug said, "Sure. You guys just stay on the porch and we'll go inside." He looked at James and Collin, still finishing their ice cream. "Hey boys, I think ya'll need a bubble bath! Let's head in the house."

In less than a minute, we had all filed into the kitchen. Matthew and Edgar sat on the porch rockers that faced each other. Of course, each of us took turns pretending we needed something from the kitchen pantry which just happened to be next to the patio door. Doug got a bottle of water, even though it was room temperature and he'd already downed two big glasses of tea. Ashley pretended she wanted a graham cracker even though she rarely eats carbs.

Sadly, I'm the worst participant in the discreet game because I always feel the need to make a full verbal explanation. "I wonder if we have enough baked beans for next week's church potluck? I'm worried about it. I guess I'll need to look in that pantry and check on our baked bean inventory." Any time someone uses the term "baked bean inventory" they're definitely involved in a massive cover-up.

Even though several of us got a good glance, none of us spoke a word about what was taking place. Edgar pulled some papers out of a manila envelope and used an ink pen to point to things on the paper."

Matthew's expression never changed. Was this bad news? Sad news? Good news?

In less than ten minutes, Matthew opened the kitchen door. He was carrying the manila envelope and he looked almost exactly the way he looked at the beginning of his speech downtown. Nervous but resolved. "You guys can come out now. He's gone."

Dusty moved quickly toward the door and patted Matthew on the arm. "You okay, man? Everything alright?"

His voice cracked a bit. "Yeah, fine."

Dusty made one more attempt. "Anything we can help you with?"

"No. I'm good. Just need to get back to Chester and Ida's and help with the yard. Chester's arthritis has been bad lately."

Sarah did the same thing Sarah did every Sunday afternoon. She even said the exact same words. "I can give you a ride. I'm going right by there."

I hugged Matthew and whispered, "If you need anything, you know we're here, right?"

"I do. Thanks."

I handed him the tray of leftover sandwiches. "Tell Chester and Ida we said 'hey.'"

He dropped his head. "I will."

It's weird to watch Sarah and Matthew drive away every Sunday afternoon. Kind of like watching an old married couple. He opens the driver's side door for her. She smiles and says, "Thanks." Then he runs around the back of the car and gets in on the passenger side. One of them must say the same funny thing every week, because they always look at each other and laugh as they fasten their seatbelts. I wish I knew what they were saying. I wish I knew why Edgar Morgan came all the way from California too. Oh, and I definitely wish I knew where Matthew Prescott went last week…and why he went there. But mostly? Mostly I wished, prayed, that Matthew Prescott could find a home. I had a feeling his original one had burned to the ground.

Chapter 23, SARAH: Unraveling the Mysterious Matthew

I tried to put a positive spin on the mysterious visitor. "You must be really important, Matthew."

"How's that?"

"A personal messenger? I mean, we don't get very many of those in Sharon."

He smiled and nodded. "Yeah, I guess." He moved his hand to rest on the middle console. Working man's hands. Strong. I so wanted to reach over and place my hand on top of his. I wanted to tell him it would all be okay, no matter what.

He moved his legs and I asked if he needed to scoot the seat back. He shook his head and we sat in silence. I wish it took longer to drive from Carlie's to Chester and Ida's house. I wish it took hours every Sunday to get there. But it doesn't. It takes all of nine minutes and that's only because I drive five miles below the speed limit.

Matthew cleared his throat and looked out the passenger side window. "I guess you're wondering about that back there."

"I am. But I'll live even if it remains a mystery. No pressure."

"Thanks."

Soon we were in front of Chester and Ida's house. I was glad they weren't out front. Maybe Matthew would linger. I turned toward him. "I hope you have a good week. I'm sure you're tired. Maybe you can squeeze in a nap after the yard work, or some reading anyway."

He tapped his hand gently on the console. "Yeah, maybe so. Can I ask you a question, Sarah?"

"Absolutely. If it's about times tables, I'm a genius. Anything else, well, it's up for grabs."

He turned to face me. "Your mom, you said she never finished grieving for your dad, like it happened yesterday. But why is that? It's been what? Seventeen years?"

"Eighteen last month. I don't know really. I'd say it's because she loved him so much. But it's not that. I mean, I've known people who've loved, and lost, and managed to move on."

"Yeah, Dusty's first wife and baby. I think about that a lot." He looked out the front windshield. "But they weren't killed by…they weren't killed by a person really."

"I don't know. Dusty took a lot of responsibility for that whole scenario, saying if he'd been there, he would have heard the tornado alarm, gotten them to safety."

Matthew's voice grew softer. "Right. But it's still not…it's not…like someone directly killed them. It's not like what Jim Hill did to your mother, right?"

"Or what you feel like you did? To your parents, I mean?"

He looked directly into my eyes. Anguish. Tiny tears forming in the corners of his dark brown eyes. Then I did it. I can't believe I did it, but I placed both my hands gently on top of his left hand, still resting on the middle console.

"Matthew…Mary, she would have forgiven you. Completely. She'd want you to go on. She'd want you to live. Live well."

His face turned red as he leaned forward a bit. "Thank you for that." His right hand touched the side of my face as he whispered, "Sarah..."

The screen door slammed and he quickly drew his hand back. I was dizzy and could barely see Chester and Ida waving enthusiastically from the front porch. It's like they were in a fog. Matthew opened the car door as he took a deep breath. "I better go see what Chester and Ida have planned for my afternoon." He leaned into the car before closing the door, face still red. "Thank you, Sarah. Thanks for the ride, and for your help. You have no idea."

I couldn't speak, but managed to wave. He turned to look at me one more time and then he was gone.

I only live five minutes from Chester and Ida's house. Right on Mill Street. Left on Main. Soon, without remembering the drive, I was sitting in my driveway, wondering what just happened with Matthew Prescott. Or what didn't happen, what could have happened. I closed my eyes and leaned the seat back. George Strait was singing about crossing his heart and making promises, making her dreams come true. I couldn't even remember having dreams anymore. Busy teaching. Tending the rose bushes. Eating dinner with Mama every Wednesday and Friday night. But one thing I did remember. I remembered what his hand felt like on my face. Wonderful. Beyond wonderful.

There was something depressing about walking into the little yellow house, the house Papa and Granny loved for more than half a century. For the first time in my life, I realized why they loved it. It was life to them, the place they raised a family, cooked sausage every morning, built a fire every winter evening. The place Granny grew award-winning roses.

The place she tended memories. Memories of real life and love.

For me, the yellow house had become a place of frozen dinners, old appliances, and a tote bag of flashcards sitting by the door. Loneliness. I wanted to turn the car around and go right back to that driveway. I wanted to politely tell Chester and Ida to go inside so Matthew Prescott could kiss me. But I couldn't help but wonder what Granny and Papa would say about that, about him, about me. Good or bad, sadly, they were no longer alive to say it.

Chapter 24, SARAH: For the Love of Chester

I sat out on the porch all afternoon, holding out some odd sense of hope that he would come walking by. I'd be reading a magazine and he'd walk onto the porch. I'd ask if he wanted lemonade. He'd say it sounded good. I'd stand up to go inside and he'd stop me. He'd touch my face again. He'd tell me he couldn't stop thinking about me. He'd wrap his arms around me and kiss me before I even had a chance to touch the screen door.

But evidently Matthew Prescott has nothing in common with a high school girl who drives by the band director's house, just to drive by. So none of that happened. At 7:30 I got up to go inside just as Bart and Charlotte Nelson pulled into the drive. Bart rolled down the window. "Sarah, we came by to tell ya that Chester's in the hospital! Heart attack. Dang fool won't take his medicine. We're goin' up there, if you'd like to go with us."

"Yes. Absolutely. Let me grab my purse."

The hospital was quiet. Sunday evening, I guess. Well, it was quiet until Charlotte Nelson got there. The receptionist never looked up from her computer. "Can I help you?"

"We're here to see Chester, of course!"

"Chester who?"

"How many Chesters you got in here? Lord, you got less than 50 beds, Hon, and most of em's empty. There can't be too many old men named Chester who had a heart attack this afternoon!"

The receptionist scowled. "Room 145."

"Thank ya, Baby."

Bart grabbed Charlotte's arm gently. "Down this hall."

Brother Dan and Doug were talking quietly, leaned up against the wall down at the end of the hallway.

Aunt Charlotte started shuffling her feet more quickly as she reached her arms out to hug Doug. "Baby, what do you know? Can we go in?"

"No. Only three at a time. Ida, Carlie, and Matthew are in there right now. Carlie's getting Ida situated for the night. We told her we'd all take turns, that he'd never be alone. But she refuses to leave him."

I broke in. "How's he doing? I mean, what's the verdict?"

Brother Dan shook his head. "Not good. His heart's weak. They're keeping him monitored. He'll be here at least a few days."

Carlie walked out of the room, dabbing her eyes with one of those brown paper towels from a public restroom. "He's resting right now. Brother Dan, I told him you were here. He's asking for you."

Matthew followed Carlie into the hallway. His jeans and gray t-shirt were marred with dirt and sweat stains. He looked at Brother Dan. "I thought I'd give you some time with the both of 'em."

"Thank you. There's a waiting room across the hall, if you guys want to go sit in there."

Charlotte bellowed, "Just be sure to tell Ida and Chester we're here. And we'll be here all night long if we need to be. Oh, and tell her not to worry about makin' that cake for Imogene's birthday on Tuesday either. We've got it took care of."

Brother Dan laughed. "I will, Charlotte. I will."

The waiting room was empty. Doug and Carlie sat on two green vinyl chairs with an end table between them. Charlotte grabbed an old "Good Housekeeping" magazine and sat with Bart on a black vinyl couch. Matthew and I stood nervously near the door. He put his hands in his pockets. "I'm sorry for being so dirty. I was in the middle of yard work, obviously."

"Oh, no problem. What happened?"

"Ida just came running outside, yelling my name, saying Chester had fallen in the hallway. When I saw him, I knew he was in trouble. Breathing real hard. Covered in sweat. I probably should have called the ambulance. But...." He looked around and then shook his head.

"But what?"

His face grew solemn and his voice quiet. He leaned away from the group. "I drove him here. I shouldn't have. Ida was screaming to get him to the hospital. I knew the keys were in the bowl by the door. So...I just did it."

"Are you in trouble?"

"I don't know." He smiled. "If you hang around long enough, you'll probably find out."

"I'm sure there are special circumstances, right? I mean, it's not legal to stab someone in the throat either. But if you're doing an emergency tracheotomy to try to save someone's life, there's a special provision, right?"

"Uh, yeah, if you're a doctor. But if you have a felony record related to stabbing people, you're probably not gonna get off that easy."

I smiled as I gently hit him on the chest. "You don't have a felony record related to driving old men to the hospital, do ya? So there. No problem."

He dropped his head and frowned. "I have a felony record related to doing things without thinking them through. I should have called an ambulance."

I touched his arm. "You did what Mrs. Ida wanted you to do. And that's what any man, any good man would have done."

He looked into my eyes and whispered, "I'm not sure what a good man would have done. The men I've known haven't been the best, the best role models, I guess."

"Well, you did the right thing."

"Thank you, Sarah."

Doug stood. "Who wants coffee? Doughnuts? Hamburgers? I'll make a cafeteria run."

Matthew answered, "Let me get it. I need to walk around a little. What does everyone want?"

Charlotte yelled out, "I ain't supposed to be eating anything good, so can you get me a bran muffin? And a banana? And a carton of milk? And a pack of Juicy Fruit? Bart, give the poor boy some money."

Matthew laughed as Bart handed him a five. "Absolutely. I can do that, Aunt Charlotte."

Doug said, "We're easy. How 'bout two cups of black coffee? But here, I'll come help ya."

"I was hoping Sarah could help me." He looked at me. "You available?"

"I am." No truer words were ever spoken.

Chapter 25, SARAH: Heart to Heart

We walked down the long hallway. I could smell the odd combination of freshly mown grass and expensive men's cologne. Matthew walked at a fast pace and I wondered if it had something to do with being in prison so long. Did they make them walk quickly? Or did he learn to walk quickly to stay out of people's way?

I broke the silence. "Are you worried? About Chester, I mean?"

"He's pretty tough. They both are. But yeah, I'm concerned. At least he's stable now."

"Mrs. Ida tells me you're quite the reader. I saw all those books piled up by your bed."

"Snooping, huh?"

"Hey, I never even walked in the room. I can't help it that you leave this big messy pile of books laying around."

He laughed. "Messy?"

"Okay. I'll admit the room looked pretty neat and clean. And yes, I was impressed that the bed was made. So you get nine points out of ten. How 'bout that?"

"I'll take it."

"You mentioned that Jim Hill probably never slept well after...after what happened. I mean, is that why you have all those books there? Insomnia?"

He cleared his throat as we entered the cafeteria. "I guess. I never sleep all night, no. The sleep problems are probably more about prison than the accident. Traded one trauma for the other, I guess."

"What's it like? Prison, I mean."

He shook his head as he stopped and faced me. "You don't want to know."

"I do actually."

"Yeah, but Aunt Charlotte's waiting on that Juicy Fruit, Sarah." He smiled and turned toward the cafeteria line. "Maybe we can talk about it another time."

"Yeah, maybe."

My heart ached. Matthew was shutting me out. And that made sense, I guess. Rejected by his own parents, not to mention fourteen years of seeing God knows what every day. He was just trying to survive. Survive and get Charlotte's Juicy Fruit. Soon we were entering the waiting room again.

Matthew spoke with gentleness as he handed Charlotte a brown paper bag, "Sorry, Aunt Charlotte. No bran muffins. We got you a banana nut."

"That's fine, Baby. Did you happen to bring any butter?"

Matthew looked away in an effort to keep from laughing. "Butter? Um, no. I didn't."

"Yeah, a big hunk a butter makes a muffin go down a lot easier, Darlin'. But your people, your California people may not have raised you eatin' butter on muffins. And that's okay. It is."

I handed Doug the coffee cups just as Brother Dan walked into the room.

Everyone jumped to their feet. Aunt Charlotte hollered, "Tell us he's okay, Hon. Go ahead. Tell us."

"He's resting comfortably right now. Ida seems pretty resolved and comfortable too. Bart and Charlotte, he definitely wants to see you. Both of you. But first…well, first he's requested a meeting with Sarah. Alone."

"Me?"

"Yes."

"Oh, okay. Yeah. I'll be right back."

I slowly opened the door. "Hello. It's me, Mr. Chester. Mrs. Ida?"

A weak but familiar voice said, "Come on in."

I approached the side of the bed and instinctively straightened the blanket. Chester looked tired and so did Mrs. Ida. She only weighed 110 pounds probably. Hair solid white. She never wore make-up or made any attempt to soften the many wrinkles brought on by more than 85 years of living. She held his hand gently, but pulled away just long enough to bring a yellow plastic cup to his mouth.

"How are you two doin'?" I pretended to hit him on the arm. "I think you gave us all a pretty good scare, Mister."

He smiled. "You're sweet for coming."

"I wanted to come, to check on you."

"Sarah, I'm sure I'll get better." He looked at Mrs. Ida. "With a good lookin' nurse like this, how could I not?"

"Right. Oh, absolutely."

"But just in case I don't, I want to tell you something."

"Mr. Chester, you're gonna be fine. Brother Dan says you're stable now."

"Yeah. But stable don't keep me from being 88 years old. I'm an old man and old men don't live forever."

"Well, none of us live forever."

Ida brought the yellow plastic cup back to his mouth and he took a sip of water. She wiped his mouth with a tissue and then kissed his bald head. The entire exchange seemed to give him strength. "It's about Matthew. You know how much we like the boy. It's only been a few months, but he's family to us." His voice weakened as though he were about to cry. "Family Ida and me never really had."

"Yes."

He reached for my hand. "We're giving him the house, Sarah."

"What?"

"The house. We've talked about it. It's what we both want. We're not gonna live forever. If I go on to Glory, Ida will

121

need someone to help her. He'll be good to her. But when she's gone, we want him to have the house. We done got it drawed up with Jimmy Smithson this week."

"That's wonderful news. Really. You guys are amazing. But what does that have to do with me?"

Chester grabbed my hand and looked into my eyes. "That house would have been nothin' to me without..." He paused and then wiped his nose with a wadded up tissue. "...without this woman right here."

My face flushed.

Chester continued. "He's a good man, Sarah. A good man. And he needs someone to love him. 'Course he's gun shy. Makes sense, don't it? He's known a lot of sufferin' in his life. A lot of sufferin'. Some of it he brought on himself, but no matter. That's all in the past. What's done is done. Most of what the boy has seen we'll never understand. But I know he's healing. And we was wonderin' well, we was wonderin' if you have any feelings about...about Matthew?"

"I doubt Matthew has feelings for me."

"That's not what I asked ya, Sarah."

I felt tears coming to my eyes as I patted his arm. "Just concentrate on getting better, okay? I promise we'll all take care of Matthew. I promise."

He held my hand tighter. "Matthew likes you, Sarah. You gotta know that."

Before I had a chance to answer, Janie Evans burst through the door. She had been a nurse since before I was born. "Mr. Miller, how are we doing?"

"I been better, Janie. I been better."

"Your visitors need to go home till tomorrow. You need your rest. I told Bart and Mrs. Charlotte they could come in for two minutes. But we need to clear the room after that."

I stood and placed my hands gently on his arm. "You are an extraordinary man, Chester Miller. And you have an extraordinary wife too."

He smiled at Ida and shook his head. "Ain't that the God's honest truth?"

Mrs. Evans was busy organizing pills by his bedside. "Sarah, the doctor is getting ready to meet with the rest of your group across the hall, if you want to say your good-byes now."

I walked around the bed to hug Mrs. Ida. "Look after this ol' man, will ya?"

She wiped her face and smiled. "He's looked out for me all these years." She paused and grabbed my hand. "And they been good years, Sarah. Not perfect. But good."

I patted Chester's arm. "I'm sure. Good bye…'till tomorrow."

I tried to compose myself in the hallway. I dabbed my eyes with a Kleenex, applied some clear lip gloss, and put my hair up in a clip. When I walked into the waiting room, Carlie handed me a bottle of water. "How is he?"

"He's a trooper."

"Sarah? Sarah Simpson?" The voice was familiar but I couldn't quite place it. I turned to see a face I hadn't seen since probably 8th grade.

"Brian?"

He extended his hand. "You remember. Yes, Brian Carter."

Remember? Who could forget? Brian Carter was the smartest kid in the middle school. He would have been Valedictorian had his dad not gotten that job that moved them to somewhere, somewhere I couldn't remember. But the Brian I knew had braces and acne. Shy. Had he not been so brilliant, I probably wouldn't have remembered him at all. This Brian was none of those things. Handsome. Confident. Clearly, the only thing he had in common with 8th grade Brian was the brilliance, as was evidenced by the white coat.

Chapter 26, CARLIE: Doctor, Doctor, Give Me the News...

What a night. Chester nearly died of a heart attack. Matthew broke the terms of his parole by driving him to the hospital. Aunt Charlotte ate and drank at least 750 calories in the waiting room, all the while explaining how hard it is to be on such a strict diet. And just as things were heating up between Sarah and Matthew, a doctor came in and threw a wrench into the whole thing. I know. You'd think the mechanic would be the one throwing wrenches, right? Wrong. Trust me. This doctor knows how to wield some serious fire power.

Janie Evans told us the doctor needed to come in and explain what was going on with Chester. I'm sure Janie told the doctor that Mrs. Ida was really old and she sometimes forgets to take her own blood pressure medicine. Plus, in such stressful circumstances, she might forget the details of Chester's condition and treatment plan. We were more than glad to be the conduits for information Mrs. Ida might need later.

But when the doctor came in, none of us recognized him. That's not unusual for me, but Doug knows everyone in the county. Finally, we recognized him from his picture in the paper. Dr. Brian Carter. New to the area. Well, not new really. He lived in Sharon a long time ago, until his mama and daddy moved to Knoxville for some kind of high falutin' academic job. When they moved, Brian wasn't even in high school yet. He moved back here last month because evidently Dr. Beaumont messed up Bill Watson's medication and nearly killed him. And after that, several people lovingly suggested Dr. Beaumont should retire. Well, I don't know if their suggestions were loving or not. Love or a lawyer? We'll probably never know for sure. But there was a doctor opening anyway. I figure Brian Carter moved here 'cause he probably didn't have much chance to go anywhere else, seein' as how he's young and everything. I saw a PBS special on this once, how young doctors sometimes have to "do time" in small towns in order to get part of their student loans forgiven. I don't know if that's the kind of deal this is or not. And I don't know if I like people referring to small towns as a place to "do time" either.

When he introduced himself, he didn't say, "I'm Dr. Carter." He just said, "I'm Brian Carter." Doctors do that sometimes when they want to come off as being humble and noteworthy. And people were making note alright. People were definitely making note.

Turns out he and Sarah went to school together back in the day. So they quickly reminisced about the drama club and the spelling bees and all the things nerdy kids did in the 90's. But then he efficiently redirected and explained Chester's situation to all of us. He used very practical wording we all could understand. At one point, he looked at Matthew and said, "So, you live with the two of them, yes?"

"Yes."

"When he gets released, he'll need a lot of help and support. I have some instructions I'd like to give you. Nothing complicated or hard for you to understand."

Matthew remained silent. Just because a man has dirt all over his shirt doesn't mean he can't understand simple instructions. I couldn't help but wonder if he wanted to tell the good doctor that he was plenty smart, that he graduated from a private college in California, that he'd even gotten into Vanderbilt Law. But of course, he said none of those things. He just nodded his head.

"Any questions?"

Aunt Charlotte spoke up. "Are you married, Darlin'?"

He smiled. "I'm not. Are you available?"

She laughed and pointed to Uncle Bart. "Nope. Not me. This here's my man and no young doctor is gonna come in and sway me from my vows."

"That's good. I respect a woman with priorities."

As our group was breaking up, Uncle Bart and Aunt Charlotte walked across the hall to say their hellos and good-byes. Brian Carter put his arm around Sarah. "Great to see you again, Sarah! I'd love for us to get together sometime. I'm off on Tuesday. Any possibility there's a spelling bee in town?"

She turned bright red. "Afraid not. We'll be going over spelling words in my class though. Trust me. It gets pretty exciting."

"I'm sure. How 'bout dinner instead?"

She hesitated, but only for a moment. "Uh, yeah. Sure."

"Great." He quickly removed a business card from the pocket of his white coat. "Text me your number and I'll make a plan and let you know. Looking forward to it."

Doug extended his hand. "Thank you, Dr. Carter. Thanks for all your help with Chester and Ida."

"You're welcome. If you need anything at all, call my office. It was nice to meet you, all of you."

And then he was gone. I found myself wishing Sarah had never gotten that front tooth fixed. Oh, and I was mad that she'd finally gone to one of Emma's Mary Kay parties at the community center too. Mabel had invited her for what? Two years? But no. She had to wait 'till now. And who says highlights look better than natural mousy brown? Oh, and what's wrong with long denim shorts or a loose-fitting t-shirt from the Soybean 5K Run? Nothing, that's what. Nothing at all.

Matthew's face was pale. He looked like a kid who'd gotten the wind knocked out of him in a fight on a school playground. He pulled Doug aside and spoke quietly. "I better just leave Chester's car here. Can you give me a ride home?"

"Sure, absolutely."

"I want to say bye to them. I'll only be a minute."

"No problem. We'll just wait."

But before Matthew could get out of the waiting room, Sarah said, "The Nelsons and I, we'll be goin' right by your place. Really. They won't mind."

Matthew barely spoke as he moved across the hallway. "Okay. That's fine, I guess."

Chapter 27, SARAH: Bad Times in the Good Times Machine

Charlotte Nelson sometimes has a hard time distinguishing between what should be shared and what shouldn't be shared. When Matthew and I climbed into the second row captain's chairs of the Good Times Machine, she began her monologue with enthusiasm. "I like that Dr. Carter, Sarah. Sure do. I remember now who his mama and daddy is. His daddy was a tall, skinny fella. Taught at UTM. Sure seems like a nice boy, don't he, Bart? Smart too. Real smart. And Sarah, your mama is gonna be right pleased that you're goin' out with him too. I mean, gosh darn it, Honey, we all love Jerry Conner. Who don't love 'em? I've known that pudgy little doll baby his whole life. But you done right to break his heart, Baby. You done right for sure."

Before anyone could get in a word, Bart had pulled into my driveway. "First stop. Sarah Simpson."

Matthew opened the door and got out so I wouldn't have to step over him. He reached back into the van and took my hand. When I'd arrived safely on the pavement, he said, "Nelsons, thanks for the ride. It's a nice night. I think I'll just walk home from here." He closed the door and waved.

Charlotte rolled down her window and protested. "Baby, we don't mind takin' you over to Ida's. We don't."

"Oh, I know. But really. It's not even a ten-minute walk. It'll do me good. Clear my head a little. Thank you."

Bart yelled, "Charlotte, he's a grown man! Leave the poor boy alone."

We both waved as they pulled out of the drive. Matthew headed toward the sidewalk. "Good night, Sarah."

"Wait! It's still early. And you're right. It's a nice night. Do you want to sit on the porch a while?"

He never even turned around. He just called out over his shoulder. "I've gotta get up early! Better not." I stood there, watching him walk away in the dark. A few times he removed his cap and shook grass clippings out of it. Part of me wondered why he didn't at least wait to leave until I got inside the house. Wasn't that what a gentleman would do? Wait until the lady got safely inside. But then I realized it was Sharon, Tennessee. I didn't remember the last time a felony crime was committed downtown. And it was definitely not committed at 9:30 on a Sunday night. Plus, it had been a lot of years since Matthew had had to think about social graces, especially social graces involving a woman.

I plopped onto the porch swing. Brian Carter. It had been forever since I'd even thought of him. I recalled every part of tonight's conversation. His sense of humor. Handsome face. But I didn't text him with my phone number. Not right now. I'd wait until tomorrow. Give him some time to ponder. Give myself some time to…I don't know, think about what it would be like to go out with someone whose main goal in life didn't involve surveillance of some kind.

Carlie pulled into the driveway and barely opened the car door. "Want a little company?"

"Sure. Come on up. The rocker's got your name on it."

"Good. I need a little rockin' time. Maxine got James to sleep before we got home. Doug has some work to do for a meeting tomorrow. So I thought I'd drop by and see a friend."

130

"So this is just a friendly visit, eh?"

"Of course. Well, that and I'm dying to know what you're thinking."

"About Chester? Brian Carter? Matthew breaking the terms of his parole?"

"Any and all of the above."

"I'm sad for Mrs. Ida. If he passes, I can't see her makin' it, Carlie. She'll be one of those who dies of a broken heart."

She rocked back and forth like an old woman imparting wisdom. "She loves him. That's for sure."

"When it comes to Brian, it wasn't really as much of a shock as I made out like it was. I mean, I'd seen his picture in the paper. But I figured he was married with kids by now."

"And?"

"And what?"

"Are you excited? About Tuesday?"

"I'm nervous. I haven't really dated since Jerry. And obviously, that whole thing went south in a hurry. You should have heard Mrs. Charlotte railing about it in the van. Said Jerry was a good guy, but I did the right thing, breakin' his pudgy little heart and all."

"She said that? In front of Matthew?"

"Yeah, he was right there. He probably didn't even know I'd dated Jerry at all."

131

"And now he thinks you're a small town heart breaker, huh?"

"Who knows what Matthew thinks? Does anybody know?
He goes away without telling anyone where he's going. He
gets a message from his father without telling anyone what it
was about."

"It'll take a while, to trust people. He'll come around."

"Yeah, I guess."

"Funny, I was startin' to think there was somethin' goin' on
between you two. He was starting to look at you like…"

"Like what?"

"You know, like a man looks at a woman."

My face grew warmer. "I doubt that. I just asked him to
come sit on the porch a while. He walked down the sidewalk
like he couldn't wait to get away from me."

"Well, duh! You're getting ready to go on a date in two days.
With someone else. That doesn't exactly foster confidence in
a man, right?"

"He's had plenty of chances."

"He doesn't need chances. He needs confidence, confidence
you'll say yes."

"Are you kidding? After that speech the other night, every
girl and woman in town was pawing all over him. Now he's
going to be on TV and that will be multiplied by what? A
million?"

"Mark my word. He's not asking because he's unsure of the answer."

"And he told you that?"

"Uh, no. Not exactly. Look, I know these things, Sarah. I do."

"Oh yeah. I keep forgetting how you have that special intuition when it comes to matchmaking. What are you going to call your matchmaking book? 'The Principal and the Pomeranian'? Or is it 'The Principal Overcomes Pet Dander'?"

"Keep laughing, friend. Keep laughing. Everyone likes to make fun...until they need me. And you do. You need me."

"Okay. So, Matthew and I have eaten together, what? Ten times at least? Your house, Ashley's place, church several times. And you're saying there was never a time when he could have said, 'Sarah, would you like to walk to the diner with me tomorrow night?' Or 'Sarah, would you like to go to a movie?' No. I'm not giving him an out. He's had plenty of chances."

"You're right. But have you ever thought about it from his perspective? No car. No family, really. He's trying to get on his feet. Plus, we don't even know all the things that went on in prison, things that would still haunt him."

"I guess. Chester and Ida sure think a lot of him."

"They do."

"Carlie, I have a question that requires your matchmaking expertise."

"Oooh, I can hardly wait. Hit me."

"What should I wear Tuesday night?"

Carlie jumped to her feet. "Oh, yes, I can help you! Let's hit that closet, Girlfriend!"

I opened the front door and said, "You first."

She immediately started mumbling something about the miracle of push-up bras and how chunky scarves were invented by women who hate men.

Chapter 28, SARAH: There's More to Life than Good Salsa

There aren't that many places to go for dinner in Weakley County. Brian texted me last night asking if I wanted to go to Paducah or Jackson. I said I wasn't picky and a local place would be fine. Carlie picked out a black pair of pants and a bright red shirt for me to wear. I felt red was a little too...I don't know. But Carlie said red indicated an openness to romance and adventure. I think she reads too many women's magazines.

I found myself pacing, waiting for the knock on the door. Mama called at ten till six to remind me to be friendly and not to talk about the school kids too much. Her exact words? "No doctor wants to hear long drawn-out stories about kids fighting on the playground or costumes for the Thanksgiving play." Thanks, Mom. I was gonna try to wow him with a question about what a 3rd grade Miles Standish should wear. But now you've given me serious cause to reconsider. Good night. I know she was just trying to be helpful. Everyone is just trying to be helpful. Now it's too late 'cause the knock on the door finally came.

"Brian, hey, come on in. Let me grab my purse and we'll be ready." He looked even better than I expected. Ironed khaki pants, probably done at the dry cleaners in Martin. Blue and white striped oxford shirt, navy jacket. He wasn't wearing the wire-rim glasses he had on at the hospital. Must have contacts in. Eyes really blue.

"Sarah, you look beautiful. Red, it's your color."

"Thank you."

"I'm up for Mexican food in Martin. You?"

"Sure. Sounds great!"

The Mexican restaurant was crowded, which was odd for a Tuesday night. But then I remembered it was discount night at the movie theater and maybe there was a connection. We had to sit close on the little wooden bench because an older couple was sitting beside us. We talked about his parents, still living in Knoxville. We talked about my mom, still working at the nursing home. Conversation was dwindling a bit, when I heard a familiar sound. A sound I had heard all my life.

"Law mercy, what in tarnation is goin' on 'round here? Is there a convention in town? Lord, why don't these college students eat in the dorm? Their mamas and daddies done paid for all that perfectly good food."

I turned to see Charlotte Nelson with her arm around our teenage hostess. The young girl replied, "Not sure, really. But we'll get you seated as fast as we can."

"Thank ya, Baby!" She turned and immediately made eye contact with me. "Oh look, Bart, look who's here! Look at this, would ya?"

Brian stood and extended his hand. I stood because, well, I wasn't sure what to do. Brian spoke kindly because he probably didn't know what he was getting himself into. "Hello again. Nice to see you two!"

Charlotte laughed. "Thank ya, Baby. You too. We was up at the hospital seein' Chester this afternoon." She squeezed my hand. "Sarah, they think he'll go home tomorrow. Yes, Ma'am. Reckon the ol' cuss dodged another bullet. Anyway, well, Matthew dropped by the hospital on his way home from work. Offered to take us out to dinner seein' as how he's eaten at our place a few times and he ain't much of one for cookin'. He's in the bathroom right now." She whispered as though she were relaying a terrible secret. "I think he drinks a lot of that yellow Gatorade during the day. Bless him."

Brian stayed calm. "Well, it was good to see you two. We'll let you get back to your waiting, I guess."

Charlotte was not done yet. "Oh Honey, we got nothin' but time." The older couple beside us got called to a table and Charlotte squeezed herself onto the bench right next to Brian. "Baby, you smell good. Sure do. I always figured a doctor would smell like rubbing alcohol or formaldehyde. But you smell good. Oh, look! Here comes Matthew now!"

Matthew walked toward us but I couldn't tell whether his expression was one of apathy or if he was just trying to play it cool. He had on the exact same clothes he wore when he returned from the mystery trip. Plaid cowboy shirt, dark jeans, brown cowboy boots. His hair was damp which made it wavy. Good-looking without being haughty or proud. Chester's words had gone through my mind at least 1000 times in the last few days. Matthew likes you, Sarah. Now I was starting to wonder if they were just the words of an old man who thought he was dying, an old man who wished things were one way…even though they weren't that way at all.

Matthew managed a smile, as he extended his hand. "Dr. Carter."

"You can call me Brian."

"Thanks." Matthew looked into my eyes and I couldn't help but remember the day he touched my face, the day he whispered my name. I wanted so much to go back to that day, to rewind and have another chance. He nodded. "Hey, Sarah."

"Hi Matthew. Glad to hear Chester's improving. I was gonna call the hospital later tonight."

"Yeah, it's good news. Look, we're just here to eat so we'll let you two get back to your..." He paused. "Your..."

Brian replied enthusiastically, "Our date?"

Matthew turned away and looked at the busy hostess. "Yeah."

Charlotte jumped in. "As crowded as it is in here, ain't no way we're gonna get a table fore my blood sugar drops." She patted Brian's knee. "Thank God there's a doctor in the house, huh?"

She immediately yelled out to the hostess. "We saw our friends over here! So if you got a table for five, we'll take it!"

Matthew turned and looked at Charlotte like she had just blown up the Pentagon. "No. No, they don't want to do that, Aunt Charlotte. We should leave them alone. Really."

But the wheels were already in motion. In less than a minute, the hostess came back and said, "Charlotte, table of five."

I glanced at Brian, but I couldn't read his expression. You'd think he'd be sad about having to share me. Sad about not getting all my attention. And maybe he was. But he wasn't sad enough to stand up to Charlotte Nelson. And I wasn't sad at all.

Charlotte and Bart led the way behind the hostess. Matthew stayed near the back and whispered, "I'm sorry, guys."

Brian smiled. "Don't worry about it."

138

Charlotte began with her latest dieting revelations. "Dr. Carter, I figure I can eat tortilla chips 'cause corn is a vegetable and ever'body talks about the healing power of vegetables."

"I guess that's one way of looking at it. Matthew, what do you do?"

"I'm a mechanic. In Bradford."

"It's always good to know a mechanic."

Matthew glanced through the menu. "I guess. Sarah, what's the latest news in third grade?"

"Big big excitement in Ms. Sarah's class today. We got a gerbil. A real live gerbil. His name is T.G. It stands for…well, guess. Guess what it stands for."

Charlotte grinned. "Terrible George."

"Nope."

Brian said, "Theodore Girard."

I laughed. "Good guesses, all. Keep going. You'll get it eventually."

Bart said, "Tyler somethin' or other."

"No. Not Tyler."

"I named him myself. Matthew, any guesses?"

He set the menu down and looked into my eyes. "T.G., huh? I'm thinking it stands for The Gerbil."

"Ding ding. We have a winner. How did you know?"

He raised his eyebrows and looked into my eyes. "I guess I figured a no-nonsense woman would give a gerbil a no-nonsense name."

He was right. How could he have possibly known? He went right back to looking at the menu but he smiled like he was proud of himself for knowing the answer, for knowing me.

Charlotte quickly changed the subject. "Dr. Carter, how do you like being back in West Tennessee?"

"I like it. Yeah, a lot quieter. Slower pace than my residency, of course."

Matthew grabbed a chip. "Where did you do your residency?"

"St. Thomas in Nashville."

"Nashville's a great city."

"It is. Matthew, are you from around here?"

"No. California originally. San Diego area."

"San Diego? And what brought you to Sharon, Tennessee, from San Diego?"

Matthew didn't hesitate. "Prison, I guess."

The table was silent. Brian coughed and then put a chip in his mouth. Even Charlotte had nothing to add. Matthew looked straight at me and continued. "I left San Diego to go to law school at Vanderbilt. Got on drugs and flunked out. Killed two people in a car wreck." He looked back at the menu.

140

"Did fourteen years. That's where I met Dusty McConnell. And that's how I'm here. He owns the shop in Bradford."

Brian looked like he'd been hit by a meteor. "Wow, that's quite a story." He scooted his chair back and looked around. "Where is that waitress? They seem overrun tonight."

Waitress? You just heard Matthew say what he said and you're wondering where the waitress is? Wondering why we can't order our fajitas and move on with our lives? I drank the last of my water. "Matthew is getting ready to be a TV star, Brian."

"He is, is he?"

"Yeah. A & E is doing a new show called, 'Sweet Southern Freedom.' It's about Dusty's shop, his time in prison, and his hiring of Matthew. Second chances and all."

"Sounds like a smart idea."

Matthew's phone buzzed. He jumped up. "I'm sorry. I need to take this." He briskly walked outside. I watched him pacing on the sidewalk.

Brian turned to make eye contact with me. "Did you know that about him? The prison thing?"

"I did."

"And people around here, they're okay with it?"

"I don't know. Chester and Ida adore him. Everyone says he does great work at the shop. He spoke at this rally downtown and it seemed to mean a lot to a lot of people."

"Yeah, but…I mean, Sarah, I would think you, of all people…would be a little…"

"A little put out with him for driving while he was on drugs? For killing someone? Two people?"

"Yeah."

"He was twenty-one years old, Brian. He did fourteen years in prison." My voice escalated a bit. "Fourteen years. And he's still doing time. The person he killed was his own sister, his sister and her roommate. Mary was his best friend. "

Matthew ran to the table. "Uncle Bart, we need to go now. Mrs. Ida. She needs us."

Chapter 29, CARLIE: Will This Circle Be Unbroken?

Chester Miller died tonight at 7:08 pm. Massive heart attack. Less than an hour earlier, he said he was feeling better than he'd felt in years. He ate broiled chicken breast and red Jell-O from the hospital tray. He promised Janie Evans he was going to stop eating fried food and bacon. He told Dr. Burton about the time a rabid squirrel got into the old school house and Miss Henderson knocked a hole in the floor with a sledge hammer trying to kill it. He told Mrs. Ida she was prettier than the day she married him out under the pecan trees on her daddy's farm in Palmersville. Then he died. Mrs. Ida was holding his hand the whole time.

Janie Evans called us and we immediately called Matthew's cell phone. Doug stayed with James and I went to be with Mrs. Ida at the hospital. As I entered the emergency room door, I saw Uncle Bart, Aunt Charlotte, Matthew, Dr. Carter, and Sarah running through the parking lot.

Aunt Charlotte was already crying hard. "Oh Lord, I can't take it! I can't! Poor Ida. She won't make it. She won't!" Picante sauce stains were all over the front of Aunt Charlotte's Sunday dress. It was the green knit dress with the wide black belt. The one she always wore to funerals and weddings. I'm sure she thought Matthew Prescott's dinner invitation was worthy of the best she had to offer.

Uncle Bart put his arm around her as we rushed into the elevator. "She'll make it, Charlotte. She ain't got no choice. She'll make it."

Matthew's face was white but he remained silent.

As though we were somehow blaming him, Dr. Carter said, "He was 88 years old. There's only so much any of us could have done."

Sarah leaned toward Matthew and reached for his hand. "I'm sorry, Matthew. So sorry."

Matthew looked at Sarah like he'd lost his best friend, like he wanted to tell Dr. Brian Carter to go away forever. But he didn't say it. He wouldn't say it. He wiped tears from his face and spoke quietly. "Thank you."

In a few seconds, Sarah let go of his hand and moved back next to her date. All of us dreaded the elevator doors opening. Pure dread. But the doors did open. And the moment they did, we heard the quiet sobs.

Mrs. Ida was sitting in a green vinyl chair with her head in her hands. She had on light blue double-knit pants and a button-up blouse with white and blue flowers all over it. It's the same outfit meemaws everywhere wear. Except Mrs. Ida had never been a mother or a grandmother. Chester was her family. Her everything.

Matthew Prescott was the brave one. His bravery was never more evident than it was at 7:51 pm on the night Chester Miller died. He literally ran ahead of all of us. He knelt in front of Mrs. Ida and placed his hands gently on her knees. When she saw him, she wrapped her arms around his neck and cried out in pain. "Oh, Matthew, Matthew! He's gone. What am I gonna do? He's gone."

She laid her white head gently on his strong chest and he stroked her hair. Tears ran down his face but he spoke with quiet authority. "I know. I know. He was a good man. The best." She leaned back into the chair and he grabbed both of

144

her hands. "I'll take care of you, Mrs. Ida. I will. You and me, we're a team now. Family. I'll take care of everything. I promise."

Even Uncle Bart started crying. "Gall darn pollen in the air. I'm headin' to the john."

Aunt Charlotte put her hand on Mrs. Ida's shoulder. "Oh Ida, I'm so sorry. We all are."

She wiped her eyes with an old handkerchief embossed with blue flowers. "Thank ya, Charlotte. Thank ya."

We sat with Mrs. Ida for more than thirty minutes. Matthew finally got her to drink water and eat part of a ham sandwich. He stood and spoke like a father speaking to a daughter. "Mrs. Ida, we probably need to go on home now. We'll go to the funeral home as soon as they open in the morning."

She lifted her head. "He's at Groeden's. Right down there by the flower shop. Chester's had it all arranged for years."

"Yes, Ma'am. I'm sure he has it all worked out. But you need to get some rest."

Uncle Bart put his hand on Matthew's shoulder. "I'll pull the van around. Just bring her down to that side entrance."

"Will do."

Janie Evans pulled Matthew aside and handed him a small medicine bottle. Dr. Burton had already come by and given Mrs. Ida a sleeping pill.

Dr. Carter extended his hand to her. "I hope you'll be able to get some sleep, Ma'am."

She shook her head as Matthew reached over and completely enveloped her in his arms. He leaned his head forward to rest gently on top of hers. She said quietly, "Thank you, Matthew. Thank you." Matthew held her up as they walked slowly toward the elevator.

Sarah looked at Dr. Carter like the dog ate her homework. "I'm sorry, Brian. I really should go with Mrs. Ida. There are things she might need me to do for her, things Matthew wouldn't feel comfortable doing."

Dr. Carter hesitated. "Yes, well, of course. You should go. No problem. Can I call you later?"

"Sure, that's fine. Matthew, wait for me! I'm coming with you."

Chapter 30, SARAH: Learning to Live Again

I remained quiet in the elevator. Matthew had finally gotten Mrs. Ida calmed down and I didn't want to say or do anything that might resurrect the outward grieving. At one point, it almost looked like she was closing her eyes and going to sleep against his chest. She never let go of Matthew and he never let go of her.

Bart and Charlotte had already pulled the van around. I slid into the very back seat so that Matthew could sit across from Mrs. Ida in the Captain's chairs. The ten minute trip to their home was completely silent, except for the occasional sobs. As Bart pulled into the drive, Mrs. Ida spoke though her voice was weak. "Sixty-eight years. Sixty-eight years I been cookin' his breakfast, ironin' his clothes, doin' for him. So what am I supposed to do now?"

Charlotte answered, "I don't know, Ida. I don't know. Matthew'll help ya though. He will."

Bart helped her onto the porch as Matthew unlocked the front door. "Now Ida, you know we's only a phone call away. Only a phone call away."

"Thank ya, Bart."

Matthew and I were on each side of Mrs. Ida as we entered the front door. Her knees began to give but he caught her.

Matthew said, "I'll help get her to the bedroom. You think you can get her ready for bed?"

"Sure. Mrs. Ida, let's get your night clothes on."

She mumbled but we couldn't understand her words.

147

She sat on the edge of the bed and began sobbing again. Matthew kneeled down in front of her. It was the most beautiful thing I'd witnessed in a long long time. He carefully unstrapped her orthopedic shoes and then pulled them off so gently. As he removed her thin blue socks he spoke with kindness. "Mrs. Ida, Sarah is going to help you. She's going to help you get ready for bed."

Her words were slurred. "What about Chester? Where's Chester?"

Matthew looked at me, as though he were unsure what to say or do. Finally he got up the courage. "Mrs. Ida, he's gone…gone to heaven, remember?"

She began to sob quietly. Matthew wrapped his arms around her. "You'll see him again. You will."

I whispered, "Matthew, we'll be fine. I'll help her get ready." I'm not sure what Dr. Burton gave her, but it was potent. Within five minutes, I had gotten her in an old flannel night gown and she was snoring loudly. I slipped out of the room, leaving the door slightly open.

I stood at the door to the living room. The lights were all out except for the hallway light. I could barely see Matthew sitting in the brown vinyl chair. His head was in his hands. He glanced over at Chester's recliner. "Saturday night we watched an educational show about Eisenhower. Said he remembered when he was president. Remembered hearing him on the radio. He may not have been educated. But he wasn't dumb. He was a smart man, Sarah. Wise."

"Chester was a good man. Yes."

"He was."

"He thought the world of you. Really, Matthew. You were a bright spot. For both of them."

"It's funny. When Dusty first asked me about staying with them, I thought it was crazy. What older couple would want an ex-con to just move in with them? A rent house, maybe. But staying in their own home? No way."

"But they were special."

"Right. Dusty told me they trusted him…and so they trusted me. I didn't understand that really. That level of…that level of…"

"Community?"

"Yeah, I guess." He started laughing. "Not that they didn't have their moments. At first, they were suspect. They'd watch me go in and out of rooms. They'd sit outside when I was doing yard work. But after the first week or so, they both relaxed a lot. Said I was family."

"You were family…are family."

His voice got lower. "Don't know why it's so hard. I mean, I knew he was old. But…"

"But it was still a shock. It was for all of us."

"Right."

"Mrs. Ida is sound asleep and will probably be asleep for quite a while. Guess I better get on home. But if you need anything, anything at all, you know where I live, Matthew. Carlie and Mrs. Charlotte are coming by in the morning at 7:30. They said they'd be happy to go to the funeral home

149

with her when she wakes up. Dusty said you called about wanting to work in the morning, maybe till noon, when they'll be back from the funeral home, when she'll need you here for a while."

"Yeah, that should work."

"Dusty said he'll send someone for you about 8:00. Figured you'd need the extra time to get her settled in."

"Sarah?"

"Yes."

"Are you in a hurry?"

"Not really."

"If you're busy, don't worry about it. I was just thinking maybe you...you could sit a while?"

"Sure. I can do that." I moved toward the floral chair because it was closer to Matthew and I didn't want to speak too loudly. "You figure Mrs. Ida would be okay with me taking her chair? Just this once?"

He nodded. "I'm sure."

I didn't turn the lights on and neither did he. Who could have known what a truth serum darkness would be?

Matthew spoke first. "Dr. Carter. He seems real nice."

"He does."

"And you guys knew each other in Junior High, huh? Small world."

"It is. Odd how he ended up back here, after all these years."

"And even odder that Aunt Charlotte insisted we all sit together at dinner. I'm sorry about that, Sarah." I could see his head shaking even through the shadows. "It was out of line, but how does anyone tell Aunt Charlotte she's out of line?"

I laughed. "Trust me. People around here have been trying to figure that one out for years. So if you have any insight, let us in on it, Matthew."

"Everyone knows she means well. I think that makes a big difference."

"Yeah. She would do anything for any of us, for anybody. It really is true. Love covers a multitude of sins. Matthew, is there anything I can do? I figure it's been a hard day for ya."

He lowered his head as his boots shuffled against the hardwood floor. "My dad died. On Friday."

"Oh, I'm sorry. I had no idea."

"That's where I was, you know, last week. My friend, Julie, called. Said he was really sick, that maybe I should come, maybe it would be my last chance to see him…make amends and all."

"And did you get to see him?"

"I did. My mom too. Maybe it was because Julie was there, but she acted glad to see me. Well, not glad really. But she didn't throw me out of the hospital room. Probably because it would have been embarrassing. To throw me out. And they don't do anything to embarrass the Prescott name." He looked up. "I've done plenty of that."

"Matthew, I don't know what to say. I mean, I'm so glad you went out there. Glad you were able to make peace with him, with both of them. But I'm sorry he died."

He paused. "Evidently I didn't make peace. Not really."

"But I thought you said they responded well?"

"I said they didn't throw me out."

"What happened?"

"When I walked into the room, my dad was coming in and out of consciousness."

"And your mom?"

He shook his head. "You don't understand the way we do things. My mom let me go a long time ago. It's like I died when Mary died. Embarrassment. Shame. When I entered the hospital room, she looked shell-shocked. She didn't get up. Never touched me. Finally, she whispered to my dad, 'Matthew's here.' He actually came to for a bit. I walked to the bed, put my hand on his. And said…" Matthew started crying. He pulled a Kleenex from the box on the coffee table and blew his nose. "I'm sorry. I don't even know why I'm telling you all this."

"It's fine. I'm glad you're telling me. Go on."

"I said, 'I'm sorry, Dad. I loved Mary. I'll always love her.'"

"And?"

"And nothing really. He smiled and then it's like he went back to sleep. Mom said, 'He needs his rest.' Julie and I left the room. Julie said she'd bring me back to the hospital the next morning. But the next morning they had moved him home. They brought in Hospice and everything. Julie was kind enough to take me to the house and Mom was a little more open. She told me it was good of me to come. She asked about where I was living. When I told her all about Dusty and the job, she asked how I liked living in a small southern town. I told her I liked it. Dad was unconscious the whole time I was there. But I don't know. I felt like I had made progress. I knew I'd never see him alive again. But..."

"It felt like closure."

"Right. Until Sunday. At first, the guy just told me Dad had died. I figured Mom had sent him to deliver the news. Or maybe they were sending him to transport me back to the funeral."

"But there was something else."

"Yeah. Evidently they didn't want me at the funeral. Dad died Friday morning and they scheduled the funeral for Sunday afternoon, the same time the guy showed up at Doug and Carlie's to tell me he was gone."

"That's crazy. I'm sorry. That was painful, insulting."

He nodded his head. "But that wasn't the main reason Mr. Morgan came from California. His real job was to tell me I'd been written out of the will. Years ago. That my cousin, Stephen, would be inheriting the business, that there was no need to pursue any legal action because it was all finalized a

153

long time ago. He gave me all the paperwork." He paused
and his voice grew softer. "I don't care about the money.
And I never cared about the software business. But there was
something about...about the way he said it."

"The rejection. The finality."

"Right. Made me wonder if Mom thought that's why I went
out there in the first place. That I was afraid I wouldn't get the
money or something. I don't give a damn about their money,
Sarah. I never did."

"I'm sorry, Matthew. A lot of loss for one week."

"The sad thing?" He spoke louder. "I'm more grieved about
Chester dying than I am about my own father dying. How sad
is that?"

"I have a question. Your friend, Julie, why didn't she call to
tell you he died?"

"Don't know. Maybe they asked her not to. Maybe they told
her they'd already told me. Anyway, I need to move on, put it
behind me. I'm sorry for wasting all your time, Sarah. And
I'm sorry about messing up your date with Dr. Carter. I could
have helped Mrs. Ida myself." He rose from the vinyl chair
and stretched his arms into the air. "I've burdened you long
enough."

"No. I wanted to be here. I did. You didn't mess up my
evening at all. It's not like we're actually dating. I mean,
yeah, it was a date, but it's not like he's my boyfriend or
anything."

Matthew laughed quietly. "Yeah, he's no Jerry Conner.
That's for sure."

I stood but didn't move toward the door. "I can't believe Charlotte said that. That was a whole weird deal. Really. It's not like it sounds."

"And how does it sound?" He walked closer to me and I felt nervous, the same way I felt in the car that day.

"You know, like I led him on or broke his heart. I didn't."

He got even closer and looked into my eyes. "Jerry Conner still likes you, you know."

"And how would you know that?"

"The way he looks at you."

I grabbed my purse and fidgeted nervously with my keys. "How? Like I'm one of the few single women left in Sharon?"

"No. He looks at you like you're...you know, like you're beautiful."

"I hadn't noticed."

He walked toward the front door and turned on the porch light. He turned back to the living room and spoke with an air of sadness. "But you don't have to worry about Jerry pursuing you anymore, Sarah."

"I don't, huh."

He placed his hands in his front pockets and looked straight out the screen door. "No. Aunt Charlotte's right. Jerry's been outdone this time. And I'm sure he knows it. I'd offer to give you a ride home. But Chester's car is still at the hospital and I'm not supposed to…"

As I moved toward the door, high beam headlights illumined the front porch. Jerry got out of the patrol car and moved cautiously toward the steps.

Matthew smiled and said quietly. "Speak of the devil." He opened the front door. "Hey, Jerry! Come on in."

"Uh, thank ya, Matthew. I was just, well, I heard about Chester and I wanted to share my condolences with Mrs. Ida."

"She's gone to bed. Dr. Burton gave her some medicine. Been asleep for a while now."

Jerry stood on the porch, nervously looking in all directions. "Well, that was real sad about Chester. Real sad."

Matthew was still holding the door open. "It was. A hard loss for all of us."

I did something wrong. Hurtful even. I moved forward and stood as close to Matthew as I possibly could. I could even feel my left hip touching his right arm. I could smell his cologne and feel every breath he took.

"Hey there, Sarah. It was good of you to come help Mrs. Ida. Janie said you was on a date with Dr. Carter but that you quit on him because…well, because you was comin' over here to help, you know, help Mrs. Ida that is."

Matthew put his arm around me and looked into my eyes. "She's a Good Samaritan alright. Sure is." Sadly, within seconds, he let go and walked out onto the porch. "Jerry, I bet you'd be glad to drive Sarah home tonight."

156

"Oh, absolutely!" His face beamed just exactly like the first day he donned the uniform. His mama had shown the picture to everybody in town at least a dozen times. She carries the picture in an old blue envelope in her purse. "Sarah, let me run clear your seat out. I'll be glad to take you home. More than glad." And with that, he turned and skipped off the porch like he had completely forgotten the grief of Chester Miller's death, the grief that had supposedly motivated an evening condolence call.

I gently slapped Matthew's chest and whispered, "You are just looking for trouble, Mister."

He grinned. "Hey! I think we should at least give the guy a fighting chance."

"I think you should stick to working on cars."

"You're probably right." He gently grabbed my arm and I turned to face him. "Thank you, Sarah. Thank you for helping tonight." He meticulously straightened the welcome mat with his feet. "And not just with Mrs. Ida either. Thank you for helping me. You're a good listener. I'm not sure why I told you all that."

"I'm glad you did. And don't worry. I'll keep it to myself. Besides, don't you want the locals to think you were away carrying out some dangerous International espionage mission or something?"

"I guess there are worse things for them to be thinking." When he smiled, his dark eyes looked even more handsome. Peaceful. Of course, it could have just been the moonlight. Or the porch light. Or the flashlight. Wait, the flashlight?

"Jerry, what in the world are you doing?"

157

"Just sending a light signal to let you know your chariot awaits. You know, like a bat signal or a lighthouse signal. Oh, and this is no ordinary flashlight either. It's for law enforcement purposes only."

Matthew laughed. "Better be careful with that, Jerry! You could uproot the plants!" He winked at me. "You two kids stay out of trouble now!"

Chapter 31, CARLIE: "The Notebook" Comes to Sharon, Tennessee

Okay. Remember at the end of that movie, "The Notebook," when James Garner lays in the bed with his wife who has dementia? When I first saw that scene, I was in a theater and everybody in the theater was just blubberin' and blowin' their noses to beat the band. I mean, if you can watch that scene and not cry, well, you've got no soul. You probably kick dogs or make mean faces at babies or take money out of the offering plate when it comes by.

Anyway, that whole James Garner thing is called the broken heart principle or something like that. One spouse so grieved by the other one's death that he or she dies too. Some people even say there's medical evidence for it. Well, evidence or no evidence, that's exactly what happened on Mill Street in Sharon, Tennessee, sometime Sunday night.

Aunt Charlotte and I went over to Mrs. Ida's at 7:30 to relieve Matthew so he could go to work for a few hours. He said she was still sleeping peacefully. That wasn't too surprising considering the fact that she'd had sleeping medicine. But at 8:30 Aunt Charlotte got concerned and went to check on her. There was a great commotion and she hollered out, "Oh Lord, Carlie, she's dead! Come quick! Ida's done gone to meet her maker!"

We called 9-1-1. But we both knew she was gone. The whole town of Sharon was in an uproar too. The news of Chester's death had no sooner spread through Mabel's and the barber shop before folks got word that Mrs. Ida had passed less than twelve hours later. But the worst part? Well, the worst part was when Aunt Charlotte and I had to drive to Bradford to tell poor Matthew.

Dusty was on a ladder changing out a floodlight bulb. Matthew was rearranging piles of tires so he could pressure wash the parking lot. They both tried to play it cool with the whole TV show coming up. But I knew they were cleaning up the shop because shooting was to begin next Monday.

Dusty waved and stepped down from the ladder. "Mornin', ladies! I tell ya, my heart is sure grieved over Mr. Chester. That was a loss. A real loss."

Aunt Charlotte was unusually silent. I guess that odd fact in itself was enough to prompt his curiosity. "Carlie, everything okay?"

"Not really. We need to speak to you and to Matthew too."

Dusty carefully placed the old bulb in a big rusty trash barrel on the side of the shop. "Matthew! You can take a break inside. These ladies need to speak with us."

Aunt Charlotte and I remained silent as we sat down on the ugly green couch. Dusty paced nervously. Matthew opened the door as he pulled the familiar red rag from his back pocket and wiped his hands. "Where's Mrs. Ida? Is she sick or something?"

Aunt Charlotte started weeping uncontrollably. Matthew's face turned pale and his voice got quiet. "Wait, you're not telling me…"

Aunt Charlotte jumped from the couch and threw both her chubby arms around him. "Yes! Yes, Baby! She's dead. Gone to be with God…with Chester, Darlin'."

Matthew pulled away from Aunt Charlotte and threw the red rag to the ground. "No! She wasn't even sick! What did he

160

give her? That Dr. Burton? How did…" He sat in a chair and put his face in his hands. "Please God, no. She was all I had left."

Dusty kneeled by the chair and placed his hand on Matthew's shoulder. "She was an incredible lady. And she loved you, Matthew. She did. They both did."

"But I don't get it. That medicine made her sick. It must have!"

Aunt Charlotte spoke with unusual calm. "Baby, this is what she wanted. 'Member how she said it last night? That she couldn't see no life without Chester? Well, God worked it out for her not to have to go through all that. She was 85 years old. Had a good life with a good man. And let me tell ya somethin'. People always felt sorry for both of 'em havin' no kids and all." She wiped a tear as she wrapped her arm around his shoulder. "Well, look what God done. Right here…at the finish line. He gave 'em you. And they was proud too. Lord, they was proud to have ya, Matthew."

Aunt Charlotte never ceases to amaze me. One minute she seems certifiably crazy. The next minute I'm convinced she's smarter than all of us put together.

Chapter 32, Sarah: Joy Multiplied and Sorrow Cut in Half

The janitor, Mr. Billings, is the one who first shared the news. He bolted into the teacher's lounge at lunchtime. "I just got word from Jerry Conner. Mrs. Ida died sometime in the night. That's all I know." I still couldn't believe it. I'd known both of them all my life. Loved them. But so had everyone else in the school and in the town of Sharon. We mourned, yes. But unlike Matthew, none of us had ever had to mourn alone.

I couldn't wait for the closing bell. But I didn't rush to leave school. I sat quietly at my desk thinking about Chester and Ida. She'd been my first Sunday School teacher. She gave us Fruit Stripe gum every Sunday and marshmallow eggs at Easter. She used a big flannelgraph board to teach Bible stories. Mitch Smith once asked how she could tell which flannelgraph character was Jesus and which one was Paul. She laughed and said, "This one here's Jesus 'cause he don't look tired or weary."

I sharpened pencils and graded math homework. Truth is, I didn't leave because I wasn't really sure where I should go. I remembered that Sunday afternoon when Matthew walked in the door from his mystery trip. I couldn't tell who was happier. Matthew because he got to see the Millers? Or the Millers because they got to see Matthew? Tears started falling on the red ink numbers in the grade book, causing them to fade slightly. A knock at the door startled me.

I instinctively rose to my feet. "Yes? Come in."

Matthew walked in and stood by the door without making eye contact. He had on his Sunday clothes. Ironed khaki pants. Light blue oxford shirt. Looked like his cowboy boots had been polished and shined. He leaned up against the wall with one foot propped behind him. When he did, I couldn't help but think about those cowboy pictures with the cowboy leaned up against the wall in that exact position. But Matthew Prescott was far more handsome than any cowboy I'd ever seen. In his left hand, there was a familiar folder from Groeden's Funeral Home. He cleared his throat. "I just came by to make sure you'd gotten word. I mean, about..." He smiled and coughed. "Who am I kidding? It's 3:30 in the afternoon. Every person in Sharon knows by now. That's not why I came by. You're probably busy, Sarah." He started to leave. "I'm sorry to bother you."

"No. Don't go. You're not bothering me. Really." I stepped out from behind my desk. As I was walking toward him, I began crying like I'd lost my own mother. He immediately moved away from the wall, and walked toward me. He wrapped his arms around me, almost exactly the way he had wrapped his arms around Mrs. Ida in her time of grief. Fully encompassing me. Providing a place of absolute safety. Security. Warmth.

"It's okay, Sarah. Go ahead and cry." I pressed my face into his chest and cried almost exactly like I did when my daddy died. Sorrowful. He rubbed his hand gently over my head. "It'll be okay. We'll all get through it."

Finally I pulled my face back and whispered. "I'm sorry, Matthew. Don't know what came over me."

"Sadness. And there's nothing wrong with being sad. Mr. Chester and Mrs. Ida, they're worthy of that sadness."

"I guess. Gosh, I've gotten make-up all over your shirt. I'm sorry. Really."

"Don't worry about it. I'm getting ready to go home anyway. I can change."

"Well, at least you won't have to worry about supper."

"How's that?"

"Oh Matthew, there are so many things you don't know about Sharon. So many things. When's the last time you were home?"

"'Bout noon."

"Right. Well, let's see, it's almost 4:00 now. Yeah, I'd say there's a pretty good trickle by now. Did someone tell you about leaving the house unlocked?"

"Yeah. Carlie told me to be sure to leave the house unlocked when I went to the funeral home. I didn't understand that."

"Well, I'll drive you home and you'll understand."

When we got near Chester and Ida's house, James and Collin were playing in the front yard with all four of Dusty and Clara's kids and one of the neighbor boys. Dave and Ashley were sitting on the front porch with Doug and Carlie. Dusty and Clara were out by the street visiting with Lexie Lawson and her three-legged beagle. Aunt Charlotte was helping Brother Dan unload the back of his minivan. Uncle Bart was trimming the hedges.

Matthew smiled and asked, "Did I invite a bunch of people over without knowing it?"

"No. Chester and Ida invited them over. Kind of. They extended the invitation when they died. This is what we do,

164

Matthew. We don't grieve alone. It's not healthy. We grieve together. Oh, and we eat." I patted his arm. "Our grief never keeps us from eating."

Chapter 33, CARLIE: I'm Grieving. Pass the Potato Salad

Chester and Ida Miller's death was shocking and sad for all of us. But everyone in the community agreed there was a certain sweetness to their departing together. Mabel said, "Them two was joined at the hip since they was teenagers. Couldn't even say one name without saying the other. God knows His business and all is right with the world." She laughed and added, "Oh, and that Chester was so dang tight with his money, it would thrill him to death that he's gettin' a two-for-one down at Groeden's Funeral Home. Leave it to Chester to stick it to ol' Groeden."

Of course, we all brought food to the house. It's what we do. But the whole concept was new to Matthew Prescott. Monday afternoon Sarah pulled her Ford Focus in behind Brother Dan's van and Matthew's post-death small town education began. James ran to meet both of them at the porch. "Matthew, I'm sorry your Mama and Daddy are dead. They're in heaven and you are gonna miss them a LOT."

"What?"

"Mama said Mr. Chester and Mrs. Ida were like your mama and daddy and that's why you lived here. And it's why you're gonna make loud crying noises and be sad and stuff. That's why we brought meatballs and coconut cake. Right?"

Aunt Charlotte grabbed him in the middle of an escape attempt. She yelled loudly, "Yes, sir! This boy right here is the sweetest smartest little young'un around. And I am gonna squeeze the stuffin' out of him!! I sure am!" She ran from the porch onto the front yard. Her entire body jiggled like Jell-O being released from the mold. "You too, Collin! Oh, and all you McConnell young'uns is sweet as sugar too. You better watch out! Aunt Charlotte gonna get all kinds of love on you babies!!"

Mabel came walking up the sidewalk carrying a box of fried chicken from the diner and a pecan pie she swore was still warm and burning her hand. Mitch Smith brought over a gift certificate to Sammy's. Buster and Michelle brought fried catfish and cinnamon rolls and that layered salad that's made up of cold peas and sour cream and onions and a bunch of stuff that sounds like it would be absolutely and completely horrible. But it's delicious. Unless you're a kid. Kids look at layered salad kinda like they look at Cole slaw or black coffee. It's an acquired taste.

Aunt Charlotte took it upon herself to be Matthew's teacher. She pulled out the dining room chair which was probably from the 1960's. Aluminum legs and green plastic-coated seats and chair backs. "Now Baby, you sit down right here at the table with pretty little Sarah and I'm gonna fix you kids your plates." She cupped her hands together. "Ever'body, get in here!!! The poor boy's grieving and he don't need to eat alone!"

Matthew chewed on his lip to keep from laughing. The crowd gathered around the table and Brother Dan said a prayer of thanks for the bountiful food. That was all fine and good. But Brother Dan is such a tender soul. He closed with these words: "Lord, Chester and Ida blessed us. Every one of us. Every day they blessed us. They blessed us with their simplicity, their faithfulness, their love. Thank you for giving them to us as a gift. Help us to follow their example. Help us to follow your example. Oh, and thank you for blessing us with Matthew too. Thank you for the gift he was to the Millers, to all of us. In Jesus' Name, Amen."

Well, that simple prayer got the waterworks goin'. Aunt Charlotte started crying and raising her hands and wiping her face with a dirty apron. "Lord, I'm gonna miss them two. Sure enough. I'm gonna miss them two somethin' awful."

Ashley grabbed a Kleenex and said, "Chester used to always tell me he was born for the stage, just that his stage was a little smaller than mine. Uncle Bart still says he was the best storyteller at the barber shop."

Dave told the story of the Millers driving to Florence, Alabama, when he and Ashley got married. "I asked him, I said, 'Chester, at your age, you sure you can drive that far for the wedding?' I remember his exact words. 'It's never too far for family.'"

Aunt Charlotte finally said with an air of authority, "Well, ever'body's had their cry now. Chester and Ida would want us to move on and get busy with life. There's visitation tomorrow and a funeral on Friday and we'll all need our strength. So eat up! Mamas and daddies, make the young'uns their plates. I'm gonna fix plates for Matthew and Sarah. I'll fix yours too, Bart. I know just what you like. Matthew, you ain't picky, are you? Lord knows you can't be if you sat at Ida's table every night. Whew! I loved that woman but she could overdo on some green onions. Have mercy. I ain't never known a woman who loved green onions more than Ida Miller. Oh, and her meatballs? No need to lie about it. Dry as a sand box. Dry as a sand box."

Chapter 34, SARAH: The Blessing

By 8:30 Brother Dan and I were the only ones left sitting on
the porch with Matthew. Everyone else had school kids who
needed to be bathed and attended to. Brother Dan slowly rose
from the rocking chair. "I better go too." He looked at
Matthew. "Everything is completely done for the funeral on
Wednesday morning. Chester and Ida had it planned down to
the detail. Of course, at the time, they had no idea there'd
only be one funeral." His eyes filled with tears. "What a gift.
To both of them. Exactly the way they would have wanted it.
If you need anything, anything at all, Matthew, you call me.
Day or night. But before I go, there's something I need to talk
to you about."

Matthew stood. "Sure."

"Did Chester and Ida ever talk to you about, about the house?"

"The house? Not really." Matthew pointed to the porch
ceiling. "I mean, we had plans to paint the porch ceiling. See
where that's peeling right there? In all the corners? Yeah, I
figured I could do some scraping, some primer and paint.
Good as new. After things calm down a bit, I'm still willing
to do that. It'll have better resale with a fresh coat of paint."

"And where are you planning on living?"

"Not sure yet. Whoever owns it now, if they could give me
even just two or three weeks, it would help a lot. I'm sure
Doug or somebody from church knows a place I could rent
that wouldn't be too expensive."

My heart could hardly contain the excitement. Brother Dan
paused. "Well, finding another rental house is not really
gonna work, Matthew."

169

"Why?"

"'Cause that's not what Chester and Ida wanted."

"What do you mean?"

Brother Dan's voice cracked as he fought back tears. "Matthew, they both loved you. You were like the son they never had, the one they'd always prayed for."

Matthew shook his head. "You can't know how much that means to me. Especially right now."

"Matthew, this house? It's yours now. It belongs to you. Free and clear. A gift. It was their parting gift. They took care of all the details with Jimmy Smithson's law office downtown. The furnishings? All the contents? They're yours."

"What? You've got to be kidding me?"

"No. I have all the paperwork right here. They wanted me to be the one to tell you."

Matthew Prescott buried his head in Brother Dan's chest and cried like a man who hadn't cried in a long time. I figure he hadn't cried like that since, well, since Mary's death fifteen years ago. And I knew it wasn't about inheriting the house either. It wasn't about owning Chester and Ida's Coca-Cola crate collection, the outdated glassware, the ugly dining room chairs, or the old iron bed he slept in every night. No. It was about those words. Those powerful words. They loved you like a son.

Chapter 35, SARAH: Better to Have Loved and Lost...

I was parked behind Brother Dan, so after all the crying was over, I hugged Matthew and told him I'd see him at visitation. He said, "Could you just move your car? And then stay a bit longer?"

"Sure."

When I walked back onto the porch, he was sitting in the big porch swing.

"Is there room for me?"

He nodded and I sat down beside him. At first, we couldn't get the swinging motion right. I was nervous. Embarrassed. Finally I laughed and said, "No wonder I was no good at softball. A woman who can't even swing on a porch swing could never hit a ball with that little bitty bat, right?"

He smiled. "How do you know it's not me who's messing it all up?"

"You're right. Just because you're a gifted mechanic and you were an all-star college athlete, yeah, that doesn't give you license to operate a porch swing, Mister."

He leaned his head back and smiled. "That settles it. I'm the problem. What if we go sit on the porch steps instead?"

"That's good."

I sat down on the steps. He sat closer to me than he had ever sat before. I could hardly breathe. "That dress looks real pretty on you, Sarah."

"Thanks. I've had it for years. My friend says floral prints are out now, but I don't know. This dress always makes me feel happy. Hopeful."

"Did you know? About the house?"

"I did. Remember that night in the hospital? When Chester and Ida wanted to see me?"

"Yeah."

"They told me they were giving it to you. Of course, Chester thought he would go first and Mrs. Ida would live here for years. But that was one of the things he said to me…that you were the kind of man who would take care of her. He had confidence in you."

He lowered his head and clasped his hands together. "I would have."

"I know."

"So why would he tell you that? About the house? Why did he tell you but never told me?"

I knew my face was turning bright red. "Not sure really. He just wanted me to know, I guess. He wanted me to know how much they thought of you. What kind of man they thought you were."

He shook his head. "I'm going to miss them. Both of them."

"We all are." I patted him on the knee. "Oh, and when all this funeral food is gone, what do you plan to do about cooking? By my calculations, green onions or no green onions, Mrs. Ida had you kinda spoiled."

172

"Good point. I never cooked growing up. Didn't work the kitchen in prison. Ate out that failed year of law school. And yes, Mrs. Ida cooked for me several times a day. So at 35, it's high time I learn the fine art of boxed mac n cheese, at least."

"Puh-lease. We can do better than that. I'll give you lessons. How 'bout it?"

"Sounds good. The porch light's attracting bugs. Do you mind if I turn it off?"

"No, that's fine."

When he sat back down, I could feel his left arm at my side. He looked up. "Moon's pretty tonight."

"It is. Did you ever get to see the moon? I mean, when you were in prison, could you go outside at night?"

"No."

"I'm sorry."

He shook his head. "Just part of it, I guess."

"But not the worst part?"

"No. Not the worst."

"What was the worst part, Matthew?"

He never made eye contact. "I was young when I went in. Naïve."

My heart clenched in my chest. My great uncle had been a prison guard in Alabama and I remembered him talking to my daddy in the backyard about what sometimes happened to the young men when they first arrived. Had he known I was listening through the back door, he never would have said those things. At the time, I didn't even understand what his words meant.

"I'm sorry."

"It's fine."

"Well, I'm glad you're here now. We all are."

"Me too." He scooted closer and touched my hand. It startled me and I jumped. He immediately let go and stood up. "Oh, I'm sorry. I didn't mean to…to scare you."

I jumped to my feet. "No. I'm sorry, Matthew. It just took me by surprise. That's all. Really."

"No. It's my fault. I didn't give you any warning." He shook his head and walked onto the porch. "I don't know how to do this, Sarah. I don't. I never really had the chance…"

"Do what?"

He bit his lip and started pacing nervously. He pointed to himself and then to me. "This."

"Well, if you want my opinion, I think you're doing fine."

He stopped pacing and looked at me. "Thank you. For saying that. I like you, Sarah. I have for quite a while."

"I like you too, Matthew. And I have for quite a while."

He slowly walked toward me and I could barely breathe. He was more relaxed. "You're not going to jump again. Are you?"

"No. I'm perfectly calm."

"Good. I told you I'm not good at this." He took a deep breath. "And I don't ever...I don't ever want to do something that's not right. Something that hurts you."

I held out my arms. "I trust you. Completely."

He moved forward and slowly wrapped his arms around me. I leaned into his chest. Absolute euphoria. I'd never experienced anything like it. As his right hand touched the back of my head, he whispered, "You're beautiful, Sarah. In every way." I pulled my head away from his chest and looked into his big brown eyes, eyes that had seen so much pain over the years. Loss. Suffering. Rejection. But at that moment, they were filled with hope. He leaned forward and gently kissed me on the cheek. He pulled away, as if he were asking a question. I smiled and closed my eyes. His lips touched mine. It was a tiny glimpse of heaven. Better than the very best of dreams. Sadly, a bright light put an end to it.

"Matthew! Sarah! Is this your idea of grieving for the dead?" Jerry Conner pointed the flood light at our faces and we both squinted.

Matthew rubbed his eyes. "Jerry? Jerry, where's your car?"

"I parked it around the block. Didn't want to give you the heads up, Mr. Prescott."

"Uh, okay."

Jerry stumbled onto the porch like a drunk tiger seeking easy prey. "So, this is the respect the both of you have for the Millers, eh? I'm not shocked by Matthew here. But, Sarah, I thought sure you'd know better. What would your mama think? You've known Mr. Chester and Mrs. Ida all your life!"

"What would my mama think? What are you talking about, Jerry? Since when did you become the grief police? Everyone in town is sad about the Millers. Me included. The real question is why you're here at 9:30 at night. What business could you possibly have with either of us?"

He put both hands on his hips and patted the gun in his side holster. "It just seems pretty suspect to me. That's all. Matthew here, disowned by his own family. And then, in no time at all, he convinces two half-senile old people to give him everything they've got. And then wouldn't you know it. They both end up dead!"

Matthew moved slowly toward Jerry and spoke like a principal chastising an unruly student. "Jerry, get off this porch before I do something we both regret."

Jerry raised both hands above his head and yelled, "Go ahead! Kill me, Matthew! Not like you ain't killed plenty of other people. Why not me? Sarah, you better watch your back! Once a con, always a con!"

Matthew turned toward me and shook his head. "He's drunk. Go inside and call 9-1-1. I'll hold him 'till they get here."

When I got back out to the porch, Jerry Conner's gun was on the porch swing. Jerry was lying face down on a big rug and Matthew was holding his arms behind his back. I didn't ask. And he didn't volunteer any information. But as far as I could tell, no injuries had been sustained by either party. In

176

fact, Jerry looked unusually calm, like he was almost asleep. Within five minutes, a sheriff's deputy car pulled into Chester and Ida's driveway. He left his lights off so as not to cause a commotion.

I was relieved to see Bob Garrett get out of the car. I had full confidence he would do the right thing. I wasn't even sure what the right thing was. He ambled toward the porch as he shook his head. "This here doesn't seem like a very good situation. Sarah, why don't you give me your take on it."

"Yes, sir. Well, Matthew and I were just out here on the porch when Jerry came by and started shining the spot light and accusing him of a bunch of stuff. Unfounded accusations, of course. Anyway, that's when Matthew realized he'd been drinking and definitely didn't need to be carrying a gun and driving the patrol car. Jerry said it's parked around the block because he wanted to sneak up on us."

"Yeah. I saw it down by the diner."

"Matthew thought we should hold him and call you."

"Smart. Both of ya. Matthew, I'd say you exercised quite a bit of restraint in this situation. Accusations, false or otherwise, have led to many a man's angry downfall."

Jerry mumbled, "He assaulted me. Assaulted a law man. Let him rot in jail."

Mr. Garrett walked onto the porch and picked up Jerry's gun. "Good God, that smell! He's been out at Miss Lucy's. That's definitely the smell of Miss Lucy's gut rot. Don't even know how they call that stuff moonshine. Stronger than gasoline. Let me see if I can help you a bit." He carefully cuffed his hands behind his back. "Jerry! Jerry, let's see if we can get you stood up now. I'm gonna have to take you in. Don't make it hard, hard on either of us."

I stayed on the porch while Matthew helped Mr. Garrett pull Jerry to his feet and walk him to the patrol car. Jerry was spewing expletives the whole way. By the time they got to the car, he was sleepy and happy to lie down in the back seat. But he still managed to yell out, "You're goin' back to jail, Matthew. Jail!"

As Matthew came walking up the steps, he no longer looked relaxed. Or happy. "The sheriff's deputy wants to talk to you before he leaves."

"Oh, okay."

Mr. Garrett was propped up against the car. Moonlight provided just enough light to see fatherly concern on his face. He spoke quietly. "Sarah, I've known you your whole life. And you know I'm a straight shooter, right?"

"Yes, sir."

"I went to school with your mama and daddy. Good people. Both of them. And there's nobody in this county that's respected any more than you are. You know that."

"But?"

"But reputations tarnish much more quickly than they're built."

"And that means what?"

"It means be careful. I'm not saying Jerry's accusations were founded. And Lord knows Jerry's disdain for Matthew

178

Prescott has nothing to do with the Millers. Truth is, he's still sweet on ya. We all know that. But no matter." He put his arm around my shoulder. "I get that Matthew didn't do all that time for bank robbery or murder. I know he was young and it was all a terrible accident. But Sarah, fourteen years in prison? Trust me. Prison does things to a man's soul. If a man ain't a criminal when he goes in, well, a lot of times he is one by the time he gets out. It hardens him. It does. And if your daddy was still here, believe me, he'd tell ya the same thing. I better get Jerry to the tank." He walked around to the driver's side but paused before opening the door. "Look, I'm not telling you what to do…or what not to do. Just telling you to be careful."

"Thank you, Mr. Garrett. I understand." I waved as I watched his car pull away. All the joy of 30 minutes ago had now been tainted. Tarnished. Corrupted. I was mad at Jerry Conner. Mad at Bob Garrett. Or was I really mad at Matthew? Mad at him for taking drugs fifteen years ago. Mad at him for having to live with the memories of prison. Mad at Chester and Ida for loving him so much…for convincing me to love him too.

Matthew stood quietly on top of the porch steps. Still handsome but troubled now. Hands in his pockets. Make-up still smeared on his ironed blue oxford shirt. I didn't even walk up the steps. I couldn't. "It's getting late. I better get home. Can you hand me my purse?"

He didn't speak one word. Just nodded. When he handed me the purse, he managed not to touch me.

"Thanks. I'll see you at visitation tomorrow night. I'll be there around 5:00."

"That'll be fine."

"Matthew?"

"Yes."

"You did the right thing. With Jerry, I mean. A lot of men would have flown off the handle. Said a bunch of stuff they'd regret later. Or worse, punched his lights out." I laughed nervously. "Not that you weren't tempted. I'm sure you were tempted to deck him."

He shuffled his feet and looked up at the moon. "The ramblings of a drunk man aren't worth prison time, Sarah."

"I'm sure you're right."

"Look, we both know if you hadn't been here, telling what happened, they would have taken me in with him." He lowered his head. "My word against his."

"And that would have gone…"

"Only one way."

"Well, I hope you can get some rest. It's been a crazy day. A hard day for everyone. Try to get some rest, Matthew."

He nodded. "You too."

I started the car and looked through the windshield one more time before I backed out. He was still standing on the porch in the exact same place. A hopeful man now broken again. My eyes filled with tears. The gentleness of his kiss would never be forgotten. But neither would Mr. Garrett's solemn words. "Prison does things to a man's soul."

Chapter 36, CARLIE: Tuesday Morning, Full of Grace

It was 7:00 am and Aunt Charlotte didn't even bother with the knock and familiar "Yoo Hoo!" Doug and I were sitting at the table drinking coffee when she and Uncle Bart ran in the kitchen door as though they were headin' to a fire.

Aunt Charlotte's face was red and sweaty. "You been listenin' to the local news?"

Doug put down the newspaper. "No."

"Jerry Conner done got arrested last night. Drinkin' and startin' trouble with Matthew Prescott. I knew there was gonna be trouble! I did! Lord, I told that young'un to stay away from Miss Lucy." She shook her head. "He don't listen though. He don't."

Doug stood and pulled out a kitchen chair. "Here. Have a seat, Aunt Charlotte. You're gonna get overly excited and then you'll be the next one in the news."

Uncle Bart barked, "Hell yeah! That's what I been tellin' her, Doug. She don't listen any better than Jerry does."

She moved quickly toward the chair. "Carlie, Honey, I'll take some milk in my coffee and a lot of sugar, if you got it. None of that walnut sage hickory nut creamer or whatever the gall darn stuff is. Just milk and a lot of sugar."

I laughed. "And I guess you want something to eat too?"

"Yeah, 'cause you know my nerves is on edge, Baby. On edge."

"Uncle Bart, what about you?"

"Black coffee and whatever you got."

I set their cups of coffee on the table along with two big hunks of Mabel's famous banana bread.

Doug put the newspapers aside. "Okay. Start again."

Aunt Charlotte spoke more calmly. "Well, Jerry got drunk last night and decided to make trouble for Matthew. When he got to Chester and Ida's, well, guess what he found? Go ahead, Baby. Guess."

Doug replied with absolute calmness. "I have no idea."

Her voice escalated as though she were revealing the formula for a secret weapon. "Well, he done found Matthew and Sarah out on the porch, uh, well, back in my day we called it sparkin'! Yes, sir! They was sparkin', the two of 'em. Right out there on Chester and Ida's front porch."

Doug bit his lip but a small laugh escaped despite his best efforts. "Sparkin', eh?"

Aunt Charlotte looked deathly serious. "Yeah they were. Cora Belle heard the whole thang. Said Jerry went off on a rant 'bout how they wasn't neither one grievin' proper for Ida and Chester. And how it was just a little too convenient that Matthew got all friendly with Chester and Ida and then them both end up dead at the exact same time."

Doug shook his head. "You have got to be kiddin' me! Everybody in town knows Matthew loved those two. And they loved him too. That's crazy. Jerry's just jealous. And I guess he's in a lot of trouble now too."

Uncle Bart piped up. "Lloyd Cramer done fired his ass before he hit the drunk tank. Sarah called 9-1-1. Bob showed up to carry him in."

Doug shook his head. "This is gonna kill his mama. And Jerry too. A tragedy. All the way around."

Aunt Charlotte leaned forward. "You're not gonna wanna hear this next part, Doug Darlin'."

He smiled. "Oh, then maybe you better not tell me." But of course, that was like telling the wind not to blow or ice cream not to melt in the hot sun.

"Some folks been talkin'."

"Oh, I've no doubt they've been talkin'."

"Some folks is suspect 'cause Chester and Ida? Well, you won't believe it. They done left their whole place to Matthew. Yes, sir. The house. The car. The glassware collection. Reckon he could even lay claim to that 50 states quilt, if he had a mind to. 'Course ever'body 'round here knows that Ida had every intention of donating that to the Fire Department raffle."

Doug's voice was gentle as he smiled and shook his head. "Those two were something else, weren't they? I'm glad they did what they did. The way I see it, leaving the whole place to Matthew was like a final life lesson. To all of us. A reminder that they both believed in second chances. And maybe we should too."

"Well, not ever'body sees it that way, Hon."

"People see what they want to see, Aunt Charlotte."

Aunt Charlotte put the last crumb of banana bread in her mouth as she rose from the chair. "You're right about that, Baby. Well, Bart and I best be gettin' on. I still gotta make my deviled eggs and meatloaf for the funeral dinner tomorrow. And Cora Belle and I got hair appointments for this mornin'."

Doug stood and reached out to hug her. "Aunt Charlotte, do me one favor. Please."

"You know I'd do anything for ya."

"Let's try to support Matthew. If you hear talk, bad talk, come to his defense. We've spent a lot of time with him over these months. And there's no way I'm gonna believe he did anything but love and support Chester and Ida. And there's no way he tried to influence them to make him the benefactor of their place either. I mean, you believe that, right?"

"Oh, absolutely. That precious little thang been through so much. So much hurt. Disappointment. Ida and Chester was like his real chance at family. No. Matthew Prescott would have never done nothin' to hurt them." She laughed. "Especially not for a house full of soda pop junk and a car that spends more time broke down on the shoulder of the road than it does 'tween the lines."

Chapter 37, CARLIE: Let's Stand in Support of Sparkin'

At 5:00, Groeden's parking lot was already full. Mr. Billings, the school janitor and local newshound, had already filled everyone in on the latest news. Evidently Chester and Ida have two living relatives. Two great-nephews. Both live with their families in southern Indiana. After being contacted about Chester and Ida's death, they arrived in Sharon mid-morning. When they did some research and discovered they weren't in the will, they promptly left town after lunch. Mabel said they were in such an angry mood, they didn't even leave a tip. This was especially insulting because she'd already given them a 10% discount in honor of their bereavement.

As we walked through the parking lot, I wondered how visitation would go seeing as there were no family members present. When we have funeral home visitation in Sharon, Tennessee, the family members all stand by the casket near the front of the room. People stand in line to greet the family members and tell them how sorry they are. Sometimes they even say things like, "Your daddy was my favorite teacher. He taught me my times tables." Or "Your grandma taught me how to knit when I was in middle school."

Sometimes they even tell stories about the deceased that seem like they're not complimentary at all. Things like: "Your brother used to always cheat at checkers. He'd run around the barber shop every Saturday bragging that he beat me. But that ol' scoundrel couldn't have beaten a preschooler at checkers." Or "Your granddaddy was the tightest man I knew. Once tried to get me to sell 'em a watermelon for a dollar. And that man was such a talker, he nearly had me convinced."

Y'see, the point of funeral home visitation stories is not really to make the deceased person seem perfect. We all know he or she wasn't perfect. It's about, well, making the family members know that despite the imperfections, their daddy or grandma or brother was an original. One of a kind. That he or she made a difference, that they'll never be forgotten.

Mr. Groeden extended his hand to Doug and pointed toward the big room where Chester and Ida's bodies lay. At the front of the room, Matthew and Brother Dan were standing by the caskets, greeting people as they came by. Matthew wore the same clothes he wore when he spoke at the rally downtown. Dark pants and a burgundy striped shirt that Doug had helped him pick out at the men's store. He looked tired, like he hadn't slept well. Brother Dan wore a dark suit and looked like he'd slept just fine.

A few times Brother Dan patted Matthew on the back. I felt confident he was saying stuff like, "Mrs. Eula, Matthew here was such a blessing to the both of them during their final months. He took good care of them. He did." I only hoped that Brother Dan, with all his tenderness and kindness, wasn't overselling Matthew...especially to the customers who weren't quite ready to buy.

I remembered Aunt Charlotte's early morning declarations about Matthew and Sarah on the porch last night. I scanned the room but she wasn't here yet. Doug was busy visiting with Maxine about interest rates when I noticed Matthew looking around the room too. I felt confident he was looking for Sarah. Y'see, there are some things I don't know anything about, a lot of things actually. Algebra. Geography. Physics. How to find my car in the Wal-Mart parking lot. But I do know about people. About men. About women. And blessedly, I know about love.

When there were only about five people in front of us, Matthew startled a little. Then he smiled and nodded. I turned my head just as Sarah greeted Mabel and stepped into the line. She was beautiful. More beautiful every time I saw her. She had on black pants and a black sweater. Her hair was down and her make-up flawless. I made eye contact. She waved. I grinned and raised my eyebrows. I felt confident she understood my signals. After all, everyone in town had heard the news by now. Chester and Ida died within twelve hours of each other. The TV folks were to arrive in three days to start shooting the reality show. Jerry Conner no longer works for the Sheriff's department because he got drunk last night while he was on duty. And Matthew and Sarah? Well, evidently they were caught sparkin'. Sparkin' on Chester and Ida's front porch.

Chapter 38, SARAH: Let's Give Them Somethin' to Talk About

Mama called this morning right before I left for school. Wondered if I knew the whole town was already talking about me and Matthew, and about Jerry getting arrested. I didn't know. But I wasn't surprised either. She asked if I regretted making a fool of myself with an ex-con I barely knew. My answer was definitive. "No, Mama. I didn't make a fool of myself. I don't regret it either. And no, Matthew isn't someone I barely know. I've known him for several months. He works hard at Dusty's Shop. He took good care of Chester and Ida. Besides, we all thought we knew Jerry Conner, right? And look what happened there. Who's the law breaker, Mama? Matthew or Jerry? I think you're a bit confused."

Mama didn't buy it though. And I figured she wasn't the only one. I could feel the stares as I entered the funeral home. Carlie is the only one who looks like she's happy to see me. Happy enough to lose her place in line to come speak to me.

"Hey! Sarah."

"Carlie."

"Why don't we go outside for a minute? Visitation's just getting started. We'll have time."

"Sounds good."

"I'll run tell Doug. He'll be happy sitting on the pew a while anyway. He and Maxine are talking interest rates."

"I'll meet you outside then." But I didn't go outside. Maybe I should have. But I didn't. I made eye contact with Matthew. He looked tired and sad. But even in the sadness, he managed

188

a smile. So I walked to the front of the room. I could feel all eyes on me but it didn't matter anymore. In fact, it almost gave me courage. Sarah Simpson. Hometown girl. Girl who never crossed her mama or daddy, went to local college, became a teacher, moved into her Granny's house. That Sarah Simpson was gonna make a scene in Sharon, Tennessee. Not a bad scene. A good scene.

Mitch and his wife, Judy, were up next. I pleasantly asked if I could break line just for a moment. They stepped back and smiled. I reached out for Matthew and, though he looked surprised, he put his arms all the way around me. I whispered, "I'm sorry I left so quickly last night. Don't know what I was thinking. I know this whole situation is hard. But I want you to know I'm here for you. I am. I'm going outside but I'll be back." I pulled away and then leaned forward and kissed him on the cheek.

His face turned red as he smiled. "Thank you, Sarah."

The walk to the back door was empowering. I even stopped several times to greet fellow teachers and parents waiting in line. I saw my mama standing between Cora Belle and Mabel. Despite her slight scowl, I reached out to hug her. I whispered, "It's fine, Mama. You don't have to trust him. You have to trust me. Surely you can do that."

Carlie and I sat on a wooden bench in a little garden area behind the funeral home. Nights were getting cooler now but I didn't mind. The funeral home seemed warm and stuffy. The garden air was refreshing.

Carlie's voice was unusually serious. "So, to hear Aunt Charlotte tell it, there was quite an uproar last night."

"Just Jerry being stupid."

"And now he's been fired?"

"Yes. But that had nothing to do with Matthew or with me."

"Agreed. So, I take it by that little public kiss just now, you're no longer interested in Dr. Carter."

"No. I never really was. Mama tried to tell me all the reasons I should be."

"But that didn't matter?"

"Not really."

Our short conversation was soon interrupted. "Excuse me. I hate to bother you. I'm looking for Matthew Prescott."

Chapter 39, CARLIE: Here Comes Trouble

Sarah and I were visiting in the garden when a strange woman walked toward us. Oh, I don't mean strange like odd or weird-looking. I just mean we didn't know her. I knew she wasn't from Sharon. In fact, I felt pretty darn certain she was with the new television show in some capacity. Tall and beautiful with a really deep tan. And not the kind of tan old people have who own Chihuahuas and live in Florida either. No. I felt certain it was a California tan. Her hair was dark and pulled into one of those really smooth pony tails, like rich people always have in movies. Her make-up was perfect. Skin? Flawless. The beige pant suit looked like it came from something on Rodeo Drive. And then she opened her mouth. "I'm looking for Matthew Prescott."

Sarah and I immediately stood. Sarah's face turned pale. But I managed a few words. "Matthew? Yes, we know Matthew. We know him well. He's just inside. We'll show you the way."

She smiled. Her teeth were the most perfect teeth I'd ever seen on a human being. We're not talkin' braces. We're talkin' veneers. Movie star teeth. Her voice was pleasant and kind. "I asked down at the diner and they said he'd be here. I thought that was a bit odd. I don't want to interrupt. Is he attending a funeral?"

"No. Tomorrow is the funeral and tonight is visitation. The older couple Matthew's been living with? Sadly, they both died. So the people of the community are coming to pay their respects and he's greeting them."

"Oh, that's sad." She looked toward the front door and then turned back to face us. "I'm sorry. I didn't even introduce myself. I'm Julie Crawford. I've been friends with Matthew since birth."

I extended my hand. "Carlie Jameson."

"THE Carlie Jameson? The author?"

"Absolutely. Well, unless you represent a law firm for an outstanding speeding ticket or something."

"I'm a huge fan. Really. A huge fan. The books. The movie."

"Thank you. Would you like to sit a while? I mean, it's pretty crowded in there right now because people are getting off from work. The crowd will thin pretty soon and it will be easier to have a conversation with him."

"Sure. Thanks."

Sarah put her hand out. "I'm Sarah Simpson. Not famous. At all. Just a third grade teacher here in Sharon."

"Nice to meet you, Sarah. And no offense to Carlie, but teachers are the real stars. So don't ever apologize for changing the world, okay?"

"Thank you, Julie." Sarah looked like she just found out her dog got run over. Julie's physical beauty was one thing, but her kindness? Her kindness seemed like an overpowering death blow.

"You're welcome. Carlie, I just started re-reading 'A Single Woman's Guide to Ordinary.' Even better the second time around. Seriously. Matthew was in California recently. He told me it was an odd setup around here. A small town filled

with famous people? Who would have thought? It's no
wonder the networks found him and decided to do a show.
Ashley Harrison Robertson spends a lot of time here too,
yes?"

"Yes, believe it or not, she does."

Sarah cleared her throat. "You mentioned Carlie's first book.
Are you single, Julie?"

"Well, as Carlie's book says, 'Yes, but not by choice.'
Married for nine years. Investment banker. Ran off with the
receptionist. Yada yada. Same old story. Divorced for a year
now and still not used to it."

Sarah nodded her head. "I'm sorry. So, did you travel from
California? Is that where you live?"

"Yes. Matthew's been through a tough time lately with his
family. Thought it might be fun to have a surprise visitor from
home. A familiar face, maybe."

Sarah rose to her feet and reluctantly straightened her sweater.
Her voice cracked, but I felt certain Julie didn't notice. "Well,
let's not keep Matthew waiting. Here, Julie, we'll go ahead
and show you the way."

"Thank you. It was a pleasure visiting with you both. Really.
I see now why Matthew loves it here. He's right. Southern
hospitality at its very best."

The three of us walked toward the front door. Mr. Groeden
opened the door and his eyes grew large, like he'd never seen
a beautiful woman before. Poor Sarah. Moments earlier, she
had the world by the tail. Full of life. Courage. She'd even

kissed Matthew in front of the whole town with no regard for what people thought. Completely fearless.

The worst part? The worst part was the fact that Sarah's mama and Mabel were the ones visiting with Matthew and Brother Dan up front near the caskets. I knew how to avoid this train wreck if I could just get the train cars to cooperate. "Julie, let's sit back here on the last pew until a few more people get through the line. Some of them have waited for a while and we certainly don't want to stretch their southern hospitality to the limit, do we?"

She laughed. "Absolutely not."

Sarah looked relieved. As her mama and Mabel came walking up the aisle to leave, I prayed they would smile and keep walking right on out the door. Smile and wave, people. Just smile and wave. But Mabel came to a complete halt.

"I don't believe I know you, dear."

"No, you probably don't. I'm Julie Crawford." Oh Julie, please don't do it. Don't say it. Don't. Don't say…and then she did. "I'm from California. I'm here to visit Matthew."

Sarah's mother, Deloris, snapped her head. "Matthew? Are you kin to him?"

"No. A friend."

Deloris looked directly at Sarah. "A friend, huh? Well, he's pretty good at makin' friends. That's for sure."

"Oh, we've been friends since we were babies. Neighbors growing up in San Diego."

194

Mabel removed her glasses and adjusted her blonde wig slightly. When she did, a big brown piece of hair came flying out the side. Deloris tried to discreetly tuck it back in. But Mabel's face turned red and she gave Deloris a look like she'd disrespected her mama's grave or something.

There was something about Julie Crawford's presence that made us all feel a little undone. Not good enough. Mabel was the only one to actually voice it. "You'll have to pardon my appearance, dear. My good clothes are at the dry cleaners and Buddy Garrison's on vacation and his nephew is runnin' the place and he's slow as molasses. Oh, and my Avon lady has been in the hospital too." She leaned toward Julie and whispered, "Poor Gertrude. Shingles nearly killed her. But I need some fall lipstick colors bad. I mean, here I am stuck wearin' this dang watermelon color from the beginning of the summer. I must look frightful."

Mabel did look frightful. But Mabel always looked frightful. She was old but insisted on wearing big blonde wigs. She had a huge behind but wore stretch pants in bright colors. She had lipstick on her teeth more than half the time. And none of us cared whether the lipstick shade was watermelon or autumn bronze. Her frightful appearance was normal. We'd all accepted it. And I'd certainly never heard her apologize for it.

Julie patted Mabel on the arm. "Oh, no apology necessary. I think you look fine." First black mark on Julie Crawford's name. Kind and sweet, yes. But she lies.

Deloris added, "Well, I'm sure you need to get on and see Matthew. Sarah can haul you up there. She's been comin' to visitation at this funeral home her whole life. She knows how it's done."

"Thank you. Really. Everyone has been so nice to me." Julie stood and looked at Sarah, having no idea what she was really asking of her. No idea about the kiss on the cheek less than an hour earlier. No idea about what happened on the porch last night.

I interceded. "Sarah, don't worry about it. I'll take her." I stood and pleasantly grabbed Julie's arm, giving her no choice really. We began to walk slowly down the long aisle. I knew Matthew hadn't seen her yet because the room was filled with people. Once the folks came forward and paid their respects, a lot of them sat in the pews to visit. Matthew was turned toward the caskets with his arm around Aunt Charlotte. Uncle Bart was standing to the side telling Brother Dan about the time Chester dressed up like Daniel Boone for the Christmas parade.

I touched Matthew gently on the arm. "Matthew, you have a special visitor."

I decided to make special note of his reaction. This would give me the clues I'd need to decide if this truly was a friendship. ie. We made mud pies together. Or if it was something else entirely. ie. We made...well, I don't want to think about it.

Sadly, his face lit up in a way that wasn't very mud pie-ish. "Julie?"

She reached out and threw her arms around him. "Surprise!" He happily reciprocated. She was nearly as tall as Matthew and her head leaned over his shoulder a bit. For the first time, Matthew seemed completely out of place in our tiny town. He and Julie looked like they were cut from the same cloth. Beautiful people. Perfect teeth. Expensive cologne. Even his years in prison hadn't changed the fact that he and Julie had grown up with backyard pools, expensive vacations, and house staff. Suddenly, the town of Sharon seemed provincial. Backward even.

Aunt Charlotte, never one to mince words, extended her hand and threw it all out on the table. "Hello, Honey. I'm Charlotte Nelson. And I do think you might be the purdiest woman I ever laid eyes on. Lord, have mercy, they grow 'em big out there in California, don't they? Oh, I don't mean big like big around. No. Who am I to talk about big? No, I mean, tall and purdy and all fancy like. You look like you could be in one of them perfume commercials!"

Matthew laughed. "Julie actually did a few TV commercials back in the day."

Aunt Charlotte beamed. "See, I knew I could spot talent a mile away. Welcome to Sharon, Baby!"

"Thank you. Thank you very much. I'm so sorry about the deaths. Uh, about..."

Matthew replied, "Chester and Ida Miller." He shook his head and glanced toward the caskets. "The greatest couple you'd ever meet, Julie. Seriously. They both reminded me of Simon and Jean Carmichael. Absolute sincerity."

Julie put her arm around his waist. "You heard that Simon and Jean are both gone now, yes?"

"I did. Sad. They held the neighborhood together. I can still taste her homemade carrot cake."

Julie smiled as she moved her hand from his waist to his back and leaned in closer. "What about that year that Simon dressed up like Santa Claus and fell in George Clifton's pool?"

Matthew laughed. "The red dye from the Santa suit put pink streaks in the water and George threatened to sue. Gosh, I'd almost forgotten about that. Been a long time."

"It has been a long time."

Matthew and Julie's conversation might seem innocent and mud pie-ish to the average observer. It might seem like two neighbors just reminiscing about childhood. But when it comes to observations, well, I'm able to tell the difference between average neighborly interaction and "My husband left me and I think you look awesome in blue jeans" interaction. And I can assure you of one thing. Julie Crawford didn't put on her best cologne, a tight-fitting tan pant suit, and fly all the way across the country to talk about the time Simon Carmichael fell into the neighbor's pool.

Chapter 40, SARAH: I'm Not Julie...My Name is Sarah

Whatever I thought was going on between Matthew Prescott and me, well, evidently it wasn't. An hour ago, I kissed his cheek. In front of the whole town too. Now he's standing in that same exact place at the front of Groeden's Funeral Home with his arm around a woman he's known all his life. From California. Beautiful. Kind. Sophisticated. Recently divorced. She says she came to Sharon, thinking he might need a friend right now. But she doesn't look like a friend.

I'd get up and leave except that would be too obvious. To everyone. Childish even. I'll wait, wait for Carlie to tell me what to do next. I can tell by watching her up front that she's crafting a plan. I don't have the heart to tell her it's destined to fail. Looks like people are starting to leave now and the three of them are coming back up the aisle. Matthew's trying to make eye contact with me. But I can't do it. I can't. I'll pretend to be searching for something in my purse. A lost receipt. A business card. A life.

His hand touched my shoulder and I looked up. "Julie, did you meet Sarah Simpson?"

"I did. Yes. Third grade teacher extraordinaire."

I lowered my head again, unable to look at any of them. I prayed the tears wouldn't come.

Carlie's voice broke the silence. "Julie, where are you staying?"

"Not sure yet. Where's the nearest hotel?"

Carlie laughed. "Well, you'll not find a hotel in Sharon. We're far too hospitable to need one of those. There's a few in Martin. One in Dresden, I believe."

Julie looked at Matthew and showed every tooth she owned. "Where do you live, Matthew? Have an extra room for an old friend?"

I stood up and spoke quickly without thinking. "You can stay with me. I have a guest room. It's all made up and everything. Matthew just lives a few blocks away. You can see him as much as you want." Tears were forming in my eyes but they hadn't fallen yet. I looked at Matthew for the first time since Julie Crawford's appearance. He looked at me and smiled like nothing had changed between us. But he was wrong. I grabbed my purse. "Well, I'm gonna get on home. I'm sure you and Matthew have a lot of catching up to do. And I still have food to make for the funeral dinner."

Julie turned toward me. "You're a caterer too? You must be the local renaissance woman, Sarah."

I shook my head and smiled. "Caterer? No. We don't cater funeral dinners around here. We all pitch in and cook and it's like a big potluck. You'll see tomorrow. Best food you'll ever eat. I mean, if you like country food."

"Well, I'm sure I'll love it." She opened her jacket and patted a completely flat stomach. "My waistline might not love it, but I'm sure I will."

That was it. The end. I knew my tears were coming soon, so I quickly said my final words. "Julie, the door will be unlocked and I'll leave written instructions on the table, if I've already gone to bed when you get in." I started for the door but turned around briefly and managed an insincere smile. "Matthew knows where the house is. Make yourself at home." I walked as fast as I could out the front door.

I could hear Matthew walking quickly behind me, like he was trying to catch up with me. But I was crying now so I walked even faster until I was almost running. I heard his boots stop at the sidewalk near the garden. His voice called out, "Sarah, it won't be late! It won't!" I flung my head back and waved.

I drove straight to the grocery store and filled a cart without speaking to anyone. When the check-out clerk, Mrs. Cramer, bragged about the good weather we'd been having, I managed a nod. It was only 8:14 when I got home. I wanted to get out my IPod and play a bunch of romantic songs and have a good cry and eat a ton of ice cream and then watch, "While You Were Sleeping." But I decided to do the mature thing. Cook. And clean.

The living room was already clean and neat because of my date with Brian Tuesday night. Unlike Chester and Ida's place, my house isn't crowded. I cleared out all the old furniture and knick knacks when my granny died. Some of it is in the attic. The rest is at my mom's house (a bit of a hoarder) or at my cousin's new apartment in Jackson. We donated a few things to We Care in Martin. My living room couch is almost brand-new. Tan leather with big burgundy pillows. I kept one brown plaid wingback chair because it reminded me of my grandparents. But the lamps are plain white. The coffee table and end tables are mission style. It's not that I wanted to forget my grandparents. I didn't. I never could. I guess it's just that I wanted it to seem like my place. But it doesn't. Not really. Every corner seems lonely now, longing for a time when the house was full.

The one thing I like about the old yellow house is the layout. Most older homes have a lot of little rooms. But my living room, dining room, and kitchen are all one big open area. When you walk in the front door, you can see the dining room table, the kitchen, as well as the living room. This motivates me to keep the kitchen clean. Or at least it should.

I walked into the guest room. It was the one room in the house that still looked like my grandparents. Old quilt on the bed. Round white lamp with raised bumps all over it. Even though I had just changed the sheets and dusted the furniture, the room smelled musty. I sprayed some fancy lavender spray a student had given me for Christmas. It had been years since I'd slept on that bed. My cousin, Marcie, slept on it last week. Said the mattress was getting thin and you could feel the springs. I laid down on top of the old quilt. Yeah. There's what she meant, just on the left side. I scooted to the right and all was fine. The ceiling had one brown spot but it was in the corner. I looked at the end table. Just the old white lamp and two books. Granny's Bible and "To Kill a Mockingbird." First run. Hardback. Granny bought it at an auction years ago. Probably never read it.

I cleaned the bathroom. Straightened the rugs. Clipped pink and red roses from the rose bushes to make a bouquet for the table and the guest room. Probably the last ones I'd get for a while. When the house was in order, I headed to the kitchen and donned Granny's favorite apron. "Kiss the Cook" in big black letters on red gingham. I would normally put on pajamas before doing the cooking. But I didn't. I put on lipstick and combed my hair, hoping he'd soon make his appearance. But of course, that was naïve and it made me feel like that seventeen-year-old girl again. Sadly, even though thirteen years had passed, there wasn't much difference between her life and mine.

I made cupcakes because I promised James and Collin I'd make white cupcakes with white icing the next time we had a potluck. I put the broccoli on to boil and stirred soup and cheese and a bunch of other stuff in a bowl. I always brought two broccoli casseroles to the funeral meal. It was only 9:30 when I heard a knock at the door and Matthew's strong voice. "Sarah?"

"Come on in!"

Matthew and Julie walked in, all smiles, and immediately wiped their feet on the rug. Matthew spoke with enthusiasm, "You've got the house smelling great!"

"Thank you. I'm sorry I didn't answer the door. I've got soup and cheese all over my hands. Let me just get this washed off." I pointed to the table. "Please help yourself to a cupcake. I've got plenty."

Julie sighed. "Oh, I better not. But gosh, they look wonderful."

I walked toward the table. "Not to brag, but they are wonderful. My granny's icing recipe. The best. Bart Nelson says this icing recipe should be kept in a vault somewhere. A national treasure. Julie, let me show you to your room."

Matthew looked around. "You have a nice place, Sarah."

Julie's voice grew louder. "You've never been here, Matthew? I thought small town folks were always at each other's houses, having picnics and barbecues."

I was determined not to get flustered. "Oh, we are. It's just that some of our friends have bigger places, so we tend to congregate there." I pushed the guest room door open. "Well, here's your room. There are empty drawers in that white dresser, if you need them. The bed has a few uncomfortable

spots, but it won't be too bad, as long as it's just one person."
My face turned red. "I mean, the left side here has some
issues, but anyway…"

Matthew set a large suitcase near the door. Julie took off her
jacket and laid it on the bed. I had a feeling her teeth weren't
the only things that had been altered. "It's a beautiful room,
Sarah. Thank you."

"No problem. The bathroom is just right next door. Towels
and wash cloths on that white shelf." I turned to leave. "I'm
gonna finish up these casseroles, but if you need anything at
all, let me know. TV is in the living room. It's a lovely night
to sit on the porch. I can show you how to make hot cider, if
you want."

Julie's face brightened as she grabbed Matthew's arm. "Porch
sitting sounds great. What about it, Matthew?"

"No, I better not. Dusty and I are going to the shop really
early to do some paperwork before the funeral. So I'll leave
you ladies alone. Julie, you've got Chester and Ida's number,
yes?"

"I do."

"If you need anything, call. Sarah, thanks so much for
hosting. I appreciate it."

"No problem." I walked into the kitchen, but could still hear
the faint sounds of their light-hearted chatter. I poured the
casserole mixture into two pans and covered them both with
foil. I heard the bathroom door close. As I was putting the
pans into the refrigerator, Matthew walked to the dining room
table and peeled the paper off a cupcake. "These look great

and I'm not one bit worried about my waistline." He put almost half of it in his mouth at one time.

I closed the refrigerator door. "I'm warning you. Those are addictive."

He looked at me and mumbled. "No doubt."

I walked toward the table but stopped before I got too close. "Would you like some milk? Water? Sweet tea?"

"Water. Thanks."

I put some ice in a glass and ran the faucet for a while. "It's just tap water, y'know. I don't believe in all that bottled water nonsense."

"Yeah. I remember you saying that once on the way home from Carlie's." I could hear his boots shuffling across the kitchen floor and it made me nervous.

I kept letting the water run until he was directly behind me. I filled the glass and turned. I was standing only a few inches from his chest. My face was warm and I felt dizzy. Dizzy and happy and sad all at the same time. I set the glass on the counter and glanced at the floor.

He spoke in almost a whisper. "Sarah?"

I still didn't make eye contact. "Yes?"

"Tonight, at the funeral home, when you…"

I finally looked up. "Kissed you?"

"Yeah. That had me confused a bit because last night, after Mr. Garrett left, it seemed like you had…regrets or something."

"No. I'm sorry. I was just confused. But no…I don't have regrets. At all."

His whole face relaxed. "Good. I don't either."

"But now?" I pointed toward the hallway and spoke even softer. "Do you have regrets now that Julie is here? 'Cause if you do, it's fine. I understand. Really."

He gently grabbed both my arms and pulled me toward his chest. He laid his head on top of mine and whispered, "What? No. Sarah, Julie's not my girlfriend. She never has been."

I pulled my face back. "But she wants to be."

"And how would you know that? You just met her tonight."

"Remember when you told me Jerry Conner still liked me?"

"Yes. And obviously, I was right about that."

"You said, 'It's the way he looks at you, Sarah.' Well, that's the way Julie looks at you, Matthew. You may not see it, but I do."

The bathroom door opened and Julie, with freshened hair and lips, approached the kitchen. "What a quaint little bathroom! And you've had all those antique fixtures installed. Where in the world did you find them?"

"My grandparents found them. Probably about fifty years ago. They're original to the house. But I'm glad to know they're quaint. I always just thought they were really old."

"Oh, no. They're precious."

Matthew patted me on the back. "I best be gettin' on to the house now."

Julie clapped and cheered. "Look at you, Matthew! All country talk and everything! 'I best be gettin' on to the house now.' It's downright adorable!"

I smiled and winked at Matthew. "Oh, Julie, you think that's quaint? I don't even drink bottled water. Nope! Straight out of the tap. I'm a serious rural risk taker."

She moved toward Matthew and placed both arms around his neck. "You guys are just too much! So, was my visit a good surprise? Yes or no."

He carefully removed her arms. "Yes. You're definitely a woman who needs to learn how to drink tap water and make cupcakes. So, yes. This will be a life-changing visit, Julie."

"Oh, Matthew. You always were such a kidder. So tell me more about this older couple, Chester and Ida. They were your landlords, right?"

Matthew shook his head and frowned a bit. "No. They weren't my landlords. I lived with them. In their own home. Ate meals with them. Mrs. Ida, she cooked. She even got up early and made sausage and pancakes before I left for work. She'd pack leftovers and homegrown tomatoes for my lunch. I sat in the living room with them nearly every night. Worked in the yard with both of them. We went to church together.

No. They weren't my landlords." Matthew paused then smiled. "They were my family."

Julie used his sadness as another opportunity for a big hug. "Oh, Matthew, I'm sorry. I had no idea. That you were so close, I mean. No wonder their deaths were such a terrible blow."

"I wish you could have known them. They were the most genuine people. No pretense. No games. Brutally honest sometimes. But still." Matthew started laughing. "When I first arrived, like on the very first day, Mrs. Ida said, 'Now Matthew, we ain't hidden away any of our valuables 'cause we figure you're looking for a fresh start and you got no use for troublin' two old people like us. Plus, people 'round here get pretty protective of each other. And if you was to harm us, well, let's just say ain't no neighbors gonna bother with callin' 911. No, sir."

Julie slapped Matthew on the chest. "What a character! Sarah, did you know them well?"

"Yes. All my life. And that story? I can totally hear Mrs. Ida saying it. Every word. They were something else alright. Both of them. They'll be greatly missed. By all of us."

Matthew opened the door. "They will be missed." He turned back and his eyes met mine. "Good night, all."

I smiled. "Good night, Matthew."

Julie stretched out her arms like she was leading an exercise class. "Whew! It's been a long day. Thanks for everything, Sarah." She headed toward the bedroom. "I'm gonna take a nice long bath."

"Just make yourself at home!"

As the guest room door closed, I heard a light knock at the front door. I couldn't help but smile as I opened the door slightly and whispered, "If you're selling cookies, I'll take two boxes of Thin Mints. And three boxes of Samoas. And those little peanut butter thingamajigs too."

Matthew pushed the door open gently and looked around as though he were preparing to pull a prank. He smiled and reached for my arm. "I'll try to remember that." His voice got quieter. "Can you come out here for a minute?"

"Sure." I grabbed a blanket from the couch and wrapped it around my shoulders as I tiptoed out onto the porch. "Yes?"

"I just wanted to see you for a minute. Alone." He bit his lip and hesitated. "Look, if I did anything tonight, anything to make you feel sad or…or less than, I'm sorry, Sarah. I meant what I said last night. I like you. Julie's visit hasn't changed anything. And I'm not going to be spending any more time alone with her. I want you to know that. And if you're right, what you said about her intentions, well, I'm going to make it clear she might as well go back to California."

I leaned into his chest. "Thank you."

"But what you did at the funeral home tonight?" He smiled and shook his head. "That was a pretty bold statement to the folks around here. Just don't be surprised if you receive a little push back." He paused. "And it may be from the people you'd least expect."

"Meaning what?"

He leaned against the porch post. "Tolerance is one thing. Acceptance is another. Let's take your mother, for example. She's a nice lady. Respected here in Sharon. But I'm guessing she's not thrilled with the idea of you and me."

"Mama's just embarrassed by the whole Jerry Conner thing and the fact that everybody was talking about it. Had Jerry not done what he did, most folks in town wouldn't have known or cared what we were doing on the porch."

He shook his head. "I want to believe that."

"But?"

"But I know how things are. Whatever Mr. Garrett told you last night that got you so scared, that made you not even want to touch me...there's probably some truth to it. Maybe even a lot of truth. I don't sleep well at night. I still jump when I hear loud noises. There are things that happened." He shook his head. "Things I can't talk about. With anyone." He walked toward the steps and looked up at the moon. "Think about what Aunt Charlotte was saying the other night. How proud your mother would be about you dating Dr. Carter." He looked at me and sighed. "Do you think she'd be equally proud to tell the people around here that you're dating me? You think she'd go around saying, 'Did you hear the news? Sarah's dating that guy who was in prison for fourteen years. He's not even allowed to drive a car. I couldn't be happier.'"

I reached for his hand. "I don't know what she'd say really. I haven't asked. But I know what Dusty says. And Chester and Ida, I know what they said. I know what Doug and Carlie think about you. Dave and Ashley. And Brother Dan."

His eyes met mine. "And that's enough?"

"It is."

He placed his hands gently behind my head. Even in the moonlight, I could see his beautiful dark brown eyes shining. "Thank you, Sarah. Thank you." He moved forward and kissed me like no man had ever kissed me. Gentle. Soft. Passionate but not aggressive. I thought sure I would faint. He pulled his face away. I used my finger to wipe the lipstick smudges from his mouth. He kissed my hand and whispered, "You are beautiful. In every way. Don't ever doubt that. I better go before we get busted out here." He walked down the steps but turned back briefly. "We seem to get in a lot of trouble on porches."

"So I've noticed."

He quickly walked back up the steps. "Actually, Sarah, there's something I haven't told you. Something I want to tell you."

"Oh no. You're an angel who came down to earth just to teach me some kind of moral lesson about pain and disappointment. This is all just a dream. I had a feeling you were too good to be true."

He laughed. "Hey, I may be a lot of things, but an angel isn't one of them."

"Then go ahead. Bare your soul."

"A few weeks after we met, I knew I liked you. A lot. But I'd been in prison since I was a 21-year-old kid so I didn't know how to pursue you. Not really. So, one night, over dinner, I just said to Chester and Ida, 'How should I go about telling Sarah how I feel about her?'"

"And?"

"Chester looked me square in the eyes, and said, 'Matthew, I have no idea.'"

"Ha ha ha. That's Chester."

"And then he said something I'll never forget. He reached for Mrs. Ida's hand, and said, 'Truth is, I can't even remember a time when I didn't love her. Guess I've loved her all my life.'"

"Wow."

He leaned against the post and looked down. "And I envied him, Sarah. I envied Chester Miller. Every day. He never had to go through the process of cleaning up messes from the past, never had to explain away a bunch of mistakes." He hesitated and looked right at me. "Never had to try to convince a woman he was trustworthy. Mrs. Ida knew she could trust him, even in eighth grade."

"I'm sure Chester made his share of mistakes."

Matthew looked up at the night sky and shook his head. "Maybe so. But to me? His life was pretty close to perfect."

"Or maybe Ida was just a really good forgiver."

He smiled. "Probably so. And tomorrow we honor that."

"Yes, tomorrow. And don't worry. I'll be there. With you. And I don't care who knows it either. Oh, and Matthew, one more thing before you go."

He moved close to me and I laid my head on his chest. He whispered, "Yes?"

"If things don't work out between us, I'm convinced Charlotte Nelson has a terrible crush on you. Face the facts. You're the whole reason she's trying to lose weight. Bart seems worried. He does."

He laughed as he wrapped his arms around me tighter. "Tempting as it would be to date a woman who literally holds the magic secret to pickle-making in her hands, I'm already taken." He began to kiss me again. My heart was beating faster. Like a dream. The kind of dream where you pray the alarm clock never goes off.

The front door opened without warning. I jumped and Matthew pulled away, almost tripping over the porch rug.

Julie was wearing a long, black, silk robe and showing way too much cleavage for Sharon, Tennessee. Her face bore one second of disappointment but then she covered it like a pro. "Well, well, well." She smiled and pointed her finger like she was almost congratulating us. "Looks like you two are up to somethin'! And to think, I almost bought that whole scam about how Matthew had never been inside your house. Tsk, tsk, tsk. I thought church-goers weren't supposed to lie."

Matthew was always so articulate and well-spoken. But he stuttered as he backed away. "I hadn't. I mean, I didn't. Not that anyway. No. Not ever."

"Wow, Matthew. Sounds like you've been drinking. Sarah must be more intoxicating than we know. That whole Betty Crocker deal is just a cover, huh? A cover for what's really cookin'."

I knew what it felt like to be her. I'd been there. Many times. I made a conscious effort to be kind. Maybe even ease the pain a little. "Busted. The word is out now." I pointed to Matthew and then to myself. "Truth is, we met on a prison dating site. I lured him to Sharon with the promise of cupcakes and small town charm. And he bought it. Hook, line, and sinker. He bought it."

Matthew started laughing. He didn't even look Julie's direction, which I appreciated more than he could ever know. He stared straight at me as he moved in close. "Yeah, I'm all about the cupcakes." He kissed me on the cheek and then stepped off the porch, never looking back. "Good night, ladies. See you tomorrow."

Chapter 41, CARLIE: The Little Black Dress

There's an order to funeral day in a small town. Steps really.
Step #1. Make food. Lots of food. Step #2. Take the food to
the church basement or fellowship hall for the after-funeral
meal. Step #3. Go to the funeral. (Some people look at the
deceased and say, 'He looks good, don't he? So good.' I
never do that because, first of all, it's grammatically incorrect
and secondly, well, just because, and I'll leave it at that).
Step #4. Go to the cemetery. On the way to the cemetery, try
to explain to little kids a concept which will be very hard for
them to understand. Just because we're outside doesn't mean
we can run or make loud noises. We can't run or make loud
noises at the cemetery because it's disrespectful. If you have a
smart kid, he or she will say, "Mama, why? Will it wake up
all the dead people?" Then a smart parent will say, "No, but it
might make the old people who are still alive want to hit you
with a cane. So it's a dangerous risk, at best." Step #5. Go to
the funeral meal in the church basement or fellowship hall.
Step #6. Try to convince the bereaved to eat because they'll
need their strength. This is kind of an odd thing to do because
most people know bodily strength is not usually found in
buttery casseroles and high carbohydrate desserts.

Today the funeral home is almost full. I knew it would be.
Matthew and Brother Dan are sitting on the front row. Doug
and I are sitting with Aunt Charlotte and Uncle Bart about
halfway back. Aunt Charlotte keeps us informed with a
running commentary on all the pre-funeral proceedings.
"Well, good for him! Homer Crittenden done walked in with
Jane Johnson. Mabel said she's been sweet on 'em for a few
months now and that that's why she been goin' to the beauty
shop so much and wearin' her teeth every day." "Look at Bill
Norton's girl. She done growed up so purdy. Little ol' Clint
Buford can't keep his eyes in his head." "Glad to see

Gertrude's here. Must have finally gotten free of them shingles."

We got a break from Aunt Charlotte's blow-by-blow commentary when Sarah tapped me on the shoulder and we all scooted over to make room. She and Julie both looked beautiful, but in a completely different way. Julie's make-up was perfect and her hair was straight and smooth. She looked like she stepped right out of one of those Paul Mitchell hair products commercials. Her black skirt and tan blouse were skin-tight and her shoes were so pointy, the Wicked Witch of the West would have been downright envious.

Sarah had on a solid black dress that hugged her curves appropriately. She didn't have big 1987 Texas hair, but it wasn't straight and flat either. Perfectly highlighted. Loosely curled. Beautiful. She wasn't dressed immodestly. But she was definitely making a public statement that, when it comes to Matthew Prescott, she wasn't flying the white flag just yet. You go, Sarah! If this were a horse race, the announcer would say, "Beautiful hometown Sarah comes around the bend and takes the lead." One thing's for sure. Sarah Simpson looked much more relaxed and happy than when she went running from the funeral home last night.

When she and Julie had gotten situated on the pew, I leaned over and whispered, "I wanted to call you last night. Are you okay?"

"Yes, and I'm glad you didn't call. I was busy."

"Busy? Busy MAKING food or busy EATING food? I've been worried, Sarah. I once ate nearly a half-gallon of Blue Bell ice cream when Doug and I were on the outs. Threw up in an airport bathroom and everything. Seriously. It was terrible."

She smiled and winked. "I wasn't making food or eating food. Not the whole time anyway."

When I was just about to lean in to get the whole scoop, Matthew appeared at the end of the pew. He was dressed in a gray suit and white shirt. Solid black tie. Aunt Charlotte yelled out, "Have mercy, Baby! You clean up real good!"

Matthew nodded and winked at Sarah. "Thank you, Aunt Charlotte. So do you." He looked directly at Sarah. "Did you girls rest well?"

Sarah smiled in that same way people smile when they have a secret. A really really good secret too. "I did. How 'bout you, Matthew? Did you sleep well?"

He returned her smile and stared at her like she was the only woman in the room or for that matter, the world. I started wonderin' if these two had run off to Vegas and gotten married by an Elvis impersonator without telling any of us. Good night. The heat between them could have cooked a frozen turkey in less than ten minutes.

Matthew pretended to clear his throat. "I did sleep well. I mean, I was a little restless at times, but yeah, I slept fine."

That's when we all learned Julie Crawford wasn't flying the white flag yet either. She took a deep breath. "Well, I could hardly sleep at all. Just tossing and turning. All night long." She put her hand on Matthew's forearm. "I was thinking about old times, I guess. Remember that summer Daddy rented the house at Catalina? Right after high school graduation?"

He nodded. "I do. You spent the whole time trying to get Billy Crenshaw's attention."

217

She laughed. "I wore that little bitty white bikini all summer long." She turned and grabbed Sarah's arm. "I was getting nowhere. Nothing. Finally, at the end of the summer, Billy's sister told me he wasn't interested in girls at all." She let go of Sarah and turned to Matthew. "It was a relief really. I mean, there for a while, I was worried, worried I didn't have what it took to get a man's attention."

My word. She can't be serious. Julie Crawford may not be able to make pickles or clean out a fence row. She may know nothing about gardening or other domestic endeavors. But one thing we all know for sure. Even without the fake teeth, she definitely has what it takes to get a man's attention.

Matthew smiled but not at Julie. "Sarah, would you be willing to sit with me and Brother Dan? Upfront."

She stood and straightened her dress. "Absolutely. I'd be glad to." He reached for her hand.

She hadn't even stepped into the center aisle when loud noises erupted from the back of the room. Mr. Groeden's voice was unusually firm. "No! Get out! You're not filming in here. I won't allow it."

We all turned as Dusty moved into the center aisle. "What are you guys doing here? We're not supposed to start shooting until Monday." Matthew quickly joined him in the back of the room.

A young red-headed cameraman dressed in khaki pants and a black shirt was adjusting a tripod at the very back of the center aisle. "The producer told us to get footage of the funeral. Reality is reality. You can't always pick and choose."

Mr. Groeden's voice escalated. "Well, I haven't agreed to any reality show. And I am able to pick and choose. This is my business and we want you out."

"Look man, I don't want trouble. I'll go to the very back corner. How 'bout that? You'll never even know I'm here."

Mr. Groeden paced nervously. The whole community was watching so he tried to speak in softer tones. "No filming inside this building. If you want to go out to the street, I can't stop you. But I can keep you from filming inside this room. I'll call the law, if I have to."

The young guy held up both hands. "Okay, okay. You made your point." He looked at Dusty and Matthew, as he folded up the tripod. "But you guys are gonna have to vouch for me with the producer. Tell him this old guy was livin' in the dark ages and evidently didn't want anyone to see what kind of voodoo ritual he performs in here every day." He looked at Mr. Groeden and laughed. "But hey, that's fine with me, man. Hold on to all your secrets." He walked toward the door. "I'm out. And yeah, I'll be camped across the street. So you better pull the shades."

Mr. Groeden's face was bright red as he waved pleasantly to the crowd and said, "We'll get started in about thirty minutes." Dusty put his arm around Mr. Groeden and whispered what I felt certain was an apology for the chaos.

Matthew started walking back down the aisle toward Sarah, who was still standing next to the pew. Aunt Charlotte jumped to her feet before any of us had the chance to stop her. Not that we could have stopped her. When she gets something on her mind, she's a dad gum freight train. And she spoke so loudly, I felt certain the young cameraman across the street heard every word. "Well, none of us should be troubled by

219

what happened just now!" She pointed to the back of the room. "That horribly rude child was only doin' what his boss told him to do. And he didn't have the good sense nor the proper raisin' to understand the error of his ways. Lord, bless the poor boy, that's what I say! And keep him from bein' knocked out cold and left for dead by someone not as understandin' and hospitable as our own dear Mr. Groeden. And that's all I aim to say about it."

Matthew leaned over the pew and said, "Nicely done, Aunt Charlotte. Nicely done." Sarah was still standing in the aisle. Matthew put his arm around her waist. "Why don't we head to the break room for a few minutes, before the service begins? I think we've got time."

"Sure."

There was time alright. Time for me to take a matchmaking victory lap around Groeden's Funeral Home.

Chapter 42, SARAH: If This is a Dream, Don't Wake Me Up!

We were alone in the break room and I was thankful. Matthew sat in the corner chair and loosened his tie a bit. I walked to the table to investigate the food and drink options. "Matthew, can I pour you some coffee? Or juice? Would you like something to eat? Looks like CO-OP sent sausage biscuits. I'd be glad to warm one up for you. Or there's fruit salad, if you want something lighter."

He smiled and motioned for me to sit next to him. I sat down and he put both arms around me. "I have a question. Why do you always do that?"

"Do what?"

"That thing where you always ask if I want something to eat or drink. At Carlie's, you're always refilling my tea glass or asking if you can get me something to eat. I'm just curious as to why you do that."

"It's called hospitality, Matthew. I mean, surely your mother did that, right?"

"No. Not that I can recall. I mean, even when the kitchen staff wasn't there, I never remember her…well…"

"Serving?"

"Yeah, serving. I mean, she served on committees, boards, plenty of non-profit things. But no, I never remember her saying, 'Matthew, would you like me to warm you up a sausage biscuit?' Or 'Can I get you some more sweet tea?'"

I laughed and patted him on the chest. "Well, you probably just didn't have any sweet tea in the house or any sausage biscuits for her to warm up. See, that's the problem right there. You don't come from a tea-swigging, pork-eating family and that's where the whole serving thing broke down from the get-go, see."

He laughed. "Oh, that's it. Yeah. I can see the whole thing clearly now."

"Does it make you uncomfortable? My filling your tea glass or offering you food?"

"No. No, not at all. I like it actually. It just feels weird. I didn't grow up that way. And prison? Well, that wasn't exactly the most service-oriented place either. You can imagine what that was like."

"No. I can't really."

"Good. Don't try."

"Matthew, I've been thinkin' about somethin'."

"Yes."

"I figure the first part of your life, the first 35 years, well, maybe those years were the warm-up for your real life. The one that begins now." I looked into his eyes and he gently touched the side of my face. "Maybe all the painful things that happened were a way of making you thankful for the second half of life. An honest day's work. A sausage biscuit. A glass of tea. Things most of us take for granted."

He took a deep breath. "A good woman?"

I blushed and looked away. "Yeah, I hope so."

He touched my hand. "Look at me, Sarah. I know it took me a few months to...well, to tell you how I feel. But I want you to know something. This is the happiest time of my life. And it's not the sausage biscuits or the sweet tea. Not the job. It's not even Chester and Ida making me a member of their family, though that was tremendous. It's you, Sarah. It's been you for a while. And I get that I'm probably not the kind of man you envisioned. But I want to thank you. For taking a chance on me. For believing in me. I want to be worthy of that kind of trust."

"Thank you, Matthew. And you're right. You're not the kind of man I envisioned. At all. You're beyond what I could have envisioned. Smarter. More diligent. Forgiving. Tender. And well...uh, you're..." My face turned red.

He smiled. "What? Annoying?"

"No. Forget it."

"You can tell me. I can take it."

"Good-looking. Like, 'out of my league' good-looking. 'Keep a girl up at night' good-looking. 'Who turned up the heat in here?' good-looking. Seriously. Sometimes it's scary. Well, scary and wonderful at the same time."

He placed his hands on my face and looked into my eyes. "Sarah Simpson, you are the most beautiful woman I have ever known. Period. Trust me. You're in a league of your own."

"You don't know how much it means to me, for you to say that."

223

"It's true. And before we go back in there, I want to ask you something."

"Anything,"

"Will you go out with me? On a real date? I've been trying to get up the nerve to ask for a long time."

"I will."

"Tomorrow night?"

"Yes."

"Seven?"

"Yes."

"You know I can't exactly pick you up in a car. But would it be okay if we walked to Mabel's? Maybe sit on the porch a while?"

"That would be perfect. Oh, and do you want me to invite Bart and Charlotte Nelson? 'Cause they love to be with us, Matthew. They do."

He winked. "Maybe next time. Well, we better get back in there."

"Yeah. The funeral should be starting in a few minutes."

He tightened his tie. I walked toward the door. I could feel his eyes on me. It was like a dream. Please, God, don't let me wake up.

It's odd how peaceful I felt being at Chester and Ida's funeral. I'd miss them, yes. But they had the rare privilege of dying together, the way they would have wanted. I also felt this tremendous sense of appreciation. At the very end of their lives, they'd given me a gift. They told me to trust Matthew, give him a chance, open myself up to the possibilities. They told me to be patient and try to understand why it all had to move so slowly. Now I believed all that and more. And it was beyond wonderful. Matthew and I moved to the front of the room where Brother Dan was visiting with Mayor Perkins and his wife.

Standing so close to Matthew felt like euphoria and peace. Passion and comfort. Adventure? Yes. But not the scary kind of adventure that makes you wonder if you'll come back alive. No. The kind of adventure that's exciting but always leads back home. For the first time, I understood what people like Carlie were always talking about. That unexplainable sense of connection. I wanted to passionately kiss Matthew several times a day. And make cupcakes for him. I wanted to sit with him in church every Sunday. Listen to his opinion on world politics and the economy. Paint the porch ceiling with him on a Saturday morning. Learn how to disagree. Practice the art of making up. Compromise. Make homemade chicken soup when he's sick. I wanted to be Matthew Prescott's wife and make mad passionate love to him every night.

"Sarah? Sarah?"

"Oh, uh, yeah. Sorry. Zoned out there for a bit." I shook hands with the mayor and tried to nod pleasantly.

"The mayor was wondering if we'd be willing to come to the Fire Department banquet in a few weeks. I'll be presenting Mrs. Ida's quilt. Would you like to join me?"

"Oh, yes. Absolutely. Thank you, Mayor. We'll be there."

As the mayor turned to sit in one of the pews, Jerry Conner entered from the back door. He had on his nice Sunday clothes and there was no indication he had been anywhere near Miss Lucy or her toxic "recipe". Several people in the crowd turned and then tried to pretend they thought nothing of it. Matthew leaned toward me. "Let's try to be as pleasant as we can."

"Oh, absolutely."

He placed his hand on Brother Dan's shoulder. "I think Sarah and I should sit this one out. We'll go ahead and sit down."

Brother Dan whispered, "That's probably wise."

Matthew asked, "When do I do my reading? After the first hymn or before?"

Brother Dan handed him a schedule. "It's right after 'Trust and Obey.'"

"Okay, thanks." We both looked up and pleasantly nodded at Jerry as he strolled down the aisle. Then we sat on the front pew.

Jerry shook his head and looked at us. "You two don't have to sit down on my account. Go ahead. Stand up and be proud of what you're doing." He pointed to the caskets. "Go ahead and be proud of what you did to these two as well. You're why they're here, Matthew."

Brother Dan moved forward and extended his hand as he stood between Jerry and front row. "Jerry, hey there. Glad you could make it today."

"I wouldn't have missed it. The Millers did right by everybody in town." He tried to make eye contact with Matthew but Matthew was staring at the funeral program. "Too bad they were too old and trusting to do right by themselves. Damn shame what happened to them both." He looked back at Matthew. "And not a charge being filed by anybody!"

Brother Dan put his arm around Jerry and said quietly, "We're about to start. Let me help you find a seat."

Jerry pulled away. "Why in the world are you trying to protect him?" He pointed at Matthew. "Why is everybody in town trying to protect this man? He's a damn felon!" Jerry turned to me and my heart skipped a beat. "And you? Sarah, why in God's name are you runnin' around with this guy like you've lost your mind or somethin'?" His voice escalated as he moved toward me with both hands out. "Huh? Why? God, were you that lonely, Sarah? That desperate?"

Matthew stood and it's like I could hear the crowd take a deep breath. I did too. He moved between Jerry and me. "Look, Jerry, if you've got a problem with me, take it up with me. But this is not the time or the place. And leave Sarah out of it."

"Oh, you're trying to protect your WOMAN now, huh? I'm surprised you can even get a woman, Matthew! Pretty boy like you? In prison all those years?" He started laughing as he lightly touched Matthew's chest. "C'mon, we all know you were some old man's boy toy!"

And that was the single moment in time. The moment Matthew Prescott's patience ended. Completely. He lunged forward with the strength and sheer force of an injured lion. Jerry Conner was on the ground and bleeding before I could even get to my feet. At one point, I heard a cracking sound. I prayed to God he wouldn't kill him. Brother Dan tried to intervene but was no match for Matthew's strength and will. By the time Dusty and Doug reached the front, Jerry's head was being pounded into the carpet. They managed to pull Matthew away, but it took both of them. Every ounce of energy they could muster. Matthew's white shirt was covered in Jerry's blood. His lip was busted and bleeding slightly. Dusty pulled him up against the wall, trying to calm him. But Jerry? Jerry lay lifeless on the ground.

Mr. Groeden yelled, "Jimmy, call 9-1-1! We need an ambulance."

Janie Evans moved quickly to kneel beside Jerry. Brian Carter ran from the back of the room to join her. He took off his suit coat and wiped the blood from Jerry's head and face. I could hear him calling out Jerry's name. But he wasn't responding. Janie sighed and whispered, "Thank God. He's alive."

Bob Garrett ran to the front just as Dusty was releasing Matthew from his grip. "Mr. Prescott, I'll need to take you in. Don't make this hard on yourself, Son." His right eye was starting to swell as he turned and put both hands behind his back.

When Matthew turned, I moved in front of him. "You'll need a lawyer."

He lowered his head. "No. Don't get involved, Sarah."

Mr. Garrett handcuffed him and yelled, "Mike, pull the car around!"

I spoke one more time. "I'm coming with you."

"No. Stay with Doug and Carlie. Please. Doug, help me out here."

Carlie hugged me. Doug wrinkled his brow and whispered, "He's embarrassed, Sarah. It'll only make things worse if you go. Give him time. I'll talk to Mr. Garrett and keep you posted."

Then there was the walk. The walk of shame. In front of nearly every citizen of Sharon. Matthew's lip was still bleeding a bit so Janie carefully used some wet wipes to clean up his mouth. He smiled slightly and thanked her. She patted his back and said, "No problem, Honey."

Mr. Garrett grabbed his right arm and they walked slowly toward the back of the room. Matthew bowed his head. Mama and Mabel were sitting at the end of the pew on the last row. I could clearly see Mama's facial expression. It was the same expression she had when I made a "D" in College Algebra. The same expression when she told me she got laid off a few years ago, right before Christmas. The same expression she had when Officer Thomas came to the house that evening and told her Jim Hill wasn't gonna do any time for Daddy's death, that it was all just a terrible accident. Yeah, her expression today was like that last one most of all.

The EMTs came down the aisle about three minutes after Matthew left. They put Jerry on a stretcher. He was still out cold and there was blood everywhere. Jerry looked like one of those mafia guys who had been roughed up pretty good by another mafia guy. But after they wheeled him up the center aisle, Janie put her arm around me and whispered, "I feel certain he'll be fine. He'll have some recovery time. But unless there are internal injuries, he should be alright. Oh, and don't tell anyone I said this, but Lord, Sarah, he deserved every blow." She shook her head and leaned in closer. "There's not a man in this room who wouldn't have done the same thing. Sad, really. The whole thing. Everybody loses with this one."

Brother Dan was always the voice of calm. "May I have your attention, please? We are going to have the funeral today. But we're going to take an extra twenty minutes or so. So, just know we're going to try to start around 2:30. Thank you."

Mr. Groeden and his dressed-up worker men were busy scrubbing the carpet with stain remover. One of the men even wiped the caskets where blood had splattered. I couldn't help but wonder what Mrs. Ida and Chester would say about all the mayhem at their funeral. I had a feeling Mrs. Ida would say, "That ornery Jerry Conner just couldn't leave well enough alone. He just kept pickin' at that scab until it finally bled." I figured Chester would say, "Well, one thing's for sure, Ida. Ain't nobody ever gonna forget our funeral." And he'd be right.

Chapter 43, CARLIE: A Fight and a Funeral

Well, good gosh a-mighty. It's all broken loose here in
Sharon, Tennessee. Matthew's been hauled to the Weakley
County Jail. Jerry's been rushed to Volunteer Hospital. Mr.
Groeden is busy cleaning up blood stains. And Brother Dan's
left to direct a funeral. Bless his heart.

Oh, and I can only imagine all the unbelievable film footage
the red-headed cameraman is getting from across the street.
Matthew in handcuffs. Jerry Conner on a stretcher, out cold.
And the community folks running here and there, wondering
how all this could happen in a town where the most exciting
thing that ever happens involves Mabel putting hamburgers on
sale, 2/$5.

During the break, Aunt Charlotte came running to the front to
embrace me as though we'd both been spared injury in a world
war. "Law, wouldn't Chester and Ida have had a fit over all
this? A fit, I tell ya! I had a mind to sock that Jerry Conner
myself. But Lord knows he was gettin' plenty of all of it
without my part. Are you and Doug staying for the funeral,
Baby?"

"We would. But Doug wants to go to the jail and see how
things are goin' with Matthew."

"I reckon. What am I supposed to do with that little Julie
gal?"

"Well, she has a car. I guess she can stay for the funeral or go
to Sarah's house."

Sarah interrupted. "I want to go with you and Doug to the
jail."

"Doug doesn't think that's a good idea. Matthew doesn't want that, Sarah. And he definitely doesn't want you to see him in a situation like this. We'll find out what's happening and what needs to happen and let you know. I promise."

"Okay. Call me tonight."

"That's fine. Oh look! Seems your house guest is busy getting to know the good Dr. Carter."

Sarah sighed. "That doesn't surprise me in the least."

Doug arranged to meet Jimmy Wilson at the jail. Jimmy's a good lawyer and one of Doug's best friends. Matthew was released by supper time and I didn't ask Doug for all the details. It may have involved us posting bond or setting a hearing date or I'm not sure really. But I know this for sure. When Doug walked through the door, his countenance was certainly not one of victory. Neither was Matthew's. There was a definite assumption that Jerry Conner would be pressing charges. Considering the fact that Matthew was out on parole, it could be a very strained situation, at best.

Doug didn't even sit down. "Carlie, Matthew needs to eat and drink something. I'm heading to the hospital. Jimmy said the extent of Jerry's injuries has a lot to do with what we're facing."

I handed Matthew one of Doug's t-shirts. "I thought you might want to change."

"Thanks."

Matthew walked into the bathroom slowly, like an old man whose joints were hurting. Doug shook his head and put his arm around me. His voice was quiet. "Pray Jerry's not hurt bad. If he's hurt in a permanent injury kind of way, Jimmy said Matthew's going back to jail. He's almost certain."

When Matthew opened the bathroom door, Doug tried to put a positive spin on it. "Hey man, I'll be back as soon as I can. But before I go, can I pray for you? Figure we all could use it about now."

Matthew nodded. "Yeah. And for Jerry too."

"Oh, absolutely." Doug grabbed my hand and the three of us bowed our heads. "Lord, we're desperate right now. Desperate for mercy. Mercy only you can give." He paused. "And healing. We ask for healing for Jerry's physical body. Healing for Matthew too…in whatever way he needs that. Thank you that we can ask. In Jesus' name, Amen."

Doug looked up but Matthew grabbed his arm. "Wait. There's something I need to say too." He bowed his head. "Please forgive me, God. The anger. The doubt. Forgive me for hurting Jerry. Please help me. In Jesus' name, Amen."

Doug opened the kitchen door. "I'll be back soon."

I kissed him on the cheek and whispered, "Thank you. For all of it. For caring."

An hour later, Matthew and I were drinking coffee and eating peanut butter sandwiches when we heard Doug's car pull into the driveway. We both waited silently at the table like our lives were in the balance.

The kitchen door made the familiar squeaking sound. Doug shook his head. "Not good, man. Not good."

Matthew's face grew pale as he dropped his head. "I figured. I knew he was hurt."

"The right cheek bone is broken. Doc says it may require reconstructive surgery. A few broken ribs. At one point they thought he had swelling on the brain, but he doesn't. He's conscious now. Seems to know where he is. Thankfully. They're keeping him overnight for observations. Things could change by morning. Better or worse."

Matthew looked down at a half-eaten sandwich. "Yeah. I knew it was bad."

Doug moved toward the table. "I got a chance to talk to him though."

"And?"

"And he's willing to drop all charges."

Matthew jumped to his feet. "What? You're kidding!"

"No. But there are conditions." Doug leaned against a bar stool. "And they're not good."

"Let me guess. They involve me leaving the area."

"Right."

"I figured. I guess he's thinking as long as he never sees me again, everything's forgotten, right? Back to normal."

"I talked to Jimmy to see if that were even legal. Stipulations, I mean. It is. Basically, what he's saying is, if you leave town, he'll decide not to press charges. But if you choose to stay here, he's going to follow through with the charges and all that entails."

"No. That's good. I've already been thinking about it. I need to leave anyway. It's not fair to Dusty. Not fair to…"

I broke in. "To Sarah?"

"Yeah. It's not fair to Sarah. It was already going to be tough. But now…" He shook his head. "Well, there's no reason to put her through all that. I'll talk to my parole officer about moving to California."

"But what about a job?"

"I could talk to my cousin, Stephen. He's really a pretty decent guy." Matthew let out a ragged breath and put his face in his hands. His voice cracked. "I'm sure it's all for the best anyway, right? I was never going to, you know…this wasn't my real home."

Doug stood behind me and put his hands on my shoulders. "Chester and Ida thought it was."

Matthew nodded. "They were good people. Probably a little naïve though."

"What about the house?"

"I'll sell it, I guess. If I can get a job in California, I'll donate whatever it brings to the community in some way. The fire department, maybe. The Millers would have liked that."

I took a napkin from the holder in the middle of the table and dabbed my eyes. "I, for one, don't like this idea. I'm supposed to call Sarah. Let her know what's happening."

235

Matthew stood. "I can do that. I should do it. Doug, you've already done so much for me today. More than you should have. But do you think you could drop me by her house? Maybe that would be the best way to handle it. And before we go, could I borrow your phone so I can call Dusty?"

"Sure. Phone's in the back room. And I'll take you whenever you're ready."

Chapter 44, SARAH: No Long Good-byes

Julie and I sat out on the porch most of the evening. But I was never without my phone. Carlie had already called once to tell me he was out of jail. They were waiting on the hospital report. I asked to speak with him. She said he wasn't ready to talk to me yet. What did that even mean? Whatever it meant, it wasn't good.

I recognized Doug's truck and flung the blanket off my lap. Matthew got out of the truck. He was limping a bit, wearing an old t-shirt and a denim jacket I'd seen Doug wear many times. He turned to wave at Doug and the truck pulled back out of the driveway. I ran down the steps as he started walking faster. I tried to speak as though none of it had happened. "I know you're sore, but I'm gonna hug you anyway. I am." I smiled. "I promise to be gentle."

He held out his arms. "I trust you. Completely."

I winked and said, "I'm pretty darn trustworthy. Ask anybody around here." He slowly enveloped me in his arms and I laid my head against his chest. He breathed deeply. Peaceful.

"Sarah, I need to talk to you."

"You have news? About Jerry?"

"Yeah. He's hurt pretty bad. Broken cheekbone. Broken ribs. I had a feeling. May have to do some reconstructive surgery on his face."

"Here, come sit on the porch."

Julie came running to the steps. "Matthew, we were worried sick!"

"I'm okay." He gently lowered himself into the white rocking chair. "How was the funeral?"

Julie started in. "Oh, it was the sweetest little ceremony. With Bible verses and God songs and God talk and everything."

Matthew wrinkled his brow. "They're called hymns, Julie. I thought you guys were Episcopalians."

"Oh no. Daddy just always told people we were. He said people were more likely to trust a man who had a little bit of religion in him. Anyway, after the funeral we went to the church meal. And I ate catfish and chocolate cake and this dish made out of hash brown potatoes. I must have gained at least five pounds. And I met the nicest people too. There was this one guy, the doctor. Well, he just went on and on about everything. I don't know if he was nervous or if he found me, I don't know, intimidating?"

"I'm glad you both went to the meal. These are good people, Julie."

"Well, I don't know why poor Sarah went at all. She refused to eat anything. She worked in the kitchen most of the time. And I don't know what happened back there but it wasn't good. Sarah, did you say your mama was real sick? Is that why she left so early?"

"Yeah. Uh, she just wasn't feeling well."

Matthew looked at me like a kid looks when he brings home bad grades. Embarrassment. Shame. Regret. "I'm sorry about your mama, Sarah. That she's, you know, sick and all."

"Oh, I'm sure she'll be feeling better soon. No worries, Matthew." I picked up a pillow and placed it gently behind his head and shoulders.

He grabbed me by the arm and looked into my eyes. "Thank you."

"Do you want something to eat or drink? We have funeral leftovers."

"No. I'm fine. Really. Sarah, can I talk to you…" He looked at Julie. "Alone? Just for a minute."

Julie leapt to her feet. "I'll leave you two lovebirds to do whatever it is you do out here on the porch. Sarah swears up and down it's not what I think it is, but…really…I wasn't born yesterday."

Matthew nodded. And Julie slammed the door.

I stood. "Would it help if I rubbed your back or your shoulders a little bit?"

"No." He smiled. "And it might make it harder to say what I'm about to say."

"Let me guess. You're worried. About the hearing and everything."

"No. Not anymore. Jerry has agreed to not press charges."

"My gosh! That's great! No, it's wonderful!" Tears fell from my eyes. "I'm so relieved. You have no idea."

He clasped his hands together and lowered his head. "There's a catch."

"A catch?"

"Yeah. He's agreed to not press charges if I leave the area."

"What? You're kidding! That's the dumbest thing I've ever heard. You have a job and a house, and a life and…"

"You?"

I knelt by the rocking chair. "Yes. You have me. And moving? Well, that's crazy."

He didn't make eye contact. "No. I think Jerry's right. For a lot of reasons. Look, that thing today was stupid. I flew off the handle." Matthew stood and started pacing. "I could have killed him, Sarah! Killed him! And if Doug and Dusty hadn't gotten there when they did, I probably would have killed him. And that kind of anger? That should scare you! Don't you think that's what your mama's scared of? What happened today, don't you think that's what keeps her up at night? And if it didn't worry her before, oh, I can assure you it does now! And it should worry you too."

"No. Jerry was the one who showed out today. He's even the one who touched you first. There are witnesses, Matthew! Look, you've got nothing to worry about. Let it go to a hearing, a trial, if need be. But don't walk away with your head down. Please. Don't."

"Sarah, this was all just a fantasy. Don't you see?" His voice grew softer as he pointed to the street. "They weren't going to accept me. Not really. I'm not one of them. I'm not going to be one of them. You know that. Your mama knows it, even if you don't."

"No! Some people might talk. But the people that matter? The people that matter do accept you."

He turned and faced the street as his hands nervously tapped the porch railing. "Look, I'm moving back to California. I've already talked to Dusty and he's supportive of the idea. He gets it, Sarah. He knows what it's like!"

"And what about the TV show?"

"I guess the cameraman squealed pretty loudly about everything that went on this afternoon. Shayla has already talked to Dusty about it. She knows I'm moving. Evidently, they're gonna switch it up, do this contrasting thing between the life of an ex-con in Sharon and one in San Diego. I don't know. I couldn't care less. I'll do what they say and leave it at that."

"And your work?"

"Dusty will find help at the shop. He's connected. I'll talk to my cousin, Stephen, about getting a job with the company maybe. I still have a business degree and he knows people in San Diego. Surely one of them needs to make a big community service splash by hiring an ex-con. Kind of the 'in' thing to do right now, I guess. Especially if they think they'll end up on TV. I have friends I can stay with for a while." He moved toward me and placed his hands on my arms. "And if you want to visit me…"

"You'll what? Introduce me as an 'old friend'? Like Julie here? Someone you knew back in the day?"

He leaned back on the railing. "No. That wasn't what I was going to say. You're not an old friend, Sarah. And you're nothing like Julie."

241

"I can't believe you're letting Jerry Conner ruin your life like this! That you're giving him this much power! Power to change, to change everything."

Matthew walked down the porch steps. He turned back to face me. I couldn't tell if it was sadness or anger that burned in his eyes. "You wanna know the truth, Sarah? Huh? Do you want me to stand here and tell you the REAL truth about all of it? About why I'm moving?" He raised his hands in the air. "Why I'm running? 'Cause I assure you it's not about Jerry Conner at all. Jerry Conner is not the one running me out of town. Not by a long shot."

"Who is then?"

He took a deep breath and spoke calmly. "The past. My past." He walked quickly to the sidewalk. Then turned back briefly. "I don't expect you to understand, Sarah. But I can't stay. I won't put you through that."

I stood at the top of the steps and watched him walk away. I knew he was heading straight to Chester and Ida's house. Except he wasn't. Not really. It was his house now. He was going home. But sadly, he no longer believed it.

Chapter 45, CARLIE: Saturday Morning Sharon Report

I knew Aunt Charlotte would be at our house by the crack of dawn. But I was wrong. She waited until 8:30. She even knocked this time. Doug and James were eating cereal and watching cartoons in the living room. I was making coffee in the kitchen.

"Come in!"

She moved more slowly than usual. Tired. "Bart dropped me off on his way to Co-Op to get chicken feed. The way I see it, we got a lot of trouble brewin' 'round here, Carlie. A lot of trouble."

"Agreed. But this time there's nothing we can do about it, Aunt Charlotte. So, if you're here to present one of your schemes or uh, plans, or whatever you call it, don't bother. We're over our heads this time."

"Well, I 'spect you don't know what's happened in the night."

"In the night?"

"Yes, Ma'am. Seems Julie and Matthew done hit the road. Headin' for California. Sure as shootin'."

"In the middle of the night?"

"Well, to hear Cora Belle tell it, Julie showed up at Matthew's at about 10:30 last night. Said she knows it was 10:30 'cause that's when she always takes Bozo out to do his business. Bozo is the right name for that Chihuahua alright. Dumber than a stick, I tell ya. She tried to put him in the dog show last year. But right before the judging, well, do you know what that dumb dog did?"

"I have no idea."

"He jumped up and grabbed little Becky Sanford's funnel cake. Knocked it to the ground too. Yes, Ma'am. And Lord, that little Becky just cried and cried and dumb ol' Bozo just over there sittin' next to the judges' stand chewin' on a funnel cake bigger than he is with no concern for nothin'."

"Aunt Charlotte, back to Matthew."

"Yes. Well, seein' Julie over there got Cora Belle all worried and torn up and she couldn't sleep no way. So she kept watch. About 10:45, Bobby Jones shows up. You know, that's his parole fella or whatever they call it. Anyway, accordin' to Cora Belle, Bobby and Matthew sat on the porch about fifteen minutes."

"And?"

"Well, after Bobby left, Julie and Matthew started loading stuff into her car. Well, it ain't her car really. It's a rental car. From the airport. And it has one of them sun roofs too. And she was tellin' us all about how the rental car place at the Nashville Airport didn't have no more sports cars which made her mad 'cause she always likes to rent sports cars 'cause her ex-husband wouldn't never let her drive his 'cause he feared she'd wreck it. What an ol' rascal that fella must be."

"Aunt Charlotte, get back to the story."

"Okay. So, Cora Belle said they put some stuff in the car. And by midnight, they was both gone. Gone, I tell ya. Cora Belle and Bozo walked over this mornin' and she said the whole place was locked up. She looked in the window though. Says she was lookin' in there to make sure there were no dead bodies or nothin'. And I said, 'Good grief, Cora

Belle, you watch too many of them detective shows. Ain't no dead bodies in there. Besides, if they was to kill somebody, you'd have seen them carry out the body in a big barrel or a garden trash bag or somethin'.' I don't think she even pays attention half the time when she watches NCIS."

"So, you guess they're gone for good, huh?"

"I 'spect so, Baby. I do. Cora Belle said he had the whole place lookin' neat as a pin. Even cleaner than when Chester and Ida was alive. Bless him. Oh, I'm gonna miss that fella somethin' awful."

"Sarah must be devastated."

"Well, I reckon so. Poor girl."

"So, I guess there's nothin' you and I can do to fix this situation, right?"

"Well, that's why I'm here, Darlin'. I figure we need to put our heads together." She grabbed my hand and looked into my eyes. "I 'spect you and I could get in the hospital with no trouble bein' as how we have such fine upstanding reputations and all."

"And do what?"

"Hit Jerry Conner over the head with a shovel. What else? They'd never suspect the two of us. Clean records and all." She grabbed her stomach and laughed like a chubby hyena. "Oh Baby, you know I'm messin' with ya. Just messin' with ya."

Chapter 46, SARAH: Better to Have Loved and Lost...

I rarely sleep late. They say it comes with age. As a teenager, I remember sleeping till noon. But most Saturdays now, I'm up by 7:30. Habit, I guess. But this morning I slept till 9:00. Probably because I didn't sleep well last night. Woke up about 2:00 and lay on the couch till 5:00. Thinking. Praying. Wondering.

Julie packed up all her stuff and left town about 10:00 last night. Said she was just getting in the way here and needed to go home. She wasn't in the way. And I had a feeling nothing was waiting at home either. I asked if she were going by to see Matthew before she left town. And how did she put it? Yeah. She said that, of course, she'd drop by and see him before she left. Her mother would kill her if she didn't have any better manners than that.

Manners. That was the least of Julie Crawford's concern last night. She must have overheard our conversation. She had a plan. She would go by the house, explain to Matthew that she'd be glad to take care of all the details of his move. She'd offer him a ride to the airport. And a place to stay. And maybe even a job with her daddy's company. And that would be that.

How quickly things change. Yesterday morning I woke up with all these ideas. Grandiose plans. Love and marriage and sex and happily ever after. Possibilities. But Matthew was right. It was a fantasy. Handsome California ex-con falls in love with lonely small-town teacher. Doesn't even make sense really. Mama tried to convince me from the beginning. I can only imagine her relief when she hears the news today. Matthew Prescott. Gone for good. An answer to her prayers.

I grabbed a blanket and a cup of coffee and headed to my morning spot. My heart beat faster when I saw it. A long white envelope taped to the screen door. I held out hope that this whole scene would be like a Friday night Hallmark movie. The note would say, "I love you, Sarah Simpson. I can't go to California. Not without you." Then, of course, Matthew would come springing out from behind the hedges, flowers in hand, explaining that Jerry dropped all the charges because an angel appeared to him in the hospital room and told him to forgive. Matthew, of course, would be wearing those sexy jeans and the blue and white western shirt. We'd kiss. Get married. Probably even get a dog and a cat, a couple of kids. Brother Dan would share our testimony at every youth rally in the country. The story of restoration and blessing in a small town.

I sat on the porch swing and unfolded a faded blue piece of paper that looked vaguely familiar. Ida had recently given me a meatloaf recipe written on the same paper. The blue and yellow flowers on the top of the page were so faded, I felt certain the stationery had been purchased before I was born. Oh, and sadly, I didn't hear any sign of life coming from the bushes either.

Dear Sarah,

I'm leaving tonight. This will make it easier for everyone. I'm sorry for what I did to Jerry. So sorry. No excuses. Thank you for everything you've done for me. You are a wonderful woman, Sarah. I meant every word I said yesterday. Don't sell yourself short. You deserve a man worthy of your respect.

Matthew

I thought about going inside first. But I didn't. I went ahead and had a good cry right there on the front porch. In front of God and everybody who might happen by on the way to the barber shop. And it was a loud one too. Complete with runny nose, red eyes, snorting into the blanket, the whole nine yards. Carlie's SUV pulling into the driveway didn't even thwart me.

Aunt Charlotte ran onto the porch steps. She tripped on the last step but caught herself by grabbing the porch rail. "Whew! Old fat woman nearly took a tumble. Oh, Baby, looks like you was cryin'. Your face is all a great big mess. Was you cryin'?"

"Yes, Ma'am."

"Well, yes. Of course you were. We heard the news this mornin'. How Matthew done blew right on out of town with that tall woman."

"What's done is done."

Carlie joined us on the porch now. "Sarah, you know we both love ya and want the best for ya. So go get some clothes on and clean up your face. Aunt Charlotte and I are taking you to breakfast at Mabel's. No need in puttin' this off. It's time for you to hold your head up and eat some gravy, friend."

I laughed through the tears. "Best offer I'll get all day."

Chapter 47, CARLIE: Gravy Covers a Multitude of Heartaches

Doug and I are both snugglers by nature. Now don't get me wrong. We're all about the sex when it's time to be all about the sex. But on the nights when it's late and that's off the table, we're all about the spooning. I even read in a magazine once that that kind of physical contact will make you live longer. See? That's why I'm a matchmaker. It's really no different than being a brain surgeon or an oncologist. I want to help people live longer. If the principal at Martin Primary School dies young, well, we'll all know he should have gotten on some allergy pills for pet dander. Stubbornness does not lend itself to good health, people. Anyway, snuggling time is also talking time. And on this particular Saturday night? Well, we had some serious business to attend to.

"Doug, I have a proposition. And no, not the kind of proposition I had early this morning."

"Yeah, that morning proposition still has my head spinning. Good night, Carlie. I'll be daydreaming about that for…."

"Years."

"Decades."

"Well, I hope you'll remember that little rendezvous when I forget to clean the house or when I burn food or lose my keys or back into the truck with my SUV."

"You mean you forget to clean the house sometimes? Impossible! You burn food? I had no idea! Lose things? Not you, Darling. Not you." He laughed. Then his face grew more serious. "Wait, Honey, you didn't really back into the truck, did you?"

"Me? No. I'm just saying it's certainly not out of the realm of possibilities. You know I have almost no hand/eye coordination. Ask my high school basketball coach, Doug. I'm 5'11. Couldn't even average two points a game. Seriously. I'm the worst. There are short people in New Guinea who have never even seen a basketball, and they could beat me at basketball. I'm that bad. So, If and when I do hit your truck, well, I need to know your memory of this morning will help ease the sting a little."

He laughed. "Absolutely. Okay. So what's your current proposition?"

"I'm sure you know what I'm gonna say before I even say it. We need to go to California. Both of us. Oh, and Dusty and Clara, if they can. This whole thing with Matthew is just plain dumb. Dumb. I'm sure he's hurting. I know Sarah is hurting. But what I'm gonna say next? Well, it indicates a lot of personal growth on my part so be prepared to brag on me. Are you prepared for that?"

"I am."

"I don't think we should go right now. No. We should let him flounder a little first. Give him a chance to miss all of us."

"And what if he doesn't? Miss us, I mean."

"I'm going to pretend you didn't say that. Are you kidding? Think about it. Think of all the things he's missing. The uncomplicated and enjoyable aspects of working at Dusty's Shop. The peaceful Sunday afternoons sittin' on Chester and Ida's porch. Church potlucks. Brother Dan's sermons. Mabel's hamburgers. The City-Wide Yard Sale. Afternoon barber shop banter. And of course, well, what's really gonna

250

haunt him day and night is Sarah Simpson. Sarah, with all her extraordinary beauty and intelligence and kindness and sense of humor and educational fervor and oh, her cupcakes too. That icing alone would be a siren song to a man's soul. Your own son wants to marry her and he's in Kindergarten, Doug. Kindergarten!"

"The Jameson men have always had a weakness for sugar and good women."

"Doug, Honey, I've seen the way Matthew looks at Sarah. It's really just impossible that the poor boy won't be cryin' in his root beer within a few weeks. So, just at the right time, well, I figure we walk in the door. He runs to us crying and pleading to come back home. We tell him there's still a place for him here in Sharon. And there you have it. Done. Well, not quite done."

"Go on."

"Well, there's one more little detail that needs to be taken care of first. And according to Aunt Charlotte, it involves sneaking into the hospital with a shovel."

Chapter 48, SARAH: Not Ready to Shake My Groove Thing

Carlie made me promise to show up at church and Sunday dinner. Her exact words? "If you're going to pine for Matthew Prescott, you might as well do it with friends."

When I pulled into the church parking lot, Brian Carter was the first person I saw. He was getting out of an immaculately clean white Toyota Camry. He must have thought no one was looking because he squatted down to look at his hair in the side mirror. It made me think about what Carlie always says. "Never date a man prettier than you."

Brian had never visited our church before. And I immediately tried to think of the top five possible reasons he was there today. #5. He's not very connected and he thinks Julie is still in town. #4. He knows Julie has gone but he thinks I might have her phone number. #3. He knows Matthew left me and thinks I need a shoulder to cry on. #2. He wonders if there will be another physical altercation of some kind, and a doctor will be needed. #1. He wants to attend church and this is a good one.

I'm sure that's it. He's new in town and looking for a church. That's all it is and that's all it will be. Well, until Carlie gets hold of him anyway. She'll probably be fixing him up with the poor girl at the animal shelter any day now.

I decided to take Carlie's advice and be as friendly as I could. At breakfast yesterday, she said, "Look, the sooner you get out among the people, the better. You've got nothing to be ashamed about, Sarah. Hold your head up high and get out there and shake your groove thing."

Okay. So I'm not going to take the advice about shaking my groove thing. I never really have shaken my groove thing. And I'm not going to start now. But I knew she was right about the other part. I definitely didn't need to go into hiding. I waved at Brian as I walked across the parking lot. "Beautiful day, Dr. Carter!"

"Yes. It is. Looks like the rain is holding off."

"Yeah. Glad you're visiting with us today. I'm sure you'll love it. Brother Dan's a good preacher. The best."

"So I hear."

Doug and Carlie waved at us both from the front porch. I knew what she was going to say next before she even said it. She yelled like she was at a ballgame. "Dr. Carter, please come to lunch at our house! We're ordering pizza today and there's plenty! Say you'll come!"

Brian waved and yelled back, "Yes, thanks!"

Chapter 49, CARLIE: From the Mouths of Babes...

Sunday lunch crowd is a bit slim today. Uncle Bart and Aunt
Charlotte are in Palmersville at his great niece's baptism.
Dave and Ashley are in California preparing for her new
movie. Dusty and Clara are home with sick kids. So it looks
like Sarah Simpson and Dr. Brian Carter are the only pizza
partakers today. When Doug and I pulled into our driveway,
Sarah and Dr. Carter were already sitting on the porch. Sarah
was sitting in her normal Sunday spot and Dr. Carter was
sitting, well, in Matthew's spot.

Doug pulled two extra-large pizza boxes from the backseat. "I
hope you guys are hungry!"

Brian stood. "We are! Thanks for the invitation."

James ran onto the porch. "Doctor man, you're in Matthew's
chair!"

Dr. Carter's face turned pink. "Am I?"

"Yes. That's where Matthew sits because he likes Sarah.
Because she's pretty and she makes good cupcakes."

Doug tried to redirect the conversation. "Actually, we don't
have assigned seats. Everybody's fine."

James responded, "But Daddy, you said Matthew looks at
Sarah like you look at Mommy. 'Cause you're in LOVE with
her."

Doug laughed as he patted James on the head. "Great kid
here. Little too vocal, but still. A great kid."

James scooted up even closer to Dr. Carter. "Are you in love with Sarah too?"

"Uh, no. Well, no, I don't even know Sarah that well."

James frowned and shook his head. "I didn't think so. 'Cause you don't look at Sarah like Matthew does. Not at all."

Doug opened the pizza boxes. "Pizza for everybody!" He handed a piece of cheese pizza to James. "Here, Son, take a piece of pizza. Go ahead and just put that in your mouth right there."

"But Daddy, we didn't pray yet."

"Trust me. It's God's will for you to get your mouth busy on this pizza."

I looked at Brian and Sarah. "What can I say? He takes after Aunt Charlotte. Honest to a fault."

James ate cheese pizza while Doug prayed. Turns out, James and his honest observations were the most interesting things about lunch. It was a dud all the way around. Dr. Carter spent most of the time asking questions about Julie's visit. Did she like Tennessee? Did she plan on returning? Didn't we all wonder if she and Matthew Prescott were an "item" back in the day? Did we hear that Julie had been in some national TV commercials?

But the last straw came when he finished his last bite of ice cream. He looked up from an empty bowl and said, "Yep, I'm thinking there was definitely something between Matthew and Julie. You know, back when he planned to be a successful lawyer. Before he became a drug addict and a car mechanic."

And that, my friends, was the final blow. Sarah stood, grabbed her purse, and handed Dr. Carter a piece of paper. "Brian, here's Julie's number. Why don't you just call her? I'm sure she'd be glad to hear from you and answer every question you've ever had. Truthfully, you two would be perfect for each other."

She thanked us both and stepped off the porch. She stood by her car for a brief moment. First time in months she'd stood there alone. Eventually she slid into the driver's seat. Before she fastened her seatbelt, she looked at the passenger seat and dropped her head. The little joke they shared every week was no more.

ONE WEEK LATER:

For a whole week, the television folks have been all over town. They shot footage at Dusty's Shop, Mabel's Diner, and even at Dusty and Clara's house. But the biggest announcement? The biggest news was that the pilot of "Sweet Southern Freedom" was debuting on television this Thursday. People began making plans for viewing parties. The convenience store owner, Mr. Freeman, ordered twice as many crispy chicken tenders as usual, preparing for the Thursday night rush. Homer Crittenden called the radio show nearly every morning reminding people to clean up their yards and call their out-of-town relatives.

Mabel even bought an expensive ad on the morning radio show. Mitch Smith did the voice-over and Conway Twitty provided faint background music for the ad:

"Thursday is the start of something new.

'Sweet Southern Freedom' makes its debut.

We're all on TV and we want to celebrate.

So come eat at Mabel's. The show starts at eight.

Come down to Mabel's this Thursday night.

We promise there's not going to be a fight."

Okay. So it might have been just a tad bit slanderous to use the whole fight analogy, considering the circumstances of Matthew leaving town. But what can I say? At least the TV show buzz has distracted her from obsessing about the government spy program and ketchup companies making the bottles smaller.

On Sunday, Brother Dan announced that anyone was welcome to come to the fellowship hall Thursday night to view the show on a big screen Doug was setting up. When Brother Dan realized he was competing with Mabel's business, he promptly said, "I'll be ordering a big take-out platter of burgers from Mabel, so bring a side or dessert and invite your friends."

When I picked up James from Sunday School, Sarah didn't look like herself. Hair in a messy pony tail. Very little make-up. Her voice was weak. "I need to take a rain check on lunch. I haven't been sleeping well and I need some rest."

"Anything I can do?"

She turned away and began straightening the little wooden chairs. "Not really."

"Matthew?"

"Yeah. It'll get easier though. Everybody says it."

257

"Have you heard from him?"

"No. I didn't expect to. Have you been by Chester and Ida's?"

"No."

"For sale sign went up yesterday."

"And how did that feel?"

"I don't feel anymore. Or I try not to anyway."

"And the show? Are you gonna watch the show?"

"I am. But not with a group. Too...I don't know. Too embarrassing."

"Painful?"

"Yeah. That too."

"Well, call me crazy. But I haven't given up on you two. I haven't."

She wiped her eyes and reached out to hug me. "Thank you, Carlie. Thank you."

Chapter 50, SARAH: Suffering Through "Sweet Southern Freedom"

Every third grader seemed convinced they would make it into the pilot one way or another. On the way to the playground, Randall Glover said, "Ms. Simpson, I know for sure I'll be on TV tonight 'cause I was doin' card tricks outside the furniture store and one of them cameramen said I was sure to be a star someday."

"Well, someday might not be tonight, Randall. I just don't want you to be disappointed."

He stopped mid-stride and looked up at me with his big brown eyes. "I don't want you to be disappointed either, Ms. Simpson. I mean, with Matthew Prescott not livin' here no more."

I had a feeling Randall and I were both in for some disappointment. I was certain his card tricks had hit the editing floor. And Matthew Prescott not living here? It would never stop hurting.

I poured some sweet tea and put on my favorite gray sweat pants. I dimmed the lights, hoping no one would drop by. I knew most people were at church or Mabel's. They all understood why I wasn't at either place. I instinctively smiled as the catchy opening song played against the visual backdrop of West Tennessee cornfields, men in overalls, and the scene of prison doors being opened. And then came the searing pain, the pain I fully expected. The pain I couldn't have adequately prepared for. Dusty and Matthew standing in front of the sign at the shop. Both men smiling, wearing their blue shop shirts. A sign over their heads. "We believe in second chances." When the camera closed in on Matthew's smiling face, the tears came. I missed him. The conversations in the car. The porch sitting. Sunday dinners. The feel of his lips on mine. The way he cared for Chester and Ida. I was glad they weren't here to see how it all ended.

Carlie told me the narrator was going to be that guy from "America's Funniest Home Videos" and "Dancing with the Stars." The opening monologue was perfect: "This is the story of two remarkable men, two men whose lives couldn't have been more different. Dusty McConnell grew up in West Tennessee farm country. Dirt poor with an abusive father and a severe learning disability. Matthew Prescott grew up in San Diego. Wealth and privilege. Academic accomplishment. Law school student. What could these two men possibly have in common? Both made tragic errors in judgment. Errors that led to years in prison. And that's where they met. Cell block 9. This is their story. A story of crime and punishment? Yes. But also, a story of mercy and redemption. A story of sweet southern freedom."

I cried through the whole hour. All of it. I cried when they aired Matthew's speech at the rally. I cried when I saw Chester and Ida makin' homemade ice cream on the front porch. I had to blow my nose when Dusty talked about the death of his first wife and baby. But when did I cry the most? When Dusty put his arm around Clara and said, "This woman has changed my life. Every morning I wake up and have to pinch myself. Every day I want to move forward as a husband, a father, a businessman. She makes me want to love people more. Oh, and she's beautiful too. Absolutely beautiful."

I had to chuckle when the music started playing and they rolled the credits. There was Randall Glover, on his bike outside the furniture store, doing card tricks for Bart and Charlotte Nelson. Charlotte waved to the camera and nearly hit the poor boy in the face with her arm Jell-O. Randall laughed. She pinched his cheek. It was perfect. A perfect ending.

I threw in laundry and graded some papers. I'm usually in bed before the 10:00 news. But for some odd reason, I stayed up. I couldn't believe it was the top story. Mark Cameron announced it with fervor: "Tonight was the debut of 'Sweet Southern Freedom,' the reality show that follows two men who were once cellmates in a Nashville prison, but now live productive lives on the outside."

They showed several clips from tonight's episode. Then they went to a big room where a test group of people from Jackson were ready to be interviewed about the show. Every woman between twenty and ninety had the same comment, just in varying forms: "Those boys are just precious. And that handsome Matthew is single. I have a niece he should meet." "My new man crush? That's easy. Matthew Prescott." "Is it wrong to be in love with an ex-con? I hope not." I turned off the TV and said to an empty house, "No. It's not wrong to be in love with an ex-con. But it's complicated. God knows it's complicated."

Chapter 51, CARLIE: If Only Coconut Cake Could Cure a Broken Heart

When the credits rolled, the fellowship hall erupted with applause. But then Aunt Charlotte stood and yelled, "Oh, Bart, it's us!! There we are with that little Randall Glover! What a doll baby!" But then her demeanor changed quickly. "Oh, Lawsy, I nearly killed the poor boy with my arm jiggle. Good gosh, why did you let me eat that coconut cake tonight? Oh, and that pecan pie? Why?"

I started to comfort her, but my cell phone went off. "Just let me grab this and I'll get back with you, Aunt Charlotte." I walked toward the back door.

"Hello."

"Carlie? This is Shayla McGuire. I'm dying to get your take on it. I mean, you saw the show, right? What did you think?"

"Great. Homerun. Really."

"That's what our test audience thought too. It was just like I expected. Matthew Prescott is going to be the new reality show heartthrob, Carlie! And that's going to be nothing but good for ratings."

"I'm sure. Speaking of Matthew, I take it you guys have kept up with him, yes? I mean, I guess the next episode, you'll show him moving to California and then you'll be shooting out there some, right?"

"Oh, Carlie, we've already been shooting footage of Matthew in San Diego. Great footage. He's working at an investment firm. An old neighbor hired him and he's doing well. Joined a gym. Wears a suit every day. Quite a contrast from his life at Dusty's Shop."

"Yeah. I'm sure. Does he like it? The new job, I mean? Being back in San Diego?"

"Well, I haven't really asked. But what's not to like, Carlie? No offense. You know I think your area is quaint and lovely, but Matthew is a Californian. He always has been. And San Diego? Well, that's about the best California has to offer."

"Yeah. It's great there. Beautiful. Where is he staying?"

"He's staying at a hotel downtown. His new boss is helping him out. But he's looking for an apartment. Why so many questions about Matthew? Tell me you don't have a crush on him too. Wow, Carlie, I thought you and Doug were inseparable, joined at the hip and all."

"Shayla, please. No. It's just that, well, with the way he left town, there's just some unfinished business here. That's all. I want him to do well. We all do."

"I'm sorry about him beating that man up. I am. I know he could have gotten into a lot of trouble. But that whole storyline will be killer for ratings. We couldn't have come up with something better ourselves. When the producers saw episode two, they practically accused me of setting it all up. They literally called Matthew to verify that it happened that way, and with no prompting from any of us."

"It was sad. The whole thing. He lost a lot in that deal."

"Or maybe he gained a new job and a new exciting life in California. Try to think positively, Carlie."

"I guess. Anyway, I thought the show was great tonight. We laughed. We cried. Good television, Shayla. And that's getting harder and harder to find."

"Thank you for the idea. Well, I've got to run. Daddy and I are going out to celebrate. Have a good night, Carlie. Don't party too hard in Sharon, Tennessee, tonight."

"Oh, it's gettin' downright crazy over at the dessert table. Uncle Bart and Homer Crittenden are about to come to blows over the last piece of coconut cake."

"Seriously?"

"Gotcha! They're just talkin' smack and blowin' smoke. That's what we do in a small town, Shayla. It's all in fun. Good night."

"Good night."

And that's when I knew. The time had come. California, here we come.

Chapter 52, Carlie: Livin' it Up at the Hotel California (Did using that phrase violate any kind of copyright laws? If so, contact my lawyer. I mean, please recommend a good lawyer.)

I don't remember the last time Doug, Dusty, Clara, and I went somewhere without the kids. Dusty and Clara were only staying two nights because he doesn't like closing the shop. Plus, we agreed that leaving all five kids with Uncle Bart and Aunt Charlotte was either a beautiful act of faith or a really dumb idea. Thankfully, Sarah agreed to bring over supper one night and help. Brother Dan assured us he was only five minutes away. And all of us agreed that even if they didn't take baths or brush their teeth, two days of questionable hygiene would not jeopardize their futures.

Aunt Charlotte's final words were still ringing in my ears. "Now Carlie, don't you worry none. Not one bit. I'll be sure to keep the back gate closed. I learned my lesson with Sunshine. Not that any of these young'uns are like a calf. No, these young'uns are much more important than a calf so don't you worry none." Then, just to prove that she was smarter and funnier than any of us, she yelled out, "Bart, better head down to CO-OP for more of that sweet feed! We got five extra mouths to feed."

I'd been to Los Angeles more times than I could count. But San Diego was a completely different feel. Laid back. Relaxed. Beautiful. We stayed at an airport hotel to make it easier when it was time for Dusty and Clara's return. Doug and I were planning to drive to Los Angeles for a few extra days. I had to meet with my agent. We were going to dinner at Dave and Ashley's house, as she was on a short break from the film.

Waiting in line at the rental car place, Dusty patted Doug on the back. "Okay. So what's the plan, Doug?"

"Tonight we rest. Thought we'd go have dinner at this little place Carlie heard about down on the beach. Then in the morning, we meet in the lobby at 9:00 sharp. Operation Find Matthew Prescott."

Dusty smiled. "Oh, it's an operation now, huh? Like a real military mission and everything?"

Doug responded, "Absolutely, man. There will be all kinds of obstacles. Difficulties. You better prepare yourself." He grabbed Dusty's arms and shook him lightly. "Are you prepared, Dusty? Are you?"

Dusty busted out laughing and then managed a few words. "Let me guess. Carlie's got the address of his workplace. And you've got the GPS unit in your suitcase?"

Doug smiled and turned toward the counter. "Okay. So there aren't that many obstacles. All that's left now is acquiring transportation that can withstand gunfire."

THE NEXT MORNING:

At my recommendation, the four of us even discussed what we were wearing. We all had to be in sync. Functioning as one unit. A matchmaking unit of awesomeness. Okay. That was overkill. But nevertheless, we agreed we'd all wear business casual. Not too intimidating. But not too slouchy either. Clara even pulled her beautiful red hair into a Julie Crawford ponytail. Smooth and perfect-looking. Dusty questioned whether his eye patch and a scar on his chin would look a little too suspect. Doug said, "No. You look perfect. In order to get what we want, we might need to scare the receptionist at some point." Note to self: Get Doug out of Sharon more often. He's on a roll.

The investment firm operated on the top two floors of a really tall building downtown. The elevator ride was pleasant. But then it hit me. "Oh gosh. We haven't even thought about..."

Doug put his arm around me. "About what?"

"Ever since that pilot show aired, well, Matthew's kind of...famous. They might think we're psychotic fans or stalkers or something."

Doug said, "No. We look like business people. And how often are stalkers married couples with southern accents?"

"Are you kidding? I saw a Lifetime movie about a Georgia woman who had three husbands and was stalking an Atlanta newscaster."

"Did she wear black dress pants and carry Ritz crackers in her purse?"

I started laughing. "Go ahead, Doug. Make fun. When you get hungry later, you're gonna be begging for those Ritz crackers. Ready or not, here come the Beverly Hillbillies."

The elevator doors opened to a rush of noise and activity. But one beautiful young blonde woman was calm, sitting on what looked like a bar stool behind a big counter. "May I help you?"

Doug smiled and extended his hand. Such a suave businessman. "Yes, I'm Doug Jameson and we're here for Matthew Prescott."

She cringed. "Is Matthew expecting you? Are you with the network?"

"No. He's not expecting us. We're old friends."

"I'm afraid Matthew's in a meeting right now. I'm sorry." She put a small notepad on the counter. "Would you like to leave a message for him? I'll be glad to put it with his messages."

Doug stayed calm. "No. We've come a really long way. Is there some way you can at least tell him we're here? We're more than glad to wait. We're not opposed to waiting."

"Hmm. Not really. You see, we have security policies in place. If you had called, we might could have set something up. But as it is, I'm not sure there's anything I can do."

"Doug? Carlie?"

All four of us turned our heads. But we didn't recognize the man walking toward us. I mean, we did. But he looked...different. Not better or worse. Just different. Dark suit. Shorter hair. Big smile. Shoes I recognized only from magazine ads.

Dusty ignored top-floor business protocol and ran. They hugged like it had been way longer than a few weeks. Matthew punched him in the arm. "You are a sight for sore eyes, man."

"You too. Of course, we feel like you never left seein' as how you're on TV every five minutes. Is it the Teen Heartthrob channel? Isn't that your new network, Matthew?"

Matthew shoved Dusty. "Very funny. Look who's talkin'?"
He put his hands up like he was making quote marks in the air.
"'I'm just a poor boy from West Tennessee, makin' it big on
A & E.' So, what brings you guys to town? And where are
those cute kids?"

Clara smiled. "At home. With Uncle Bart and Aunt
Charlotte. I know. We must have been drinkin' when we
made that decision. But, no. We weren't. Or I don't think we
were."

Dusty raised his eyebrows. "Honey, forgive me. You have no
idea what I put in your sweet tea that night. I just needed a
few days alone with ya. That's all."

Clara laughed and kissed his cheek. "Good move, Dear."

Doug took control of the train and moved it on down the track
a bit. "Look, we know you're crazy busy. Any chance you
have a few minutes to visit?"

"Sure. I just got out of a meeting. Why don't you guys come
into my office? Right this way."

And that's when we stepped into a scene from a movie. You
know that big office with black leather furniture and big
bookcases lining the walls? The one with the bar on one side
and a couch or two on the other? Yeah. That's when you
know the office belongs to the boss' son-in-law. Except
Matthew wasn't the boss' son-in-law. Or I didn't think so
anyway.

The rest of my party said nice things, pleasant things like,
"Nice office." Or "Great view." But I felt no need for
pretense. "Good Golly, Matthew, what has happened here?

This doesn't seem like a starter office to me. Tell me you're not involved with a South American drug cartel."

He put both hands up in the air and smiled. "Busted. You always were the insightful one, Carlie. I figured Bob Garrett got wind of my dirty dealings and sent you guys to snuff me out."

Doug laughed. "Hey, we're happy for you. Really."

"I know. And you're right. This isn't exactly a starter office. Truth is, Julie's dad felt like he owed me. He doesn't. But he feels like he does. A long time ago, right after the accident, Julie asked her dad to send his personal lawyer to represent me. He agreed because hey, it was his little girl asking, right? But evidently, my dad talked him out of it. Said it would ruin his reputation in business and that he should let justice take its course. Julie was livid. Her dad says I wouldn't have done half the time I did, if he had just followed through with her request."

Dusty sat on the couch. "And what do you think?"

"I think it's in the past. And besides, I've said before I should have served life. So, no. No one owes me anything. And I'm sure, ultimately, the hope of his company being featured on television made the decision easy for him." He walked toward the bar area. "How 'bout a drink?"

Doug hesitated.

"Hey, it's just ginger ale. I mean, it's not even lunchtime." We nodded and he poured four drinks in those really heavy glasses that make you think you should be at a fancy party wearing a long sequin gown and smoking a cigarette that's on a really long holder. Okay. Maybe it's just me that thinks

270

that. And yes, I know. Smoking is bad for you. Long holder or not. Don't smoke. End of disclaimer.

He handed us the drinks and then leaned up against the desk. "So, what brings the Tennessee contingency to California?"

I leapt from my chair. "We brought you a gift. I would have put it in one of those fancy baskets and wrapped it in cellophane, but that's not really my style. So I brought it in a Dollar General Store bag. I know. It's already pulling at your heartstrings, isn't it?"

"It is." He smiled and reached for the bag. "Thank you, I think." He peeked inside. "Great! I've been needing these! Aunt Charlotte's pickles. Mabel's banana bread. This is wonderful."

"Oh, there's more. Keep looking."

He paused and stood perfectly still. "Wow. Thank you. I mean, I don't know what to say, Carlie." He pulled out a framed picture of Chester and Ida's house. "I love it. Thank you."

"Keep going."

He smiled and bit his lip. "A journal? No. It's a book of pictures. The barber shop. Brother Dan. Aunt Charlotte." He looked up. "Let me guess. This is some kind of campaign. Carlie, it has your name written all over it."

"Guilty. But there's one more thing. At the bottom of the bag."

He sat back on the desk and pulled out a rectangle covered in tissue paper. As he pulled off the tissue paper, he didn't utter

271

one word. None of us did. He just stared at it. Finally, he looked up and shook his head. "The sad thing? She doesn't even know how beautiful she is." He turned to face the window. He placed his right hand on the glass. "She actually thought Julie was more, I don't know, more something. But look at this picture, huh? Take a good look at it. How could any woman who looks like that, who serves people the way she does, how could she ever have doubts…about anything." He set the picture on his desk.

Dusty spoke softly, "How can we help?"

For the first time, I heard sadness in his voice. "Help with what, Dusty? Look around. This is the good life, right? Or it's supposed to be. The California ex-con dream. Oh, and guess what? I even have a Facebook fan page now." He turned away and whispered, "Set up by somebody I don't even know. Somebody who doesn't know me."

Doug stood. "Look, we know you're busy. We won't take any more of your time. But you're right about our visit. We're here to say, 'Come home.' I know it might make your legal things complicated. It could mean going through a trial. But we miss you. All of us do. Some of us more than others."

"How is she?"

I set my glass down. "Hurting."

"It'll get better. With some time. Isn't that what people always say? Time heals all wounds."

"They also say, 'A watched pot never boils.' But they're wrong. If you turn the burner on high, a pot of water will boil, whether someone's watching or not. So really, sometimes those sayings are just plain wrong."

He smiled. "You'll see. Sarah will get back on her feet. She just needs a chance to move on. You guys have dinner plans tonight?"

"We don't."

"Julie's dad's hosting a big company dinner party at a restaurant that looks out over the water. It'll be fun. Come as my guests. I promise the food will be good."

Dusty jumped to his feet. "You know the West Tennessee folks are all about free food, brother."

"Well, it won't be as good as the church potluck. But we do the best we can."

He wrote down the address and we made plans to meet at 8:00 for dinner. Country people eat around 6:00 but we learned a long time ago that city folks sometimes eat as late as 9:00 or even 10:00. They'd get horrible indigestion except that they stay up late too. To quote that song from Aladdin, "It's a whole new world."

As we walked out of Matthew's office, I turned back briefly. The picture was still there on the front of his desk. Sarah sitting in the rocker on our front porch. Matthew standing beside the chair, looking at her like she was the most beautiful woman in the world. Because to him, she was. And is.

Chapter 53, CARLIE: Country Mice and the California Coast

We warned Matthew that we didn't have dressy clothes. He told us not to worry. But that's what most men would say. If I said to the average man, "The only thing I have to wear to your cousin's wedding is this ratty ol' pair of denim shorts, a brown t-shirt, and a pair of yellow flip flops," do you know what that man will say? Nine times out of ten he'll say, "Oh, that'll be fine." Except, of course, he'd be wrong. And so was Matthew.

The restaurant looked like a huge southern plantation, which I thought was odd, considering we were in California. But Matthew was right. It was right on the water. Beautiful. Classy. Pricey. Matthew greeted us at the door with a smile. I grabbed him by the arm. "Look at everybody in here. They're dressed to the nines."

He looked us up and down and smiled in that way where he shows every one of his perfect teeth. "And you guys are dressed to the…well, at least to the sevens. So really, don't worry about it."

Clara and I both had on dress pants and those sweaters you get at Wal-mart or Cato, you know, where the white shirt collar and cuffs are sewn into the sweater to make it look like you have a shirt on under the sweater. But really, you don't. It's all just a sweater/white shirt con job. Doug and Dusty had on khaki pants and button-up shirts. Julie's dad wore a suit that I felt confident cost more than our car. He approached us with a big smile, like he was trying to sell us something. "Welcome! You must be the Tennessee friends. I'm Bill McLaughlin. Welcome to our little soiree."

I put out my hand. "Oh, we like to soiree every chance we get. Yes, sir!"

Julie came running through the crowd. She had on a tight red dress that had every part of her body shoved upward in such a way it spilled over the top. She threw her arms around my neck. "Carlie! It's great to see you! All of you! Daddy, these aren't just Matthew's friends. They're my friends too. And Carlie's famous. A writer."

"She is, is she? Well, forgive my being behind the times, Carlie. I come from the Hemingway era. And sadly, when it comes to literature, I've let myself go."

"Oh, no problem."

"Daddy's all about business. And he's good at it too. He says Matthew has the makings of a great businessman. Tough and tender."

And so the evening went. Julie flirted with Matthew. Matthew acted uninterested. Julie's daddy explained in graphic detail how to make money investing in high-end clothing companies. We feigned interest with utmost friendliness. We ate shrimp and steak. We all agreed it was the best mango salsa we'd ever tasted (because none of us had ever tasted mango salsa). Julie tried to explain to her daddy about hash brown casserole. It just kept going on and on and on. Finally, Doug put an end to it. Thank you, Doug. God bless the day you were born.

"Dusty and Clara have an early morning flight, so we best be going." He reached to give Matthew a hug. "It was good to see you, man. Really. Glad to see you're doing well."

275

Matthew placed his drink on the table. "Wait. I'll walk with you to your car."

As we walked, none of us said much. I guess it had all been said. Before we got in the car, Dusty spoke for all of us. Perfectly. He put his arm around Matthew and pointed back to the restaurant. "This life? If it's the one you were meant to live, Matthew, you know we're supportive, right? And we always will be."

Matthew bowed his head. "I know. Thank you."

Chapter 54, SARAH: Sweet Southern Surveillance

Sharon, Tennessee, is now on the map. It's always been on
the map. I guess most people just didn't know it was there.
When I drove by Chester and Ida's just now, there were a
couple of young 20-something girls taking pictures of the
house from the front sidewalk. Wouldn't that have just tickled
Chester and Ida to no end? If only the girls could have gone
inside and seen their collection of Coke crates and glassware.
Maybe even the 50 states quilt. But of course, those girls
hadn't the slightest interest in collectibles or old people or
even small towns. No. It was all about Matthew Prescott.

The fire chief called this afternoon. He hemmed and hawed a
bit until I finally said, "Chief Richardson, is there something I
can do for you?"

"Well, yes, Sarah, there is. Matthew Prescott made it clear
that he had every intention of donating that quilt to our raffle.
Is there any way you can acquire it?"

"I'm sure Judy will let me in the place this afternoon. Yes, I'll
take care of it."

That's one of the good things about small towns. We don't
operate on just the letter of the law. It's the spirit of the law.
Everyone knew Matthew Prescott was the rightful owner of
the house and all its possessions. And everyone knew he
meant to donate that quilt too. So, when I went by the realty
office to ask Judy if she could let me in to get it, she didn't
hesitate. She shuffled some papers and handed me the key.
"Sarah, I can't go right now. I've gotta show a house in
Martin. Don't forget to lock when you leave." She smiled, as
she grabbed the phone. "And try to keep your hands off the
glassware."

I wasn't embarrassed for people to see me going in the house. I had business to attend to. Legitimate business that involved fire safety and fire trucks and overall fire protection for our lovely area. I could see Cora Belle and Bozo looking through her kitchen window. I waved as if to say, "Go ahead, Cora Belle. Call Mabel or Charlotte or whoever you need to talk to. Yes, I'm walking into Matthew Prescott's house. Alone. With a key."

The house smelled like that new clean-smelling Lysol. Not the kind that reminds you of when you were sick as a kid. No. The new kind that smells like flowers and clean laundry. Everything looked exactly the way it looked when we gathered here after Chester and Ida died. The dining room chairs were all neatly tucked under the table. I walked into the living room and sat in Chester's green recliner. I rubbed my hands on the worn arm rests and remembered that day he told Matthew the whole town was wondering where he was, what he was up to. But not to worry. He and Ida had set 'em straight. Sure enough. When it came to Matthew Prescott, Chester and Ida Miller set all of us straight. Or died trying.

I walked down the hallway and paused outside his room. The bed was made perfectly. Blankets folded neatly on an old cedar chest. The stack of books was gone from the end table. While I didn't feel one bit bad going in the house to get the quilt, I did wonder if it would be crossing a line to walk into Matthew's room. But I did it anyway. I looked in the closet. Empty. And then I sat on the edge of the bed. If walking into the room violated his privacy, what I did next was probably an out-and-out crime. I opened the drawer of the end table. The only thing in there was Mrs. Ida's old stationery pad with the faded blue and yellow flowers on top. No ink pens or pencils. Nothing.

As I was closing the drawer, I noticed pieces of stationery tucked loosely under the pad. I knew not to look, and not because it could be considered criminal activity. No. I knew not to look because my mama raised me better than that. Way better.

I left the room quickly and headed to the back room to retrieve the quilt. As I was walking toward the front door, lavender quilt folded neatly in a big garbage bag, I paused. I set the bag next to an old wooden coat rack and walked back into Matthew's bedroom.

I lowered myself quietly onto the edge of the bed, as though Cora Belle could hear the old iron bed creaking from across the street. I slowly pulled open the drawer and reached for the loose papers and spread them out on the quilt. I shouldn't have. But I read each faded sheet of paper. Every word.

Dear Sarah,

I wish I could write poetry. But I'm not a poet. Your beauty is beyond what I can explain with words. I don't want to leave you. The moment

Dear Sarah,

I'm not giving up on us. I can't imagine waking up every day, knowing I won't see you. I will find a way for us to be together. Please trust me. The memory of your lips on

Dear Sarah,

I need you. I want you to need me too. I want you to be able to count on me. I want to be that kind of man. It may take some time, but I want to earn your trust again. Is it possible that

Dear Sarah,

*Prison bars don't take away a man's freedom. A man's
freedom is lost when he no longer possesses moral courage.
What I did today showed a lack of moral courage. You
deserve better. So please*

Dear Sarah,

*Sometimes I have bad dreams about the night Mary died. Or I
remember things that happened to me in prison. But last night
I had the most wonderful dream. You and I were walking
down by the creek. I kissed you and you laid your head on my
chest. And all I could think about was taking care of you. You
make me want to be a better man and that*

Dear Sarah,

*I love you. Desperately. And that's why I'm leaving tonight.
Brother Dan is right. Sometimes real love requires sacrifice.
I hope you can*

My heart was racing. I slowly moved my hand over the pieces
of paper. I closed my eyes and remembered the first night he
kissed me. The night he said he didn't know how to do this.
This thing between the two of us. But he did know. Better
than anyone else had ever known. And I was convinced he
still knew.

I gathered the papers and stacked them neatly under the
stationery pad and closed the drawer. Without taking my
shoes off, I lay back on the bed. The pillow was extra-soft.
An old feather pillow. I slowly placed my hand on the space
next to me, wishing he were there. The ceiling was stained
with brown water spots and the wallpaper in the corners was
peeling. This tiny room with the old iron bed. So different

from his childhood home. But it represented a place of hope. Belonging. New beginnings. A place to heal.

My tears fell like tiny raindrops on the patchwork quilt. Tears of sadness for every nightmare he ever endured. Tears for every time he lay in this spot in the early morning hours. Unable to find sleep. Alone. Tears for the horrible memories of Mary's death. For the fourteen years he lay in a prison cell. But mostly? Tears for myself. Matthew Prescott was the only man I'd ever loved. And he was gone.

Chapter 55, CARLIE: Be It Ever So Humble, There's No Place Like Home

Dusty and Clara flew back to Tennessee day before yesterday. As soon as they got home, they called to report that all five kids were happy and healthy and Uncle Bart and Aunt Charlotte were ready for a nap. Whew! What a relief! I mean, I'm sure all the kids would now be going around saying things like, "He don't know no better." Or "Dad gum, kick a fella in the teeth!" Or my personal favorite? "Shoot a monkey in the head and call me crazy!" I'd never want to shoot a monkey in the head. But calling Aunt Charlotte crazy? Not that far-fetched.

But despite Aunt Charlotte's continual abuse of the English language, one thing is clear. She knows how to love. And love deeply.

We had a great evening with all three Robertsons last night. Ashley cooked roast and carrots. Dave made homemade rolls. Collin drew a picture of a spaceship with markers and made me promise to give it to James. We sat on their porch and watched the waves roll in. Their home was always peaceful. Never pompous. When we asked Dave if he'd become best friends with Tom Hanks yet, he grinned and said matter-of-factly, "Yes. Yes, I have. He's like an uncle to me now. We'll be spending all holidays together from now on. I mean, sure. I'm going to miss spending Christmas with you guys. But hey, it's Tom Hanks, people. That man is gonna so love our homemade ginger snaps, Honey."

Ashley laughed. "And Aunt Charlotte's magic pickles. Don't forget the pickles."

"Yes, when Tom and Rita come over, there must be pickles. They will demand pickles!"

We spent the whole evening laughing together and silently thanking God. We all had known the blessings of authentic friendship. And real love. My evening prayer was simple: "God, give Matthew courage. Courage to just take a chance."

Just as I was picking up the book on the hotel nightstand, my cell phone rang.

"Hello."

"Carlie?"

"Yes. Hey, Sarah. Good to hear from you."

"I'm sorry I'm calling so late. Am I disturbing you?"

"No. It's earlier out here, remember? No. You're fine."

"How was your visit?"

"With Dave and Ashley?" Silence. "Hey, I'm just jokin'. I know. You're calling to find out about Matthew. Yeah, it was good. He's doing well or seems to be anyway. He has a really good job. The expensive suit, fancy office, whole nine yards."

"Good. That's good. I'm glad he's adjusting. And what about your gift idea? Did that go over well?"

"It did. Yeah. He loved it."

"Good. That's good. Well, I'll let you go and I'm sorry I bothered you."

"Sarah?"

"Yes."

"Is there something else you called to talk about?"

Her voice cracked, "I don't know what to say really."

"Why don't you just admit that you love him? You do. You love Matthew Prescott, right? Whew! Feels great to just get that out there in the open, doesn't it? Wait a minute. Did I put words in your mouth? 'Cause I do that with people. Horrible habit, it is. Anyway, this is your chance. I'll be quiet. Do you love him, Sarah? Because if you do, it's okay. It's not a crime to love someone."

There was a short pause. "Yes. And every morning, I pray, 'God, help me forget about him. Help me move on.'"

"And every evening you lie in bed, thinking about him."

"Yes! How did you know?"

"Been there. Done that. Got the tear-stained pillow cases to prove it."

"So what am I supposed to do now?"

"I guess you should just head to Miss Lucy's for some gut rot moonshine." Silence. "Hey, it's a joke. No. Do not go to Miss Lucy's, Sarah. Your liver will never forgive you. Here's what I would say. Give it a little more time. I know. That's never the answer anyone wants. AUGH! I always hate that answer. But Matthew is in transition. Oh, and I know your next question."

"What's my next question?"

"Does he love you too?"

"Well?"

"He does."

"He actually told you that?"

"He didn't have to."

"Thank you, Carlie. For being a friend. For trying to help us. Both of us."

"Hey, I'm just a proponent of love, sister. I'm all about peace, love, and matchmaking. Oh, and cheesecake. Peace, love, and cheesecake. That should be the name of a restaurant."

"Yeah! You're a genius."

"We'll be home tomorrow evening. Try to get some rest, Sarah. I'll see you on Sunday."

"Okay. Bye."

"Bye."

Doug walked out of the bathroom, wearing nothing but a towel. "Who was on the phone?"

"Sarah. She just needed a little help from the love doctor."

He smiled. "And what if I told you I needed a little help from the love doctor?"

I threw the book on the floor. "I'd say, 'The doctor is in.'"

Chapter 56, CARLIE: Shoot a Monkey

Okay. So here's what we found when we got home from California. James got in trouble at school on Tuesday because in the middle of working on his math lesson, he yelled out, "Shoot a monkey in the head!" Mary Grace Anderson started crying and telling the whole class how much she loves monkeys and always has loved monkeys. And always would love monkeys. I'm starting to believe James needs to go to an all-boys school.

Several people have looked at Chester and Ida's house but nobody has put in an offer yet. Cora Belle has made it her full-time job to watch the proceedings and daily inform the rest of us: "Larry Crane looked in the windows yesterday. Not sure why. Ever since Mildred left him, he ain't got a penny to his name. Missy Johnson and her fiancé from Arkansas came by with Judy on Tuesday. But Missy's daddy spoiled her somethin' awful and she ain't gonna put up with anything less than brand-new. A man from Jackson was interested in it. Rental property. Can't imagine what Chester and Ida would think about that."

The truth? Chester and Ida aren't thinking about that house at all anymore. But I can't exactly explain that truth to someone who half-way believes her grandma came back to earth as a stray calico cat, to watch over her and her sister.

I saw Sarah at the Dollar General yesterday afternoon and she looked a lot better than the last time I saw her. She had on make-up. Her hair was fixed nice. Looked like she'd dropped some weight, which just goes to show everybody grieves differently. I always wanted to be a person who grieves by saying, "No. I can't fathom eating right now." Or "No. I'm too upset to eat. Just bring me a glass of water." I tend to grieve by saying. "Hand me a fork. No. Don't bother. I'll eat with my hands."

Today, while waiting in carpool line, hoping and praying James had not verbally assaulted any wild animal species, the cell phone rang.

"Clara? Good to hear from you, friend."

"I need to talk to you, Carlie. Are you free right now?"

"It just so happens I have a good ten minutes before James comes barreling out of Sharon Elementary School with details of who ate school glue and who splashed water in the bathroom. That boy should be a security guard. He doesn't miss a detail."

"I'm having a hard time. With the TV folks. They're starting to get a little too…"

"Intrusive?"

"Yes. That's the word. Yesterday the guys started asking questions about the kids' adoptions and how did that feel, parenting adopted kids and a biological kid in the same house?"

"Well, you don't have to answer anything you don't want to answer, Clara. You just say, 'It feels great. We love all four of them and that's all I care to say about it.'"

"See? I need to be more like you."

"Wait a second. Someone hand me a tissue. I just want to bask in this glorious moment. Clara, I've spent my whole life wishing I could be more like you and your kind. Quieter.

More reserved. I've always wanted to have a thought that didn't come flying out of my mouth a millisecond later. So, trust me. You don't want to be like me. You need to be you. You're the one Dusty loves. You're the mother of these four great kids. So, if the TV folks cross the line, call 'em out on it. Don't let this show ruin your family, Clara. Take control."

"Thank you, Carlie. I love you."

"I know. Evidently, I'm pretty loveable, despite the big mouth."

"Maybe because of it."

"Can I record this conversation for training purposes? Seriously. I may need to listen to it several times a day. No, really. I love you too, Clara. I always have and I always will. I gotta run. Aunt Charlotte's monkey-killing protégé is running for the car. Bye, friend."

"Bye."

Chapter 57, SARAH: Bury the Hatchet…and Leave it Buried

I told no one about the notes I'd seen at Matthew's house. How could I? It was a violation of so many things. But deep down, I was thankful I saw those words. Words I recalled again and again.

On days I worked afternoon carpool line, I was especially tired and unmotivated to cook. I unlocked the front door, kicked off my shoes, and flung my tote bag down near a green plant from Chester and Ida's funeral. It had been sent to the funeral home by the Fire Department. On the night of visitation, Matthew told me I should be the one to take it home after the funeral. His exact words? "I'm not a violent man, Sarah. But I am a plant killer." We laughed. Within 24 hours, he was being taken out of the funeral home in handcuffs.

I perused the freezer, looking for a frozen dinner that was full of carbs and fat and sugar. But evidently, I was being mature and sensible on my last trip to the grocery store. So I picked up the phone to order a pizza. The knock at the door startled me. Every time I heard that sound, my heart beat faster. Hoping. Praying. Wondering if someday he'd be on the other side of the door. Sadly, that day was not today.

I peeked through the lace curtains. No.

"Sarah? Sarah, I only want to talk to you. Just a few minutes. We can stay on the porch. Please. Just give me a few minutes."

Jerry's face still looked bad. Not as bad as it did at the funeral home that day. But, yes. There was scarring and still a bit of swelling on his cheek. He had on dark blue jeans and a John Deere t-shirt. He was pacing back and forth. His hair was combed neatly as he finally decided to give up the crew cut. And that was good. He looked much better with a little hair. I always thought he was such a good guy. Everyone did. That's why I felt so bad turning down his marriage proposal last year. Now I just thanked God for the courage. And prayed for wisdom.

"Sarah? Look, I'm not gonna touch you." He put his hands in the air. "I'm not. Everyone will be able to see us out here. Please, just open the door."

I hesitated but then slowly turned the door knob and walked onto the front porch. "You have five minutes."

Jerry sat in the rocking chair. I sat in the swing, as far away as I could get. He lowered his head and then looked straight at me. "I'm an idiot."

"You won't get any disagreement from me."

He shook his head and smiled. "I expected that. I came by to apologize."

"I'm not the one you should apologize to."

"Yes. You are. What I said about you being desperate? Well, it was…"

"Your own desperation."

"Right. Yeah, it was on me. It's all on me, Sarah."

"For the record, I'm sorry you were hurt so badly. We were worried."

"Thank you." He leaned back in the chair and put both hands behind his head. "Yeah, I could have taken 'em. For sure. I mean, he's not that big of a guy or that strong really. It's just that, well, he caught me off guard is all."

I dropped my head and whispered, "Some things never change."

"What?"

"Forget it, Jerry. So, that's it, huh? You came by to apologize for ruining my life. Well, you're forgiven. You completely ruined my life and you got beat up badly in the process. Looks like we're even. Everybody loses." I stood and walked toward the door.

"No, Sarah. Wait. Don't go back in."

"Jerry, so help me. If you say one more word, I'm gonna be tempted to deck you too. And there's not an officer within 100 miles who'll arrest me either. You know that."

"Look. I just wanted to tell you I'm leaving town."

I stopped. "What?"

"I'm leaving. I'm going to work for my uncle in Nashville. He owns a few grocery stores and he's offered me a job. So, I'm moving. Tomorrow."

"Moving? What about your mother?"

"She's going too." He laughed. "Said I'd never make it without her homemade mac n' cheese. So, yeah. She's going too. We're gonna rent out the house here. We'll live with my uncle at first and then find a place. Start over."

"Wow. I mean, I hope that works out well for you, Jerry. For both of you."

"Yeah. It'll be a good chance. A new beginning."

I reached for the door but then turned to make eye contact. "I believe in those, y'know? New beginnings. Jerry, I wish you the best. Really."

He grabbed my arm. My facial expression must have scared him because he let go and put both hands in the air. "Hey! Sorry! My bad! I said I wouldn't touch you. I'm sorry. I just wanted to say one more thing. Before I go."

"Yes."

"I'm done with the, you know, with the legal business of it all."

"What do you mean?"

"I'm not gonna pursue any charges against him, even if he does come back here."

I felt a lump in my throat. "Why?"

"Several people told me I was being an ass. That most men in the room would have done…well, what Matthew did. And I guess they're right. I was just so caught up in the…"

"Jealousy?"

"Yeah, I guess."

"Well, I think that's a good thing, Jerry. The mark of a real man is the ability to let things go. Bury the hatchet. Start over."

"Yeah. Thanks, Sarah." He stepped off the porch. I waved and he waved back. "I'll never forget ya, Sarah Simpson."

I didn't know what to say so I chose silence. When I got inside, the tears started falling. I leaned against the door and shouted to an empty house, "Yes!"

I couldn't believe it. It was all falling into place. The house hadn't sold yet. Jerry was leaving town. Carlie assured me Matthew loved me. I didn't even want pizza anymore.

Chapter 58, SARAH: Sweet Southern Freedom Turns Sour

I felt comfortable watching episode #2 of "Sweet Southern Freedom" at Doug and Carlie's house with the gang. Doug assured me he'd made every effort to let Matthew know about what Jerry said. He'd left phone messages at work and on his personal phone. He sent an e-mail. No response yet, but it had only been 24 hours. Doug said he was probably just real busy with work or something.

Aunt Charlotte handed out pickles that had been speared with plastic knives. "Here, everyone needs a pickle before the music starts! Bart, don't be loud with your eatin' though. We all wanna hear every word of the show."

"How do ya eat a pickle without bein' loud, Charlotte? It ain't even possible!"

"Shh. Here it comes. The music is about to start."

Narrator: "Tonight we begin in San Diego, California, with an up-close and personal interview with Matthew Prescott. After fourteen years in prison, Matthew was hired by friend and former inmate, Dusty McConnell, to work as a mechanic in Dusty's Shop in Bradford, Tennessee. But something happened that completely changed the future for Matthew. Was it a good change or a bad one? We'll let the viewer decide."

Dramatic music played and the scene cut to Matthew sitting in a director's chair across from interviewer, Mandy Vincent. The chairs sat on a pier overlooking the water. Sunny day. Matthew dressed in a tan suit. Mandy dressed in a short skirt and business jacket. Matthew smiled and adjusted his tie. I knew women all over the country were talking about how handsome he was. But there were so many things they didn't know. The gentle way he had cared for Chester and Ida. His thankfulness for the tiny room with the iron bed. The loving words he'd written on faded paper. Now he was on TV looking like a movie star or a business mogul. Nothing like the Matthew we all knew. And one of us loved.

Mandy: "Well, how quickly life can change, Matthew. Last week, I was interviewing you outside a mechanic shop and this week, well, this week, we're in sunny San Diego. Can you share with our viewers why you made such a drastic change?"

Matthew: "I won't go into the details, but let's just say I needed a change of scenery. I got a job with McLaughlin Industries here. Been on the job two days now and there's a pretty big learning curve. But I'm getting there. Yeah."

Mandy: "Let's go ahead and run the footage of what recently happened outside a Tennessee funeral home. The incident that caused Matthew to make the move and start over in California."

The footage clearly showed Matthew being brought out in handcuffs. Jerry coming out on a stretcher. They asked people on the sidewalk what had taken place. A few locals said inarticulate things like, "He nearly killed half the people in that funeral home. Maude and I was scared. We was all scared." "We weren't sure about an ex-con coming here to live. But now we're sure. Sure we want him to leave."

Aunt Charlotte yelled, "Stop! Wait a minute! Doug, stop the TV for a minute. What the heck just happened and when did we let Jim and Maude Billings speak for the town of Sharon? Them two ain't got no sense. Nearly burned down the community center last year tryin' to have a weanie roast for

295

their grandson's first birthday party. A weanie roast INSIDE the community center! Right there near the stage too. Good night. Plum embarrassing."

Doug just shook his head and said, "Pretty crazy. Okay. Let's watch the rest." He pushed play.

Mandy: "What do you think when you watch that footage? Hear those comments from the locals?"

Matthew: "I think the same thing I thought one second after I beat that guy up. It was a mistake. I shouldn't have done it. He said some offensive things about a friend of mine. And about me. But I shouldn't have done what I did. I regret it. And I sent an open letter to the newspaper, apologizing to him and to the community. I let anger get the best of me, but I'm getting help with that. And I'm not sure those people on camera speak for everyone in Sharon."

Mandy: "What kind of help?"

Matthew: "I'm meeting with a counselor here. He specializes in helping people who were in prison deal with anger problems. And I'm meeting every week with my pastor. We're talking about forgiveness, mercy, things like that."

Mandy: "I think it's public knowledge that the fight revolved around the affections of a woman there in Tennessee. Care to elaborate?"

Matthew: "No."

Mandy: "So, is the relationship with her on or off?"

Matthew: "You asked if I wanted to elaborate." He smiled and looked straight at her. "Was I unclear?"

296

Mandy: "You can't fault me for trying. This is what people are interested in, Matthew. I'm sure you know you've become a bit of an overnight celebrity. Facebook fan page with over 100,000 likes. Every female focus group we've talked to has had the same reaction. They're crazy about you. After spending the last 14 years of your life in prison, how does it feel to now have so many women in America interested in meeting you, dating you, or..."

Matthew: "They're not interested in me. They don't know me. If they got to know me, they'd probably find me way less exciting than what they've dreamed up."

Mandy: "Oh, I don't know. I think you're pretty charming."

Matthew looked down and shook his head.

Mandy: "Well, one thing's certain. You can't beat this scenery. I mean, look around. West Tennessee is quaint but it's pretty land-locked."

Matthew: "I guess." He looked out over the water and his smile faded. "But West Tennessee is farm country. They actually feed people. That's probably a little more important than just scenery, Mandy."

Charlotte Nelson yelled at the TV. "Absolutely, Baby! You tell 'em!"

Bart hollered, "And you was worried about my pickle eatin'! Shhh!"

Mandy: "Any plans to return to Tennessee anytime soon?"

Matthew: "That's not really possible right now."

Mandy: "And why is that?"

Matthew: "I'd rather not talk about it."

Mandy: "Well, why don't we talk about this picture that showed up on the VIP Social Buzz website yesterday. That's you and Julie Crawford, isn't it? So, are you and the boss's daughter becoming more than just friends now?"

Matthew: "No. Look at the caption, Mandy. That was a business meeting. She's a shareholder. Nothing more."

Mandy: "Matthew, I'm confused. This doesn't look like a business picture to me." The picture flashed on screen again. Julie in a black dress with her arms around Matthew. "I guess we'll just have to let our audience decide."

Matthew: "Why? Why would we let the audience decide if I already told you the answer?"

Mandy: "Do you not follow Julie on Twitter?"

Matthew: "No. I was in prison fourteen years, remember? I'm still trying to learn to socialize in real life."

Mandy: "Well, Julie tweeted the following words last night at 11:45: 'Great night with Matthew. Can't sleep.' Anything you'd like to say about that, Matthew?"

Matthew: "I'd say she needs some sleeping pills."

Mandy laughed as she reached out and patted his knee. Her hand lingered longer than necessary. "Oh, Matthew. Playing hard to get will get you everywhere with me." She turned to the camera. "After fourteen years in prison, Matthew Prescott begins a new life out on the California coast. Can an ex-con handle the pressures of big business? And how's his social life? The women of America want to know. Stay tuned. After break, we'll be traveling to Matthew's penthouse suite to discover who has and who hasn't been an overnight guest there. Oh, and what's his most requested room service food?"

The room was completely silent. Even Aunt Charlotte didn't move a muscle. The funny Pine-Sol woman appeared on screen with a mop bucket. I cleared my throat and stood. "I think I'll pass on the next segment. I've got grading to do. I need to stop by the Dollar General for some art supplies before they close."

Carlie stood. "Wait! Something's gone wrong. They said it was gonna be a family show. I think they're just trying to do one of those bait and switch things. You know, make us think it's one thing…but it's not really. It's all about ratings, getting people to stay for the next segment. They're probably just gonna talk about how his best friend from high school came by and slept on the couch or something. Really."

"Oh, I know. I just need to go." I tried to paste a convincing smile on my face. "Glitter glue waits for no one."

Aunt Charlotte speared another pickle. "Well, I don't like that Mandy girl. I don't like the way she touches him. I don't like the way she talks about Tennessee either. And I don't like the way her eyes is shifty. Ain't they, Bart? She got shifty eyes just like ol' Barry Ratcliff. Y'see, I always thought Barry's eyes was real shifty like. Well, one day I open up the paper and there he is. Front page. Ratcliff embezzles money from Electric Co-Op. All I'm sayin' is they better not let that Mandy girl near the money bag. She's trouble. Trouble with a capital T."

Chapter 59, CARLIE: Aunt Charlotte Needs a Shovel

The second episode of "Sweet Southern Freedom" was a little less sweet and a little more like, well, like Miss Lucy's gut rot moonshine. They hired this Hollywood reporter, Mandy, to cover Matthew and his new life in California. She tried to make us think they were gonna give us some juicy gossip about who had been staying overnight at his hotel apartment. Turns out it was just an old friend from college, a balding guy named Larry, who was in San Diego for an insurance conference.

Oh, and Dusty and Clara didn't exactly come out smelling like a rose either. They showed footage of Bill Goodman yelling at Dusty over what he called "a shoddy half-ass muffler job." Of course, they didn't mention the fact that Bill Goodman has pretty much yelled at everyone about everything since his 18-year-old daughter, Lola, ran off with the Italian trapeze artist who came through with the circus last year.

 At one point, the cameramen were at Dusty and Clara's house watching the kids play on the trampoline. Someone off camera asked, "What does it feel like to be adopted? Do you have any contact with your birthfather? He's in prison, right?" Clara ran to the trampoline and held up her hands and said, "Enough! Let them play on the trampoline. If this is not exciting enough for TV, then go somewhere else." Sadly, in the producers' minds, when Clara's patience was at the end, well, that's when it did get exciting enough for TV.

Yeah. I'd say the second episode of "Sweet Southern Freedom" wasn't exactly a banner day for the folks of Sharon. When the credits rolled, Dusty and Clara quietly collected the kids and went home. Uncle Bart sat at the table and unknowingly ate two pieces of tiramisu. I called it caramel coffee sponge cake and he loved it! Aunt Charlotte poured coffee and said, "Them producers is makin' us look bad, Carlie. And I don't take too kindly to that kind of nonsense. Dusty ain't never done no shoddy mechanic work in his life and Clara ain't nothin' but kind either. And Matthew? Matthew's just a poor soul who ain't been out in the open long enough to realize he's fixin' to get eaten by a lion. I don't know if it's the TV folks or that new boss of his that's gonna get to him first. Did you notice Julie's dad on camera? He got shifty eyes just like that Mandy girl."

"And Barry Ratcliff?"

She jumped up from the table. "Right! Julie's dad's eyes look just like Barry Ratcliff's eyes. 'Cept he's one of them powerful fellas that has a way of stayin' out of the paper. He knows people who knows how to make him look like he's on the up-and-up. But I don't know, Carlie. I got a bad feeling."

"I feel bad but not about Julie's dad."

"What do you feel bad about?"

"Well, this whole TV show thing was my idea. And I don't think it's goin' so well right now. Sarah's all torn up about Matthew. Dusty and Clara are worried about the kids. Matthew's livin' in California. This is way worse than my usual blunders."

"Yeah, this ain't no burnt garlic bread or bad matchmaking. But it ain't your fault. Somebody needs to get a hold of that little Shayla."

"I'll call her tomorrow."

"No, Baby. I meant somebody needs to get A HOLD of her. What is it they say in movies? Shake her down a bit?"

"This isn't 'The Godfather,' Aunt Charlotte."

"I know. Too bad we don't got no thugs or big black cars."
She moved closer and whispered, "And look at Bart and Doug
over there, Baby. Just look at 'em. They could never throw
nobody into the water." She shook her head. "And the creek's
only about a foot deep this time of year anyway."

Uncle Bart stood and walked toward the door. "That was
some mighty fine sponge cake, Carlie. But we best be headin'
on to the house. Charlotte, you ready?"

"I am, Darlin'." She hugged me and whispered, "Call if you
think of something we can do to help."

"Would it involve a shovel?"

She grinned, winked, and headed out the door. "Bye all!"

"Bye!"

After James went to bed, Doug and I poured two cups of decaf
coffee. He stood at the counter and looked out the kitchen
window like he was plotting something.

"You're not thinking of throwing someone in the creek are
you?"

"Huh? No. Just wondering why I haven't heard back from
Matthew."

"Yeah. Me too."

He turned and leaned back on the counter. "Is it just me or was
that pretty bad tonight?"

"The show? Yeah, it was pretty bad."

"I have a feeling Dusty is talking to the producers right now. He thought they had agreed not to show some of that. The deal with Bill Goodman is one thing. It's obvious he's just a troublemaker. But the scene with Clara and the kids? That was pretty brutal."

"I know. Did you see Will's face?"

"I did. Dusty said he's been having a hard time in seventh grade anyway. Some bullying from the bigger kids. Dusty considered not doing the show at all, thinking it might be bad timing for the family. But he talked to all of them and Will insisted. Said it would be cool to be on TV. Not sure how cool it seems now though."

"Yeah. What did you think about Matthew's part?"

"He looked good. In control. She tried to break him, but he didn't budge."

"I guess. So, he's there now, huh? For good?"

He put his arms around me. "I'm afraid so. From what he said tonight, didn't it sound like he was settling in?"

"Yeah. I guess I just wanted to believe…"

"I love you, Carlie." He kissed me on the cheek. "And it's always good to believe."

303

Chapter 60, CARLIE: The Moment Life Changed

At 11:15, the phone woke us both out of a deep sleep. Doug jumped and turned on the lamp. "Hello. Yeah."

I couldn't hear what was being said on the other end of the line. But Doug's eyes were squinting and the color in his face was fading. Anytime the phone rang after 10:00 pm it always reminded us of the night Shannon died. In a matter of seconds, he said, "I'm on my way," and he hung up the phone.

I sat up in bed, still half asleep. "What happened?"

He grabbed his pants off the desk chair and fumbled for his billfold. "It's Will. He's at the hospital. Stay with James. I'll let you know when I know something."

"Will? What happened? Do I need to go get the kids?"

"He took a bunch of pills. Aunt Charlotte's with the kids. That's all I know." In less than two minutes, Doug was in the truck and heading to Volunteer Hospital. I was praying a simple prayer. "God, please don't let him die."

Every minute after that phone call seemed like an hour. I couldn't imagine what Dusty and Clara were going through. Their beautiful little boy. The boy we all loved. The boy they both treasured. "God, please give him another chance."

At midnight, I called Sarah.

"Uh, hello."

"Sarah, I'm so sorry. It's an emergency and I, well, I needed to talk to somebody."

"What's wrong?"

"Doug left 45 minutes ago. Will took a bunch of pills. He's in the hospital and I don't know anything more than that."

"No. Look, you need to be with Clara right now. I'm coming to your house to stay with James."

"Thank you, Sarah. Thank you."

"On my way. Bye."

Forty minutes later I walked into Volunteer Community Hospital. "I'm looking for the family of Will McConnell."

"Down this hallway on your right."

My feet felt heavier with every step. As I got closer, I could hear conversation. When I walked in the door, Dusty and Clara were huddled on the couch. Both in pajama pants and t-shirts. Doug was on his cell phone in the corner. Brother Dan, dressed in old jeans and a dingy white t-shirt, was sitting across from Dusty and Clara.

Clara ran and threw her arms around me. She pulled away as she wiped her face with a paper towel. "Thank you for coming."

"How is he?"

"Alive."

Brother Dan stood. "The news we're getting is pretty positive. They pumped his stomach and Dusty and Clara have been back there. They need to run a few tests and then they're going to admit him into a room." He spoke more quietly, "But

305

under the circumstances, he'll probably have to, you know, he'll need to be under observation for a while."

I put my arm around Clara. "How's the mama?"

"I've been better."

"But they think he's going to be fine? Fully recover?"

"Yes. Thank God." Her voice started cracking. "It's a miracle, you know. Dusty always goes to bed early. But he was up late for some reason. And before he went to bed, he walked into Will's room. And he just, well, he never does that. And Will was lying on the floor." She began crying again and I reached out and wrapped my arms around her thin frame.

"And he's alive."

"Yes. The doctor said if we hadn't found him till morning, well…"

"The results could have been different."

"Oh God, Carlie, what would we have done? He's our boy. Our…"

"It's my fault, you know."

"What? No."

"That dumb TV show. I never thought about the embarrassment it could be for a seventh grader. And I definitely didn't think they'd make a deal about his birthfather being in prison or anything like that. It was all below the belt."

"Agreed. But right now? I'm just thankful he's alive."

"Me too. Me too."

Doug approached us. "Aunt Charlotte said she plans on staying with the kids for a few days. So you two can come and go as you need to."

Clara spoke with relief. "Thank God for that woman. But Doug, shoot straight. What did she really say?"

He grinned. "She said, 'I'm gonna make that Will a BIG batch of chocolate chip cookies 'cause that will heal every doubt or fear he ever had in his whole life.'"

Chapter 61, SARAH: You've Got a Friend...Lots of Friends.

I fell asleep on Doug and Carlie's couch and woke up at 6:00 to the sound of Carlie making coffee. Carlie is a morning person. Times a hundred. No. Times a thousand.

"Mornin', Sunshine!"

"You just called me by the name of Charlotte Nelson's deceased calf."

She laughed. "Oh, sorry!"

"You must have good news."

"I do. Will is alive and well. But he'll be staying in the hospital a day or two for observation."

"So, was it..."

"A suicide attempt? Yes. And we're all gonna be real honest about that too. Talk about a powerful moment. Dusty was crying and wiping tears. He reached down and kissed Will on the cheek and said, 'You'll always be my #1 son and we'll get through this. We will. Together.' But none of us are naïve to what needs to happen. Lots of testing. Counseling. Brother Dan knows someone who specializes in crisis counseling for adolescents. We'll work together. They're taking it very seriously."

"I wanna go by and see him after school. Is that okay?"

"Yeah. He can have visitors. And depending on when you can go, we might use it as a time for Dusty and Clara to take a break and go home for a while."

"Great. Tell them I'll be there around 4:00."

"I will."

By 3:50, the school parking lot was empty. As I got into my car, I asked God to help me love Will. I did love him. But I needed a special way to show him that love. I got the cardboard treasure box out of the backseat and decided on Tootsie Rolls and Pokemon cards. Sometimes it pays to be a teacher.

I knocked gently on the hospital room door. "It's me. Sarah."

Will's voice sounded pleasant. "Come in."

"Hey, Buddy. I brought you something."

He opened the brown paper lunch sack. "Wow! Thanks, Ms. Sarah."

"You're welcome."

Dusty and Clara both hugged me and thanked me for coming.

"Will, what if we send your folks home to take a shower?" I winked. "No offense. But they smell pretty bad."

Will popped a Tootsie Roll in his mouth. "Yeah. They look bad too."

"Now, now. We don't want them to get a complex or anything. Dusty, Clara, I think Will and I can handle the hospital room TV for at least a few hours."

Clara gathered her things and kissed him on the forehead. "Don't let Sarah convince you to do math problems. You know how teachers are. Sneaky."

Dusty laughed and rubbed Will's head. "Yeah. Sarah is a whiz bang at math tutoring. I have a feeling those Tootsie Rolls were just a form of bribery."

"Don't listen to them, Will. I promise an afternoon free of math. And I bet there'll even be Jell-O too."

Dusty and Clara left and we settled into some afternoon movie watching and light conversation. I'm not a counselor and I felt no compulsion to fake it. Will needed a friend. And that I could do. About an hour into the movie, he fell sound asleep. I stood up and walked to his bed. His big brown curls lay perfectly still on the pillow. Handsome. Ridiculously handsome. The nurse came in and checked his vitals. Her exact words? "I'm glad he's sleeping. He's been through quite an ordeal."

My mind went to a hundred places. Why did Will do it? He seemed so happy. Great parents. Smart kid. Standing by his bed in a cold hospital room reminded me again of a simple truth. Life is messy. I prayed, "God, help him see how loved he is. Help him realize his purpose."

The knock on the door startled me. I moved toward the closed door and said quietly, "Come in. He's sleeping." I turned back toward the bed to make sure he hadn't been disturbed. He was still sleeping soundly. I expected to hear a nurse or aide behind me, checking his IV or setting down a tray of promised Jell-O.

"Sarah?"

I turned quickly and almost knocked the Styrofoam pitcher from the food tray. At first, I thought it was all a dream. That maybe Will wasn't the only one who had been sleeping. But he spoke again. "Sarah? Are you okay?"

All I could do was stare. Surreal. I'd just seen him on TV last night. Dressed in an expensive suit. Ocean water in the background. Now he was standing in Will's hospital room wearing blue jeans and a black t-shirt. Cowboy boots. Looking like he used to look when he lived in a small town, when he worked at a mechanic shop, when he rode home from church with me in a dirty Ford Focus. He nervously rubbed his lips together and stared at the hospital bed. All I could think about were the times I'd kissed him. The times we sat together on the porch. The times I dreamed he was falling in love with me. The words written in ink on paper hidden in a drawer.

"Matthew? Gosh, I'm sorry. I'm just shocked." I slowly walked toward him. He put his arms around me exactly the way he did before he left. His hands touched the back of my hair. He smelled divine. "How did you get here? I mean, how did you know?"

"Doug called me last night when he was on the way to the hospital."

"Oh, that's good. Yeah. It was a scare. For all of us. Dusty and Clara just left an hour ago. They'll probably be back in less than an hour…if you want to wait. I mean, Will's asleep right now. But he'll probably wake up pretty soon."

"Yeah. That's good. I can wait. So what happened, Sarah? To Will."

"I don't know really. I mean, I know he took some pills. I know they're taking it seriously. I know we're all thankful he's alive."

Matthew walked to Will's bed and placed his hand gently on top of his head. "Yeah. Thankful."

Will stirred a bit. He blinked and reached for his water cup. "Matthew! How did you get here from California?"

"It's called an airplane, Buddy. It's pretty fast."

Will guzzled some water and then wiped his mouth with the back of his hand. "Why'd you come?"

"I came to see you."

Will looked down at the blanket and said softly, "Because they told you about..."

"Yeah. Doug called and told me you had a close call, man. So I knew I needed to come see you and make sure you're okay."

"I'm fine."

Matthew pretended to punch him on the arm. "Yeah, well, I'm glad."

"Can I ask you a question?"

"Anything, Will."

"Does it bother you when the TV people ask questions about you being in prison or other things you don't want to talk about?"

"Yeah. Sometimes. Does it bother you?"

"Yeah."

Matthew pulled up a chair and laid his hand on Will's arm. "Here's the deal, Will. You and me? We'll always be misunderstood by some people. There will always be people who judge me because of my past with drugs, or because I was in prison. There might even be people who think certain things about you because your birthfather is in prison. So every day, you and me, we have a decision to make. We decide whose opinion matters. The most. Some people will always reject us, man. But look at all the people who love us, who accept us just the way we are. History and all." He looked at me and in that single moment, it was like he could see into my soul, almost like he was there the day I laid on the old iron bed. Like he knew that I loved him. That I always would love him. He turned to Will. "That kind of love, it's pretty cool, right?"

Will smiled. "I guess. Wanna Tootsie Roll?"

Matthew laughed and stood up. "Of course I do! Why do you think I flew all the way out here if it wasn't for the free Tootsie Rolls?"

Dusty walked in just as Matthew was throwing the candy wrapper into the corner trash can. "Good gosh a-mighty! What have we here? Matthew Prescott? Hobnobbing with us common folk again?"

Matthew turned and embraced him. "Hey, I came to see my main man here. We gotta stick together."

Dusty smiled and rubbed Will's head. "Yeah. I hear ya."

We made small talk for ten minutes. Matthew cleared his throat. "Sarah, wanna get some coffee?"

"Sure. Will, I'll come see you again tomorrow."

Matthew patted Dusty on the back. "I'll be back, man. I need to talk to you."

Dusty plopped down in an old blue vinyl chair. "I'll be here."

We were silent as we walked down the hallway. A few times I glanced up at him. Still in shock, I guess. His face wore at least two day's stubble. Sexy beyond words. The sexiest part? The not shaving was just a matter of convenience to him. Probably didn't even realize the folks on the plane thought he was handsome. The bottom line? He came. He said he came for Will. I believed him. And the fact that he would do something like that, well, maybe that was the sexiest part of all.

We never got to the cafeteria. He stopped suddenly outside the cafeteria door. His arms reached out for me and I leaned close into his chest. As his hands touched the back of my head, he whispered, "Sarah, I've missed you. Every single day."

I didn't pull away. I stayed close to his chest. "I missed you too."

Just as he pulled away and looked into my eyes, a young nurse ran up to us and yelled, "Oh my God! It's Matthew Prescott! No way!"

Matthew extended his hand to her and said quietly, "Yes. I'm Matthew. Nice to meet you."

"I'm Bridget Mathis and I'm your biggest fan! Seriously! I am your biggest fan. I'm gonna call my cousin. She will just DIE when she finds out you're here! Just die!"

"Bridget, can you do me a favor?"

"Oh, anything!"

"Yeah. Could you hold off on telling anybody right now? I'm here to visit someone and if you could give me some time, it would mean a lot."

"Can I at least get a picture with you?"

He looked relieved. "Yeah, that'll be fine."

She shoved her phone into my hands. "Here. Would you take it?"

I winked at Matthew. "I'll be glad to. I mean, it's not every day you meet a famous California heartthrob, right?" He grinned and then scowled as though he were lovingly chastising me.

Bridget pulled some lip balm from her pocket and began applying it. "Absolutely! I can't believe it."

I wanted to throw gasoline on the fire a bit. "Okay, you two! Lean in real close now."

Matthew put his arm around her. She leaned in and smiled for the camera as her face turned bright red. I snapped the pic and she requested another. She reached up to kiss him on the cheek for the second picture. He pulled away and said, "Let's just smile and look forward, okay?" She hesitantly agreed.

With picture two completed, he shook her hand again and said, "It was nice to meet you, Bridget."

"Oh, you too!" She looked at me and asked, "Do you want me to get your picture made with him too?"

Matthew looked mortified. I bit my lip to keep from laughing. "Are you kidding? I sure do!" I handed Bridget my phone. "Do you mind?"

"Not at all! I mean, you'd kick yourself later if you met Matthew Prescott and didn't even get your picture made with him!"

I looked at Matthew and winked. "Wouldn't I though?"

She stood back and said, "Smile." He put his arm around me. She looked at the phone screen and said, "Now, let's get one more."

She held up the phone. "Ready?"

Matthew answered, "Almost." Then he turned and put both hands on my face. He kissed me gently on the cheek. I heard the phone's familiar click.

When I looked up at Bridget, she looked like she'd been hit by a train. She finally spoke. "Well, that was…"

Matthew gently brushed the hair from my face and looked into my eyes. "Surreal."

I could feel my own face getting warmer. "Bridget, thank you so much. Really. I hope you have a great evening."

"Uh, yeah. It was nice to meet you. Both of you." Matthew nodded and waved. She walked toward the elevator.

He put his hands in his pockets and looked around. "This is probably not a good place to talk, Sarah. I need to talk to Dusty for a while. Can you meet me later?"

"Sure. Where do you want to meet?"

"How about Chester and Ida's place?"

"What time?"

"How 'bout seven? Doug's gonna pick me up here and he can drop me off at the house. We'll order pizza, maybe."

"Sounds good. I'll see you then." I touched his arm and he kissed me on the cheek again.

"Bye."

He turned and started walking. I leaned up against the wall and stood completely still. I wanted to watch his every move. He was walking away. But I prayed it would be the last time.

Chapter 62, SARAH: Shepherd's Pie and the Little Black Dress

"Carlie, this is Sarah. Do you have a minute?"

"Yes! I'm glad you called. OH MY GOSH, friend! Have you heard the news?"

"That Matthew's in town?"

"Yes. You know! Oh, I'm glad you know."

"I saw him actually. At the hospital. In fact, I'm meeting him at seven tonight."

"Oh, Girlfriend, you made my day! Is this a date date?"

"Well, we're meeting at Chester and Ida's house actually. But he said he's ordering pizza. So, yeah, I think it is."

"Oh my gosh! I'm gonna faint! I am! But I'm cooking dinner and I don't need to faint or I will burn something. Plus, girl, you need to get off the phone so you can shower and smell wonderful and look alluring. So, I'm hanging up the phone now. Wait. You do know what alluring means, right? Tell me you're wearing something alluring. No mom jeans. No denim jumpers. No oversized sweaters. Don't make me starve out these Jameson men in order to come to your house and get all up in your business."

"I was actually thinking about wearing the black dress. Is that alright?"

"Alright? It's more than alright. Honey, you were filling out every inch of that dress. Perfection, friend! Okay. Gotta run."

"Bye, Carlie."

"Wait. Sarah, there's one more thing I need to tell you."

"I know. No chunky scarves."

"Well, that IS brilliant advice. But it's not what I was gonna say."

"I'm listening."

"Be fearless, friend...Be fearless."

"Thank you, Carlie. Bye."

Thirty minutes later I stood in front of the mirror. Black dress and black pumps. I knew I was over-dressed for pizza but I didn't care. I wanted to make a statement. I couldn't decide whether to put my hair up or leave it down. I smiled as I remembered what Carlie said once. "If you're going to put your hair up, you might as well go ahead and wear a sign that says, 'I'm not interested in you. I'm too busy being your accountant.'" I bent over and shook my hair. Then I stood up and let all the loose curls fall around my shoulders. I whispered to an empty house, "I'm trying, Carlie. God knows I'm trying."

7:00

As I pulled into Chester and Ida's driveway, I noticed the lamp in his bedroom was on. I remembered that day I saw the discarded letters. The day my tears fell on the patchwork quilt. I hoped he hadn't noticed any disturbance in the order of things. I was so distracted by that thought, I just sat in the car for a few minutes. He walked out onto the porch and started laughing. "Am I supposed to come get you out of the car? I'll be the first to admit I don't know how to date a woman. But I don't remember this scene in any movies."

I rolled down the passenger-side window. "Yes! Didn't you know? You're supposed to carry me inside. A guest should never have to get her shoes dirty. Are you telling me you didn't know this? That I was going to sit out here all night just waiting for you to do what any man would know to do?"

He smiled and ran off the porch. "You're gonna regret saying that, Miss Simpson!"

"Am I?"

He approached the car quickly. He was wearing khaki pants and an ironed white oxford shirt. Clean-shaven. Handsome. When he opened the car door, my heart started pounding. I got out of the car and when I did, he backed up a few feet and just stood there. "Matthew, is something wrong?"

"No. It's just that…I…well, I…"

"You think I'm too heavy to carry. Hey, you wouldn't be the first one to think that, I'm sure."

"No. I think you're beautiful, Sarah. That's what I was trying to say." He just stood there staring. "Beautiful. And believe me, I'd have no problem carrying you either. But considering the fact that Mrs. Cora Belle has been looking out the window for the last hour, if I picked you up right now and carried you into the house, I'm afraid the entire county would implode. Am I right?"

I reached into the car to grab my purse. "Wow. You really have learned the system around here, Matthew."

He took my arm and we walked toward the porch. "We're not having pizza. I hope you're not disappointed."

"Me? No. Did you cook? Is that what you're telling me?"

"I did. Have you ever eaten Shepherd's Pie?"

"Oh, Mrs. Ida's Shepherd's Pie? Yes. It's wonderful."

"I'm sure it's not as good as hers. But I took a stab at it. She showed me how to make it several times. But don't expect anything too…"

I stopped on the porch and looked into his eyes. "Surreal?"

He looked down. "I wanted to call you. I did. I can't tell you how many times. But I kept thinking if I left you alone, you wouldn't have to deal with all my…you know. Here. Let's go in the house before Mrs. Cora Belle strains her eyes."

Walking into Chester and Ida's house, I felt this overwhelming sense of peace. Happiness. Matthew was no Martha Stewart but he had made an effort. Two white Corelle plates right across from each other on the dining room table. Two paper napkins. Two forks.

He put an old olive green casserole dish in the middle of the table. "The table's nothing fancy. Couldn't even find any candles. Not that Shepherd's Pie is really a candle meal, I guess."

"You did fine."

The Shepherd's Pie didn't taste like Ida's. But it didn't matter. Nothing mattered except being there. With him. "So, when do you have to go back to California?"

"I'm not."

The room started spinning but it was a good spinning. I smiled and held on.

He wiped his mouth with the napkin and looked up. "I'm not with McLaughlin anymore. He cuts some serious corners. Dusty is ten times the business man he is. Ten times the man he is. It's a long story."

"Wow. I mean, that's great news. What about the TV show?"

"As of this afternoon, that's over too."

"Over? As in over?"

He smiled and leaned back in the old aluminum chair. "What other kind of 'over' is there, Sarah?"

"What happened?"

"Will was the final nail in the coffin. For both of us. But Dusty and I were fed up even before that. We did a conference call with the network this afternoon. Because of Will's situation, they let us out of our contracts without much fuss. We both agreed it was for the best. They wanted to go somewhere we didn't want to go."

"And what about Bridget and all those other Facebook fans?"

"Within a week, they'll move on to someone new. A TV dancer or some survivor guy." He carried the casserole dish to the counter. "Plus, when they all find out I'm just a poor felon living in a small town again, working at a mechanic shop, without TV cameras around, who would be interested in that guy, right?"

My knees were shaking but I managed to stand and walk to the counter. He reached into the cabinet to pull out a clear glass lid. I placed my hand gently on his back. "Was that a real question?"

He turned to face me. For the first time, I saw fear in his eyes. "Yes."

"I'll be honest with you, Matthew. I'm sure there are a lot of women interested in that guy. Even with the felony on his record. Even without a TV contract. I bet Julie Crawford would even be interested. And lots of women around here would be all about a hard-working guy with a kind heart. I know that for sure. So, really, trust me. You've got nothing to worry about."

His expression fell. "Let's go sit in the living room."

We walked into the living room. For just a moment, I expected Chester or Ida to come walking down the hallway. Matthew pulled the floral wingback chair forward so that it faced the recliner. "Here. You can sit in Mrs. Ida's chair. But I'm warning you. You may feel a sudden urge to crochet. Can you handle that, Sarah?"

"Look. My hands are already shaking a bit."

He sat in Chester's old recliner and reached for both my hands. My heart was pounding in my chest. He spoke quietly, "Can I re-phrase my earlier question?"

"Sure."

"I don't care about what Julie thinks or the women around here or the women on Facebook either. Would they be interested in me? I don't know. It doesn't matter. Not to me anyway." He bowed his head and bit his lip slightly. "Sarah, I'm asking what you think. I'm asking whether you could be interested in that guy. But before you answer, I want to tell you something." His voice grew quieter as he looked into my eyes. "I've been watching you for months now. And I want to thank you. You've never made me feel 'less than.' Not one time. And you serve people, Sarah. I notice that. It's the way you re-fill people's glasses. The way you take care of the kids at church. At school. None of that…none of that is lost on me. I notice. And…" He leaned in closer. "And I know you don't think this. But you're beautiful, Sarah. Not just pretty." He shook his head and smiled. "Trust me. You're the kind of beautiful that keeps a man from sleeping at night. You are. I promise. And I should know." He pointed down the hallway. "Because I've lost a lot of sleep back there. And you're to blame. Not Julie. Not Shayla or the women on Facebook. No. It's you, Sarah. It's been you. It'll always be you. I don't want a big life. Not the way some people define 'big'. I want this life. The life Chester and Ida had. Shepherd's Pie and porch sitting. Church and hard work. Friends who know how to forgive big mistakes and love you anyway. I want to live here. With you, Sarah. And I promise you. I promise I will take care of you…love you. So I don't really want to know if women would be interested in me. I don't care. I want to know if you love me as much as I love you. If you ever could?"

He handed me a tissue from the coffee table as he brushed the hair from my forehead. I felt sure someone would wake me up any minute now. I wiped the tears from my eyes and looked into his face. I remembered Carlie's words. Be fearless. "I love you, Matthew. I do. I have…and I will."

He jumped to his feet. "You have made me the happiest man on earth." He reached for me and I stood and placed my face on his chest. I could hear his heart beating. Bliss. He touched

324

my face and kissed me. Gently. Passionately. Perfectly. "Marry me, Sarah. Will you marry me?"

"I will."

Chapter 63, CARLIE: The End is Always the Beginning

My word. Some people think nothing happens in a small town. They couldn't be more wrong. Mabel got in a generous mood and put burgers on sale 3/$5 which made the morning radio show. Aunt Charlotte gave up on her diet, which never really worked anyway. She joined a gym in Martin instead. Yes. Aunt Charlotte joined a gym. She even bought gray sweat pants at the Dollar General. Uncle Bart said, "Lord, have mercy. The world must be comin' to an end. But at least we can eat fried squirrel and cornbread again." Priceless priorities.

Will has been released from the hospital. He's doing well. Extensive counseling and therapy. Back at school now. Dusty even did a school program about adoption and bullying. According to Clara, Will came home and said, "All the boys said my dad seems like a tough guy who shouldn't be messed with." Those words dripped from Will's lips like true poetry.

Oh, but the best news of all? The absolute best news is that Matthew Prescott and Sarah Simpson are getting married next month. Yep! I sure did call that one, eh? The ceremony is gonna take place in Chester and Ida's backyard. Well, it's Matthew's backyard now. Next month it'll be Matthew and Sarah's backyard. Oh, and Matthew went back to work for Dusty too and he seems way happier than when we visited him in his big office in California. I guess some people have to experience the world before they find their place in it. Dusty and Matthew have even discussed working out a business partnership. They're working with a group out of Nashville who helps convicted felons find work after they're released from prison. Mitch Smith even agreed to consider hiring one of Dusty and Matthew's new friends at his insurance agency.

Doug and I were sitting on the porch yesterday afternoon when Matthew and Sarah dropped by. They're both downright giddy. Matthew walks with a spring in his step. Sarah glows like a painting of a Greek goddess that's under big lights at the Smithsonian or something. Fearless, both of them. But the best part? Well, the best part was what they brought with them.

We were all just sitting on the rocking chairs discussing wedding details. Matthew pulled an old manila envelope from his back pocket. "I have something I'd like to read to you, if you've got a minute."

Doug pulled his rocking chair forward a bit. "I hope it's good news."

"Yeah. It is. It's something Chester wrote in the hospital. Left it with the lawyer. Only to be given to me, well…you'll understand when I read it."

"We can't wait to hear it."

Matthew unfolded the sheet of paper and then reached over and put his hand in Sarah's. He cleared his throat like he was trying to maintain composure.

"Dear Matthew,

I'm asking Janie to help me write this 'cause I can't spell worth a dang and my handwriting's never been good. I know she'll fix it and make it right.

If you're reading this, it means I'm dead. But that's okay. I know where I'm going. I'm not worried. If you're reading this, it also means you asked Sarah to marry you. Ida and I always thought you was right for each other. But we know young folks don't like it when old folks get in their business. So we tried to stay out of it as best we could. So if you're reading this, it means God answered our prayers. And He's been doin' that a lot lately.

Some people are always gonna judge you on what you did in the past. Don't ever let their judgment make you bitter. People who can't forgive are usually people you don't need in your life anyway. The one person whose forgiveness you needed most has already forgiven you. And He knows more about rejection than you ever will. He sacrificed a lot. So don't be troubling him by walking in shame. Hold your head up, Son.

I don't have an education. You know that. I always worked regular jobs. I've had a regular life. Except for one thing. Most folks probably don't know I won the lottery. Not the one they're always advertising on the radio. You've seen the bank accounts. You know on a good day, Ida and I never had more than a few thousand dollars in the bank. But that was always okay. With me and with her.

No. The kind of lottery I won is better than that. I've known the love of one woman my whole life. And when a man is dying, that means more to him than money. So in the same way I'm givin' you what few earthly treasures we have, I want to give you some advice from a dying old man that will give you a better treasure.

It's okay to fight sometimes. You won't agree with Sarah on everything. She won't agree with you. But don't ever walk out, Matthew. And if she starts walking out, run after her. If you promise to stay with a woman, you need to keep that promise. No matter what comes.

Sarah needs love. Compliment her. Lord, I'm glad Janie is writing this 'cause I got not the foggiest idea how to spell compliment. Kiss her and hug her several times a day. The greatest memories of my life are of laying down in bed after a hard day's work and knowing I didn't have to lay there alone. Well, maybe those aren't the greatest memories of my life. There are other things that happened in that bed that are even better than that. But seein' as how Janie is writing this, I better leave that alone. (Janie, you reckon we should take that part out?)

One of the greatest gifts known to man is a good woman. So don't mess it up. Treat her kindly. Take out the trash. Let her watch what she wants to watch on the TV sometimes. I don't like "Wheel of Fortune" but I've seen nearly every episode for nigh on 30 years. Still can't spell worth a dang. But Ida likes word puzzles. And her happiness means a lot to me. It always has. But it means even more to me now.

I better sign off now seein' as how Janie's got plenty of work to do that don't involve helping an old man write a letter. Matthew, I'm happy for you. You and me? We struck gold. What is it they always say, 'Even a blind squirrel finds an acorn now and then.' We done even better than that, Son. Way better.

I never told you this, Matthew. But I love you. So go out and do big things in the world. Be blessed. Be a blessing.

Love, Chester"

Some folks in the community are still not sure about Matthew Prescott and especially about Sarah Simpson marrying him. But that's fine. I always say that life is an imperfect journey with a lot of imperfect folks traveling alongside us. But sometimes God brings people across our paths. People who change the course of our lives for the better. People who show us how to love. And be loved. People who give us the courage to forgive. Chester's right. "Go out and do big things in the world. Be blessed. Be a blessing."

THE END

For Lisa Smartt info and funny small town tidbits, like her Facebook page at www.facebook.com/lisasmarttbooks and follow her blog at www.lisasmartt.com.

Book #5 in the *Doug and Carlie Series* coming November 2015.

ACKNOWLEDGMENTS

Every person lives with some regrets. I'm no exception. But there's one thing I've never regretted…marrying Philip Smartt in the spring of 1988. He has shown me what real love looks like. Every day. He doesn't live in the fast lane or do "splashy" romantic things that put him on YouTube. No. He gets up every day and loves me. He never gives up on me. He wraps his arms around our sons and shows them how to be men. He impacts the lives of college students. Day after day. Year after year. Thank you.

We prayed for children for almost eight years before God brought us sons. Stephen and Jonathan have taught me so many things about life and unconditional love. They've shown me what's important and what's not. And even though they're teenagers right now (pray for me), they still bring joy beyond words (and I'm a writer).

My mom and dad, Jack and Regina Golden, have spent their entire lives loving the Matthew Prescotts of the world. They didn't have to tell us about grace and mercy. We saw it. Up close and personal. I've never spent one day of my life doubting God's unconditional love for messed-up people. Thank you.

My in-laws, Les and Sylvia Smith, inspire all of us to never take love for granted. They love and serve each other with such grace. They serve those in need with enthusiasm. Thank you.

Merry Brown and I meet several times a week to write, encourage each other, share marketing ideas, and watch online cat videos. I could never have finished this book without her constant support, as well as her tech abilities. She reminds me to keep going.

My mom, Regina Golden, is an incredibly gifted proofreader. But her love for people is her real gift and legacy. I would have never attempted writing books had it not been for her constant support and meticulous writing skills. My love for spelling came directly from her. Every day I pray her incredible love for people rubs off on me.

"For by grace you have been saved through faith. And this is not your own doing; it is the gift of God..." Ephesians 2:8